She's the lady most
likely to drive him mad—
with desire…

"High stakes don't frighten
me," she announced.

They should," he growled, and then added beneath his breath, "Daft girl."

She heard him. Or read his lips. The hands that rested on the top of the table curled into fists. "What's amiss? Afraid you will lose?"

"One night upstairs," the man to his left blurted, boldly tossing down the gauntlet. "Winner claims one night with you in an upstairs chamber," he clarified, as though his meaning wasn't evident. The bastard then winked at Aurelia.

Max arched an eyebrow, waiting for her to flee. Now she would surely see. Now she would understand that she had gotten in over her head. He watched, waiting for her to come to her senses and excuse herself.

Her brown eyes locked on his as she asked, "And if I win?"

He slid his hands beneath the table and gripped his thighs, his fingers digging deep as he leaned forward. Mad chit. She was *not* doing this. He shook his head once at her. Hard.

"Whatever you want. Name your prize," one of the other men offered, leering at her chest as he did so.

Her gaze roamed over each man at the table, assessing. Four in all, counting him. She thought she could best all of them? She was playing with fire and she knew it.

"I'll have . . ." Aurelia paused, her gaze resting on him again, considering. "Your clothes."

By Sophie Jordan

All the Ways to Ruin a Rogue
A Good Debutante's Guide to Ruin
How to Lose a Bride in One Night
Lessons from a Scandalous Bride
Wicked in Your Arms
Wicked Nights with a Lover
In Scandal They Wed
Sins of a Wicked Duke
Surrender to Me
One Night with You
Too Wicked to Tame
Once Upon a Wedding Night

Available from Avon Impulse

The Earl in My Bed
An Heiress for All Seasons

Sophie Jordan

All the Ways to Ruin a Rogue

The Debutante Files

AVONBOOKS

An Imprint of HarperCollins*Publishers*

This is a work of fiction. Names, characters, places, and incidents are products of the author's imagination or are used fictitiously and are not to be construed as real. Any resemblance to actual events, locales, organizations, or persons, living or dead, is entirely coincidental.

AVON BOOKS
An Imprint of HarperCollins*Publishers*
195 Broadway
New York, New York 10007

ISBN 978-0-06-222252-7
www.avonromance.com

First Avon Books mass market printing: August 2015

Printed in the U.S.A.

10 9 8 7 6 5 4 3 2 1

For Lindsay.
Thank goodness for mommy/toddler gymnastic classes.
The idea that I could never have met you strikes terror in my heart. I love you, friend.

All the Ways to Ruin a Rogue

Prologue

Aurelia fell in love with Maxim Alexandor Chandler, the fourth Viscount of Camden—Max to his familiars—instantly. This portentous event occurred on the seventh day of April, one week before her ninth birthday. The moment the fire was lit, the flame burned bright and fierce in her young heart.

She recalled the actual date only because she recorded it in her journal that very night. Whenever she pulled forth that journal in later years, she stroked her fingertips to the aged parchment and marveled at the girl she had once been. Now those youthful scribblings made her cringe. Granted, she had been young, but he had owned her heart wholly and utterly.

Her brother had been home from Eton that April afternoon. Will had brought Lord Camden with him. She had been in the stables, playing with Nessie's new puppies, selecting her favorite and crafting arguments in her mind to present to Mama in the desperate hope that they could bring a puppy into the house to live with them.

She was bending over, her hair falling loose around her—it never stayed within her plaits. Breathless and huffing, she tugged a particularly feisty puppy by the hind legs in an attempt to stop him from fleeing the stall, when she heard voices.

"What have you there, Aurelia?" Will called out.

She released the puppy and shot straight up, shoving hanks of hair behind her ears as Will and his companion entered the stall.

The puppy made a mad dash right between the stranger's boot-clad legs. She gawked as the newcomer quickly whirled around and caught the squirming little beast in his hands. "Oh! Isn't he a cute fellow?" he said cheerfully, lifting the puppy up to his face so he could examine it. The puppy licked his chin and the boy laughed. Aurelia felt that sound to her core.

She drank in the sight of him, the strikingly handsome man he was to become fully seeded in his strong jaw and brilliant blue eyes. He wore his hair long. It fell low over his brow, and he tossed his head in an effort to force it back.

He was all lean lines and a good head taller than her brother.

One might say a girl of such tender years could not know real love—could not feel its truth, and perhaps that is the circumstance with most girls. But Aurelia was not like most girls. The longing and infatuation borne in that moment for Max, who was to become a regular addition to their family in the ensuing years, consumed her.

She wrote odes to the young viscount in the secret journal she hid in the loose floorboard of her bedchamber. She reveled in his kind attentions. When Will and her cousin, Declan, treated her to barbs and insults, commanding her to cease following them whenever they roamed the countryside, Max was tolerant, even affectionate, insisting that they let her tag along with them.

It was love.

Until her fifteenth year. Until the greenhouse.

When the fire burning in her heart was forever banked.

The day the fantasy had shattered dawned with all the promise of the spring morning pressing against the windowpanes of her bedchamber. Warm and bright with only the slightest nip in the air, she hadn't even donned her cloak as she skipped outside to her mother's greenhouse.

Max was to arrive that very day for Mama's annual garden party to herald in the Easter holiday. She wanted to surprise him with fresh flowers in his bedchamber . . . and alongside the flowers she intended to leave the sketch of him she had labored over since his last visit

Smiling widely to herself, she tucked a stray strand of hair behind her ear as she made her way to the greenhouse. Her fingers roamed over the rest of her hair, pinned atop her head. The heavy mass swept up off her shoulders was a new sensation. She had been waiting for this day forever. Six years. Ever since she first met Max.

Mama had agreed she was old enough to leave the plaits behind and wear her hair as a lady did. Aurelia could not wait to see the viscount . . . to show him that she had grown up since his last visit. Mama even agreed that she could attend the garden party this afternoon. A victory of epic proportions. She might not be permitted to attend balls and soirees yet, but this afternoon would be hers. Her moment to shine. The first time to see Camden in a year, and the first step in him seeing her as a woman.

She squared her shoulders, wondering if he would notice that she had grown nearly three inches in the last year. And that wasn't the only thing that had grown.

She glanced down at her bosom on display in her prim bodice. In the last year she had developed, gaining breasts that felt as cumbersome as melons strapped to her chest. And that was not all she had gained. She had grown curves, too. A surfeit of curves. Her hips, her derriere . . . all were embarrassingly *present*. She tried not to resent these changes. She had an older brother and cousin. She was not blind to the fact that men preferred such things in a female.

Finally. She was no longer a little girl, and she hoped Camden would notice.

He'd always been kindly attentive, but she hoped today would be different. Today, she hoped he would see her as more than a child. More than a friend. More than Will's little sister. She was, after all, a woman of fifteen.

Once in the greenhouse, she crouched before her mother's roses, carefully snipping the stalks and nestling them gently inside her basket, careful with the delicate yellow petals and mindful not to prick herself on the thorns.

The sound of soft laughter startled her. She had been so lost in her musings, cocooned in the silence of the greenhouse and her happy thoughts of seeing Max again, she had assumed herself alone amid the flowers and lush greenery.

She rose to her feet and moved deeper into the greenhouse, clasping her basket of flowers close as she followed the sound of voices farther back. The sun wasn't high enough to reach there yet. She could peer only into shadows. At first she thought it was a groom making free with one of the household maids, but then she identified the fine cut of dark blue fabric stretching over a man's back. It wasn't Merlton livery. She recognized the maid's dove gray skirts, however. All the household maids wore the same uniform. Clearly, this was an assignation between a maid and a gentleman *not* in her father's employ. Perhaps one of the guests had arrived early.

Leaning closer, she recognized the female's wild coppery curls as belonging to Ingrid, one of the kitchen maids. Usually her hair was pinned up and tucked under her cap, but it drew the eye regardless. Aurelia had envied it, wishing for it over her own dark brown hair.

Ingrid was propped up on a potting table, her legs dangling over the edge of the table, skirts hiked to expose her shapely, stocking-clad legs. Heat flooded Aurelia's face. It was a scandalous scene, made even more shocking when she realized the man's trousers were down past his hips. She couldn't see his backside. The fall of his jacket covered him, but from his movements between the maid's splayed thighs she had a fairly good notion what activity these two were about.

Mama had not yet explained the nature of male/female relations, but Aurelia had indulged herself in the numerous medical texts in the library. Mama had no concept as to the content of such books, but they proved illuminating for Aurelia.

Face burning, she turned to leave, feeling uncomfortable spying on the intimate scene, but then the maid's breathy sigh stopped her. "Oh, my lord . . ."

My lord?

She could go no farther. She had to know. Was that her brother dallying with Ingrid? Or her cousin? Her parents would *not* approve of that, to be certain, and Aurelia was not certain she approved either. She could think only of poor Ingrid. Did she fancy herself in love with Will or Declan? Nothing could come of it. Even she knew that a romance between a servant and a nobleman was doomed to fail. She did not wish heartache on the girl who always saved the very best sweet buns for her.

Turning, she peered again through the branches as Ingrid slid her hands down the man's back. The maid moaned and issued encouragement in a choking voice. The man's sounds were less frequent and quieter. Aurelia narrowed her gaze on him, seeking to identify him.

"Did you miss me, my fine lordling?" Ingrid gasped.

He chuckled, and something inside Aurelia twisted at the sound. "Indeed . . . I could scarcely wait to return here and get beneath your skirts again." He turned his face then. The motion cast his profile into view, and in that instant Aurelia's heart broke.

She gazed at the strong lines she had envisioned every night as she dozed off to sleep and every time she sat down to work on his sketch. It was Max. Max ravishing one of the kitchen maids whilst Aurelia had been so stupidly picking flowers for him and envisioning their reunion.

With a swallowed cry, she whirled around and fled on silent slippers through the greenhouse, leaving the sight of him behind—wishing she could leave the memory of him there, too. But that would chase her. Into the early spring day, the sight of him, the memory of him taking his pleasure with Ingrid, hounded her, nipping at her heels.

She tripped on the lawn, sending her basket flying. Roses sprawled all around her. Rising on all fours, she stared at the fallen flowers through eyes that had gone blurry with hot tears. It dawned on her that it had not been the first time. He'd been with Ingrid before. She gathered that much from what she overheard. And how many others had there been for him?

She choked on sobs, her hair falling loose all around her, as wild as the emotions roiling through her. Bile rose in her throat. *Stupid. Stupid.* How could she have ever thought he might wish to wed her someday?

She pushed herself up. Pain scored her palms. With a cry, she dropped back down. Shaking, she lifted her hands and inspected the deep punctures left by the thorns. Several wounds welled crimson blood against the pale backdrop of her palms. It was fitting that she should bleed. Her heart felt as though it was hemorrhaging inside her chest.

Still shaking, Aurelia finally regained her feet. She grabbed her skirts, smearing blood across the pale fabric of her pinafore. She staggered a few steps, trampling over the roses, leaving her basket behind, not caring that they would wilt there in the dirt. It felt appropriate that the flowers intended for him should wither and die. Just as her heart was.

She ran blindly then, emotion clogging her throat.

Too late, she forgot that the back of the house was a carnival of servants setting up for the afternoon's garden party. She darted among servants and tables and chairs and circled to the side of the building, ignoring the looks cast her way as she fled, her hair tumbling down her back in a wild banner that would send Mama into a dither.

Dodging free of the melee, she cut a path to the great oak tree where she often sat to sketch. It was a place of solace for her, and today would be no different. Today it was more of a comfort than ever.

Dropping down on the soft earth, Aurelia dug into the wide front pocket of her pinafore and withdrew her drawing pad. She flipped to her sketch of Max. She traced his image with shaking fingers, her heart clenching. She'd relied on her memories of him over the last year. Not too difficult. It was no challenge to recount every line and hollow, even though she had not seen him in a long while. He was probably even more handsome now at eighteen. Ingrid certainly thought so.

She stifled a sob as she gazed at the rendering. She had fashioned Max into a beautiful angel, his strong profile hallowed in divine light. She snorted at her fancy.

The sight of him, even on paper, hurt. He wasn't this angel. He was human. A man flawed like any other. She knew about flawed men. Her father preferred spending time away from home. He ignored her. Looked at her blankly whenever she was in his presence—almost as though he did not know her. He was little better with Mama . . . ignoring his own wife in favor of the gaming hells.

She dashed the tears from her cheeks with the back of her hand and sniffled. So she was learning early. Getting a taste for disappointment now. *Brilliant*. With a strangled sob, she flipped the pad to a fresh page and fished her pencil out from her pocket. She was never without pad or pencil. Mostly due to Camden. It was he who first encouraged her to nurture her talent. Called her talented and smart and funny. He'd made her feel special . . . her ability special.

Her fingers flexed around the edges of the pad. She had been so eager to show him her latest drawings. She had practiced a great deal over the last year. Plenty of people observed her laboring over her pad, but never inquired. Watercolors and sketching were a common enough pastime for most girls. Only Max knew the true extent of her passion. He'd listened and offered suggestions and encouragement as though he cared.

All her hopes, all her dreams . . . gone. Burned to cinders. She wiped furiously at the hot spill of tears. What a fool she was to think he would *see* her this time. But what did she expect? That he would look across the room and observe she was no longer a child? No longer a duckling but a swan?

Without thinking, her pencil flew over her sketch pad. She drew through a blur of tears, her fingers working from memory, from some hidden instinct—or impulse. She didn't know. She wasn't thinking. She worked until she felt purged, and when she finished, she dropped the pad facedown beside her.

Her head fell back against the tree and she

closed her eyes, waiting for the tumult of her emotions to subside.

She wasn't certain how long she remained like that. The chill of morning melted away and the tears dried on her cheeks. The rush of blood in her head faded to a dull pulse at her temples. There were only the distant sounds of the staff as they finished the final preparations for the impending party. She'd have to go in soon. Mama would expect her to begin preparing.

She wondered how she might excuse herself from attending. Even as the worst of her hurt and anger ebbed away and a numb sort of calm stole over her, she didn't feel ready to face the world. Especially not Camden.

Considering how much she had begged Mama to let her attend the garden party—and to allow her to discard the trappings of girlhood—she would have to invent a very good excuse indeed. Nothing short of a raging fever would convince Mama that she was incapacitated.

"Aurelia!" Her eyes opened at the first sound of her name. The second cry had her pushing up from the tree and scanning left and right, searching with eyes that ached from recently spent tears.

She would cry no more for this day's events. Or for him.

Looking up, she found Mama standing on the second floor balcony. Brushing off her skirts, Aurelia quickly stepped from the canopy of the tree and pasted a brittle smile upon her face.

"Ah, there you are, Aurelia!" Mama waved her hands with clear exasperation. "Look at you. What happened to your hair? You're a mess. We've much to do to prepare you. Inside with you now. Quickly!"

"Yes, Mama." Nodding, she hastened inside, her empty hands still brushing restlessly at her skirts.

Fortunately, no one stopped her as she moved through the house, reaching her chamber undetected. Once in her room, she moved to her dressing table and expelled a great breath. The girl who stared back at her was a wretched creature. Eyes red and puffy, nose swollen, her olive complexion waxy and sickly green. Her dark hair hung in tangled skeins around her shoulders.

She didn't like the hapless creature in the dressing table mirror. She vowed never to be her again. Never so naive. Never so foolish as to love someone incapable of loving her back. Shaking her head, she turned and gazed listlessly out the mullioned panes of her window.

Turning back to face her reflection, she picked up her brush and began attacking her hair, determined to set herself to rights—to rid herself of the evidence of the foolish girl she had been, harboring a *tendre* for a man who had no interest in her, who merely humored her childish infatuation.

Lowering her brush, she glared at herself, wishing she never had to clap eyes on Max again. Only she knew she would. There was no escaping him. As her misery ebbed, anger took its place. Anger at herself for being so foolish. Anger at Camden for being such a cad. She stirred her ire, swirling it around inside her, drawing strength as the fire in her heart died. She vowed she would be better for it. Smarter. Stronger. Immune to any handsome gentleman whose kindness masked a lecherous nature and faithless heart.

Never again would her heart burn.

From then on, her heart was encased in ice.

The garden party was no small affair. Not that he should have expected otherwise, Max thought. Lady Peregrine was not one to go about anything in small measures.

He glanced up at the sun and cloud-dappled sky. It was the most sunlight he had seen since summer. He would not be surprised if Lady Peregrine had negotiated with the Almighty Himself for this fine spring afternoon. The lawn was a verdant green dotted with linen-draped tables, livery-clad servants, and ladies in bright dresses, parasols angled demurely over their faces lest they freckle.

A pair of fresh-faced debutantes strolled past Max and his cohorts, sending them long, flirtatious glances.

"Look there now. The Pelby sisters are looking fine this day." Will nudged a scowling Declan with an elbow. "There are perks to be had for enduring one of my mother's parties."

"'Perks'?" Declan groused. "You cannot touch any of these 'perks.'" He kicked at the ground with a boot. "Not unless you want to face a parson's trap. Damned frustrating, if you ask me. It's like being shown a feast but permitted only water to sip."

Will chuckled.

Max agreed. Not that he was complaining, of course. His morning tryst had well sated him. He was now content to while away the holiday with his friends.

"I'm not jesting." Declan leveled both of them a somber look. "I say we slip away to visit the local tavern."

Max scanned the horizon of tables and guests, searching for a pair of dark brown plaits. He doubted her mother would allow her to attend the party, but he knew Aurelia couldn't be far. She was indomitable that way. If a party was afoot, she would not be one to miss it. Even if that meant she hid beneath a table.

In her last missive, she had promised to show him the progress she had made with her sketching. Not that he was any judge of fine art, but he appreciated her talent. Almost as much as he appreciated her. She might be a young girl, but Aurelia was an amusing and clever little thing. He smiled and slightly shook his head. She might also very well be the only female he called friend.

"Come." Will's voice distracted Max from his search. "I have something to take your minds off the unattainable perks of my mother's garden party." Will patted the front of his jacket. At Max's lifted eyebrow, Will lifted his jacket, revealing a glimpse of the flask inside. "Something to divert, eh?"

"That's a blasted fine idea," Declan said, nodding. "Let's get to it, lads." He led them through the thick press of guests and around the side of the house.

They did not advance very far before noticing a group of laughing young bucks near the large oak tree that Aurelia often sat beneath with her sketch pad. Apparently they'd had enough of the garden party's niceties as well.

Max marked several familiar faces in the group, including that of Archibald Lewis, the vicar's son. He could scarcely tolerate the fellow, but, unfortunately, he was a neighbor of Will's and he had to be endured.

"Who invited Lewis?" Declan grumbled.

"He's my neighbor, Dec," Will replied as they strolled toward the group. "And the vicar's son. How could we not invite him? Let's get this over with." There was no escape greeting them.

"At least hide the flask," Dec grumbled. "I'm not sharing it with the likes of Fish-Stink Lewis." Lewis had a certain unpleasant aroma that had earned him the designation among their set.

Archibald Lewis looked up at their approach. "Speak of the devil!" he chortled, waving a pad in the air.

Lewis's three companions swung around. The instant their gazes landed on Max they broke into loud guffaws. Two of them bent over, clutching their guts as though in pain. Will and Dec exchanged bewildered glances with Max. He shrugged back at them, at a loss over the men's hysterics.

"What's so blasted funny, Lewis?" Will asked.

The vicar's son wiped tears of mirth from his blotchy face. "I had no idea this garden party would be so amusing, Merlton." He shoved the pad they had been studying at Will.

Max leaned forward and stared down at the parchment, which depicted a caricature of himself. He wrested the pad from Will and looked his fill, absorbing the grossly exaggerated image. The blood rushed to his face as his gaze devoured the picture. The features were definitely his.

Even if the horns on his head were not.

Even if the tiny, minuscule cock was not.

If he had to hazard a guess, he would say that the artist's knowledge of male anatomy stemmed from observations of ancient Greek art. Michaelangelo could have fashioned no smaller a cock than this.

"What . . . who—" Will sputtered.

Dec only gaped, shaking his head in bewilderment.

But Max knew the artist.

As uproarious laughter spun around him, the knowledge penetrated Max like claws locking deep. He knew instantly whose sketch pad he held. He knew of Aurelia's penchant for drawing better than anyone. No one else possessed a thimbleful of the talent necessary for this level of skill.

"Cockless Camden!" Lewis hooted, doubling over and slapping his knee.

Max lowered the pad and glared at Lewis. Several of the others took up the chant and he saw red. A muscle ticked in his jaw. He felt it there, pulsing in violent rhythm with his fury.

Will took Max by the arm and tried to pull him away. "Come. Let us go."

He shook his head, unable to move. Unable to see anything past the haze of red. Unable to feel anything past the sting of Aurelia's betrayal flowing in his veins and settling acrid in his mouth.

Why? Why would she have sketched him thusly? She was a child . . . and his friend for all of that. His gaze dropped back to the image of himself—a horned satyr with wild eyes and a shrunken manhood. Was it mere jest to her? And how could she have left it for others to find? She had to know it would be discovered. Especially this day of the garden party.

With the blood still rushing to his head, his gaze zeroed in on Lewis's fleshy lips. "Cockless Camden, Cockless Camden, Cockless Camden," spilled out to the background of riotous laughter.

Max didn't think. His fist shot out. Smashed into Lewis's gleeful face. Bone crunched bone.

Blood spurted. Tucking the pad beneath his arm, he turned and beat a hard line for the house, intent on confronting Aurelia.

Subdued laughter followed him as he stalked away . . . coupled with Lewis's curses and the muffled mantra from the rest of them. "Cockless Camden . . . Cockless Camden."

He didn't have to go very far before spotting her. She was running directly for him. Only she had changed. Everything inside him seized and pulled up hard. This was the Aurelia he'd left a year ago, and yet it was not.

She was different. Gone were the plaits and girlhood frock. The deep brown hair was pinned atop her head. One fat sausage curl draped over her shoulder and wound itself down, the tip curling between the generous swells of her breasts. That bodice . . . those curves . . . those breasts. She was not a child. He could not stop himself from staring, from devouring the sight of her. She was lovely. Teeth-achingly sweet . . .

The rush of blood to his head intensified, and that only made him more furious. He felt as though he had been knocked a blow to the head. First the picture. Now this. He felt doubly betrayed. His friend was gone. This beautiful heartless creature stood in her place.

Based on the flush staining her face, he knew she could hear the vulgar chant at his back. Her fists knotted in her skirts, the knuckles white. His gaze held hers, the knowledge of her treachery digging deep.

In that gaze, he read more than embarrassment. Shame was there. She stood frozen, clenching her skirts as the color drained from her cheeks. Guilt was writ all over her face. She knew what she had done. She glanced from the pad he clutched in his hands back up to his face. She saw. She knew what he was feeling.

Without a word, he turned from the laughing boys. He turned from her.

He strode away without a backward glance.

Chapter 1

Seven years later . . .

Max knew it was Aurelia the instant she sat down at the table. Or rather, the moment she plopped into the chair across from him. The black gown she wore was so indecently tight she wasn't capable of sinking into her seat with any standard of grace. Her ridiculous disguise could not hide her from him.

He stilled, his entire body going rigid. The dress. *Her.* At this table. None of it was right or proper. Familiar ice chugged through his veins at the unexpected sight of her here, of all places. The most illicit of clubs. Young ladies of privilege weren't supposed to know places like this even existed, much less step across the threshold. He shouldn't be surprised. Aurelia had never fit Society's vaunted criteria for young womanhood.

The laughter and buzz of conversation faded to a dull growl around him as his gaze tunneled through copious cigar smoke to peer at Aurelia. His lip curled as though he had identified something distasteful. He tracked her every curve, missing nothing. Not the absurd wig of golden hair piled atop her head. Not the olive-hued skin. Nor the whiskey-warm eyes.

His body reacted instantly. How could it not? He was a man in possession of healthy appetites, and however much he did not care for the chit, she was thoroughly beddable in that scandalous dress. He'd known she was voluptuous, but he had no idea she had been hiding a courtesan's body beneath her clothes these many years. And that was what every man in this room thought as they devoured the sight of her. That she was a whore for the taking. A quick glance around confirmed as much.

The backside he had glimpsed before she sat

down was well-rounded, with generous cheeks that would fill a man's hands. He eyed the narrow waist that pooled into flaring hips. His mouth dried. Her body was made for sex. No quick and gentle mating that ladies with delicate sensibilities engaged in under the cover of darkness. She would take everything a man could give and revel in it. All *he* could give. Rough and fast. Base and primal. She wasn't a fragile piece of crystal that would break beneath a hard shag.

He leaned back in his seat as though needing to insert additional space between them. His hand slid beneath the table to adjust his cock where it had grown achingly hard. He huffed out a breath, furious that she should make him feel this way. He did not *like* her. He'd sooner take a viper into his bed than this chit who had caused him such grief.

No one called him Cockless Camden anymore. At least not to his face, but it took years to put an end to that. Even now he knew the slur was still whispered behind his back. People thought it. The repercussions of that caricature followed him still. Every time he got naked with a woman, he read the surprise in her eyes. The relief.

"Gentlemen," she greeted, her gaze fixing on him. The taunting light in the brown depths made his skin tighten with familiar battle-readiness. "Room for one more?"

"Always room for so beautiful a lady," the man to Max's left replied as he shuffled cards.

What the bloody hell was she doing here? He stared hard at her, letting his gaze convey his outrage.

She smiled prettily, her plump lips curving beneath her scarlet domino. The domino was a joke. As was the wig. Anyone who was more than a passing acquaintance with Aurelia would recognize her. Which only made her ten kinds of a fool for even stepping foot in Sodom. Even right now her cousin, Declan, was upstairs.

"Thank you." She treated each man at the table to her smile. "What is the wager, gentlemen?"

Everything in him clenched hard. He wanted to wrench her up from the table, drag her from the club and stuff her into a carriage for home. Only that would call more attention than necessary. Not that she didn't deserve a little public shaming. God knew, he had suffered enough of that over the years. Thanks to her. Pummeling anyone who dared call him Cockless Camden to his face and shagging half the women in the country had gone a long way in proving his virility and dismissing the moniker.

But if Aurelia's presence here went public, it

would ruin her. He couldn't do that to Will or Declan. Instead, he traced the rim of his glass as he stared at her, hoping she grasped the full extent of his fury. Hoping she was afraid.

"We play for high stakes." He raked her with his eyes. "Too high for you, I am certain."

He knew the dig would wound. He knew because he knew of her brother's dwindling funds. Her pin money could not be very prodigious.

She sniffed and pulled back her shoulders. An action that only pushed out those magnificent breasts. Everything in him twisted tight as the edge of an areola, dusky dark where it met her olive-hued skin, came into view. Reaching for his glass he downed it and signaled for another one.

And he wasn't the only one getting an eyeful. Every man at the table was looking, salivating at the sight of her flesh. Scowling, he took in each of their hungry stares before returning his gaze to her.

"High stakes don't frighten me," she announced.

"They should," he growled, and then added beneath his breath, "Daft girl."

She heard him. Or read his lips. The hands that rested on the top of the table curled into fists. "What's amiss? Afraid you will lose?"

"One night upstairs," the man to his left blurted, boldly tossing down the gauntlet. "Winner claims one night with you in an upstairs chamber," he clarified, as though his meaning wasn't evident. The bastard then winked at Aurelia.

Max arched an eyebrow, waiting for her to flee. Now she would surely see. Now she would understand that she had gotten in over her head. He watched, waiting for her to come to her senses and excuse herself.

Her brown eyes locked on his as she asked, "And if I win?"

He slid his hands beneath the table and gripped his thighs, his fingers digging deep as he leaned forward. Mad chit. She was *not* doing this. He shook his head once at her. Hard.

"Whatever you want. Name your prize," one of the other men offered, leering at her chest as he did so.

Her gaze roamed over each man at the table, assessing. Four in all, counting him. She thought she could best all of them? She was playing with fire and she knew it.

"I'll have . . ." Aurelia paused, her gaze resting on him again, considering. "Your clothes."

The man beside him choked. "Our clothes?"

She nodded, smiling pertly.

"You'll have each of us strip down to our bare arse right here?" another demanded.

"You cannot think to win. You *will* lose," Max hissed, letting that sink in her fool head. She would lose and be at the mercy of one of them. In that moment, he did not think she would prefer to be subject to him. Not as furious as he was.

She shrugged one shoulder. It looked as smooth as marble, and he imagined touching it, stroking the flesh and discovering if it was as soft as it appeared. One of the men at this table could very well win that privilege if he let her do this. Daft female. He should just walk away. Let one of them have her. It would serve her right, playing with fire.

And yet she was Will's sister. He couldn't leave her to those wolves.

"I'm in," he announced, hating to utter the words even as he had no choice. He would take the wager and he would win and save her from this fine mess.

He admitted there would be some satisfaction in beating her. She thought she could win. For no other reason would she have agreed to these terms. He would relish besting her.

The other men quickly chimed in their own accord.

"Let us begin then, gentlemen." Still wearing

that insufferable smile, she nodded for the game to commence with a magnanimous wave of her hand.

The cards were dealt quickly and efficiently. He watched everyone's faces closely as they played, reading for the slightest reaction.

He trained his features into a mask of impassivity. No expression. Even when the first two men tossed down their cards in defeat. Rising, they stripped off their clothes with grumbles.

A crowd gathered, jeering at their pale, naked bodies on display. Aurelia dipped her gaze to her cards, but not before he read the amusement glimmering there. She was enjoying herself. Bloody fool. She hadn't an inkling of the predicament she was in.

"Having a good time?" he bit out.

"Adequate," she retorted, treating him to a chilly smile.

Shaking his head, he tightened his focus on the cards he held, placing one on the table and drawing a new one with nary a change in expression. There were just three of them left now, Aurelia, himself, and the man to his left.

The stranger knew what he was about. Not so surprising, since the wager had been his idea. He was confident and hard to read. Max's gut churned uneasily, suspecting that he and Aurelia had perhaps been lulled into a swindle by a sharp. He glanced down at his hand, hoping for her sake that it was enough.

He watched the stranger draw fresh cards and then lift his gaze to Aurelia. "Well, my love?" the man murmured. "What have you?"

She toyed with the edges of her cards, bending them slightly, as she was not supposed to do. Not that any man at this table would correct her. No, she was by far too mesmerizing in her shocking gown, her breasts on full display.

Max's fingers clenched around his cards, the knuckles whitening. "Be quick about it. We haven't all night."

Her gaze shot to him. "I'm sorry. Am I keeping you from more diverting sport?"

"You'll be free to go about your diversions soon enough," the stranger smoothly inserted, locking gazes with Max. "Once the lady and I adjourn to one of Mrs. Bancroft's chambers upstairs."

"Awfully confident, aren't you?" Max asked, the silky edge to his voice deceptively calm.

The stranger smiled widely, revealing yellowed, furry teeth. "Our friend here is impatient, my fine lady. Shall we put him out of his misery and let him face his defeat?"

"After you," Aurelia insisted.

"Why not?" Furry Teeth shrugged. "Let us be done then. And on to more pleasant pursuits."

Apprehension finally flickered within her eyes. The emotion was visible for just a moment through the eyeholes of her scarlet domino. Now she feared she might have overstepped, did she? When it might be too late. Fool. Did she expect him to save her? Blast her, he should leave her to hang herself. Let the brute take her upstairs.

Furry Teeth fanned his cards out before him with a flourish. Applause erupted around them. Max stifled a curse and flung his cards down on the table. He'd lost.

Furry Teeth chuckled and wagged a finger at him. "You, my friend, best undress yourself whilst I take this little morsel upstairs and collect my winnings." Rising, he extended a hand toward Aurelia. "Come, sweetings. A wager is a wager, after all."

Aurelia lifted her bowed head just as Max started to rise. Not to undress himself but to stop that filth from touching her. Wretched girl or not, he would not let this vermin take her. He could not. Even if that meant reneging on a bet. His friendship with her kin demanded he protect her.

"Do you not wish to see my cards?" She queried softly.

All eyes turned to the table as she spread her cards in an arc. Surprised gasps rippled all around them.

She'd won.

Furry Teeth let out an oath.

She leaned back in her chair in the manner of a victorious queen and leveled her gaze on him. "A wager is a wager," she echoed. "I believe I'll collect my winnings now."

Furry Teeth began stripping off his clothes in angry movements, revealing his pale skinny limbs. Entirely naked, he quickly sank back down in his chair and sat there sulking much like the other two men who had already shed their clothes.

Aurelia lifted an eyebrow at him. "Well, my lord? Do you not honor your bets?"

"Honor?" He chuckled low and deep, the sound raw and prickly in his throat. "That is not a word I expect you to understand."

Her smile turned brittle. "Are you delaying on purpose? The hour grows late, my lord."

Max shoved himself to his feet, sending the chair skidding backward. He yanked off his jacket, cravat and vest, his eyes never leaving her face. Reaching behind his neck, he pulled his shirt over his head and tossed it aside in one smooth move.

A woman nearby made a hissing sound of approval.

The corner of his mouth kicked up in acknowledgment. He knew he was well-formed. He spent a goodly amount of time riding, fencing, swimming, fighting. He was not ashamed of his body. That said, he did not appreciate being forced to undress so that he could be ogled and made a spectacle of.

Anger, hot as molten rock, poured through him. It was in his every hard movement. The crowd fell silent around him as he removed one boot, then the next. His hands went to the front of his trousers and hesitated.

She watched him, her throat working as she swallowed.

"Is this what you want?" he demanded.

The color rode high in her face, crowding the edges of her domino. She was getting more than she bargained for. She realized that now.

He leaned across the table, flattening his palms on the baize surface and bringing his face inches from her. "This is what you've been so curious about? Is it not?"

Her breath escaped in a sharp hitch. "You flatter yourself."

"You set the stake, not I. Shall I satisfy your curiosity at last?" His voice dropped to a whisper. "Now you can infuse some reality into your artwork. That will be a refreshing bit of change, won't it?"

Her nostrils flared. Her words escaped in a low hiss for his ears alone, "There is truth in my drawings."

Her words struck him like steel striking flint. She was that same little witch who'd created that caricature and left it for public ridicule. He laughed once, hard and unforgiving. "You're about to witness the truth. Pay close heed so next time I expect you to get it right."

"I've drawn you once. No need to repeat the task."

He tsked. "Come now. I fascinate you as a subject. You know it. I know it."

"Rubbish," she spat, her gaze sparking fire through the eyeholes of her domino.

"Shall I prove it?" Shoving back off the table, he dropped his hands to the front of his trousers. Tearing loose the buttons, he shoved them down and stood naked before the room. Unlike the other men, he did not sink into his chair. He let the room have a long look. He let *her* drink her fill.

Her mouth popped wide in a little *o*. Those eyes of hers traveled over him, missing nothing. She looked everywhere. Especially *there.*

Those big brown eyes of hers grew larger yet. She looked for so long and so intently that his cock stirred. He knew he should have felt a stab of embarrassment as he grew before her eyes. Or perhaps not. This was Sodom, after all, where all manner of illicit activity happened before all manner of audience. Nothing was too shameful. Nothing private.

His response to her irked him. The stroke of her gaze shouldn't make him randy as a green lad. Any other female, fine. Only not *her*.

"Gor," a woman clucked from the crowd. "I wouldn't mind a ride on that."

Fire lit Aurelia's cheeks.

She had failed. She might have won the wager, but he was the victor. She had planned to embarrass him and failed. Satisfied, he sank down in his chair.

The crowd dissipated around them. The men hastily redressed and retreated, but he remained where he was, naked in the chair, holding her gaze for a moment.

"Not so cockless. Am I?" he queried lightly.

"You've proven that well enough," she replied evenly, the color in her face becoming less red and more pink.

"Do well to remember it in your spinster bed tonight," he flung out. "Or perhaps someday you will wed and have but a puny rod to take between your thighs. You'll think of me often then, will you not?"

"You're vile." She surged to her feet and started past him, but he grabbed her wrist, squeezing the delicate bones in his grip. She looked down at him, her brown eyes luminescent within her mask.

He rolled his thumb against the inside of her wrist, feeling her pulse flutter there as wild as a moth's wings. "Don't ever come here again."

"You do not command me."

"But that is what you need. A strict hand to lead you." His gaze raked her. "Look at you. Look where you are." He waved a hand about them.

"I command myself."

"Do you? Very well, then," he sneered, flinging her from him as though he could not stand the feel of her a moment longer. "Next time I'll let any manner of man take you upstairs and claim your virtue. If, in fact, you're still in possession of it—"

His words hit the mark. A stricken look crossed

her face before disappearing and giving way to a cheery smile. "You forget yourself, Camden. You did not rescue me. It is *you* who lost the wager to *me*."

Still wearing that bright smile, she turned away, her hips moving in a way he had never noticed before, swaying as she took small, tight steps in her black gown. A gown that he suddenly envisioned wadded up in a ball at the foot of his bed. That would be one way to *command* her, he thought, watching hungrily as she disappeared through the crowd of Mrs. Bancroft's sitting room. Indeed, he could command her in his bed. Beneath him. If he didn't find her so detestable, that would be the perfect place for her.

Chapter 2

One year later . . .

"Come, Aurelia. Must you dawdle? Usually you are the one urging *me* to make haste, but here you sit staring into space with half our guests gathered belowstairs."

Aurelia feigned an innocent expression and met her mother's blue-eyed gaze through the dressing table mirror. She had been lost in one of her drawings—a depiction of Lord Edderton with the body of an octopus manhandling several young girls whilst munching iced biscuits. She had been on the receiving end of his attentions once, during her first season out, and decided to make him the subject of one of her caricatures when she spotted him up to his old tricks a few evenings ago.

Edderton would not be the first to find himself featured in one of her notorious caricatures. What happened all those years ago with Camden, however accidental, had led her to this vocation. *Cockless Camden*. She winced, knowing she was to blame. His caricature had started it all, however inadvertent. It was talked about for years and had earned her his eternal enmity.

True, she did the drawing in a fit of impulse, but she had not meant it to be discovered. She couldn't change that day, but she hoped using her talent for good, to give those without a voice a voice . . . perhaps it was atonement of some sort. Now her sketches appeared all over London. They turned up at balls, the opera, the dressmaker's shop. She deliberately deposited them in the most public place. For the edification and titillation of the *ton*.

She adjusted her weight on the bench in front of her dressing table, hoping her skirts hid the pad from view. She'd barely had time enough to shove her sketch pad beneath her before Mama stormed into the chamber. It wouldn't do for the

Earl of Merlton's sister to be unveiled as the artist responsible for the ribald cartoons that poked fun at so many members of the *ton*.

"Go on without me, Mama. I'll be down directly."

Mama gave her a lingering look before nodding. "Very well." In a whisper of amber-gold skirts, she turned and left Aurelia alone in her chamber.

Aurelia returned her gaze to her reflection. Her dark eyes stared back at her pensively. She looked nothing like her fair-haired mother. Or her brother, for that matter. With her dark eyes and hair and skin, she looked more like a foundling her family had adopted into its fold. The bloodlines of her Spanish grandmother ran strong and true within her—a fact that did not win her much favor among the *ton*. Even her mother bemoaned her swarthy looks, though she had never been so unkind to voice such criticisms openly. No, she was more discreet than that. Instead she constantly supplied Aurelia with various powders to help dim her countenance.

Smiling wryly, she reached for a beaded bracelet and then set it back down with a sigh. A bracelet would make no difference to the night's outcome. Another dinner party filled with empty chatter. And tomorrow morning she would wake to yet another day of activities planned by her mother. Luncheon with the ladies from one of Mama's many charitable societies. Teas. Shopping. A ball or the opera or a dinner party in the evening. Her days stretched out before her in familiarity. All planned in the hopes that she would make a good match for herself. For the family. Even if she had not succeeded yet, it was expected she would.

Without her drawings, she would go mad. Her work gave her more than comfort. It gave her purpose.

Aurelia turned from her mirror and stood up from the dressing table, smoothing out her pale yellow skirts and trying not to think how poorly the color complemented her. Mama still tried to pretend she was a pale English rose who looked ethereal in all things pastel.

At least they needn't travel from home tonight. If she grew weary of it all, she could simply escape upstairs to her chamber, change into her nightgown, climb into bed with her sketch pad. There was solace in that.

She glanced at her bedchamber window. Rain sluiced down the mullioned glass. Abysmal weather plagued London this season—even more than usual. Another advantage for staying in tonight.

Squaring her shoulders, she departed her chamber before Mama sent someone to drag her down to dinner like a recalcitrant child and not a woman full grown. Lifting her skirts, she descended the staircase. Voices and laughter floated up from the drawing room. Hopefully, she was not the last to arrive. It would make her goal of slipping inside and finding a chair in the corner to observe the guests Mama had seen fit to invite all the more difficult. She liked watching people, listening to them, memorizing their characteristics to later catch on paper.

It was a safe assumption that Mama had selected the guests. Her brother was a married man now. His wife was the new countess and, thereby, the new hostess over all events taking place beneath this roof. Only Mama sometimes forgot that fact.

Living in the same house with her brother and his wife—no matter how much she liked Violet—was awkward. Under normal circumstances, she and Mama would have taken up residence at another property . . . a dowager estate or town house. Only her brother had sold the additional town house in London. He had, in fact, sold all properties that were not entailed, to help satisfy the nasty debts Papa had left behind after his death.

Papa had ruined them. It was a burden made only more onerous when Will fell in love with a woman who brought no dowry to the marriage. Aurelia couldn't begrudge him, however. He was brilliantly, ridiculously, in love with Violet. Aurelia was happy for both of them. And when Will assured her that his investments would soon reap benefit, she pretended to believe him. Perhaps he was correct and not merely delusional.

In the meantime, they all lived under one roof. She and Mama guests in the home that had once been their own. Her mother was merely the Dowager Countess now. And she was the unwed, cheeky sister. One breath from spinsterhood. No one knew of her secret vocation. Nor did anyone know that she secretly longed for more. For adventure.

She'd had a taste of it with her friend Rosalie, before she went off and married Declan. Now Rosalie was no longer a fit companion for illicit activities. There would be no more sneaking out in the middle of the night together. No more visits to Sodom, where she engaged in scandalous card games. Her face heated as she recalled Max that night. The vile man with his vile words and his impossibly wicked body had made her feel achingly alive.

Aurelia stopped outside the drawing room, listening to the hum of voices and clink of glasses as libations were dispersed and consumed. With a bracing breath, she entered the room to find that it was, indeed, brimming full. Declan and Rosalie were present, as well as Violet's parents, Mr. and Mrs. Howard. Mama's good friend, Lady Agatha, and her son, Lord Buckley—or Freddie to his familiars.

Aurelia fought a smile at the sight of Freddie's expression. He always wore a grin even when he stared vacantly into space. As boys, Will, Declan, and Max had pranked him mercilessly—nothing mean-spirited, just foolishness. A hidden shoe. A frog in his bed. Freddie had smiled through it all. Now, Freddie's gaze landed on her. He sat up straighter on the sofa and looked at her in that puppy dog manner of his, patting the space beside him for her to occupy. The fact that he resembled a hound dog with his long face and loose jowls only added to the visual. He would make an excellent subject for a caricature, but Aurelia wouldn't dream of depicting him in a less than flattering fashion. He was a kind soul. Once upon a time, Mama and Lady Agatha had anticipated a match between Freddie and herself.

Aurelia's lack of a dowry had put an end to that

notion. Lady Agatha might be her mother's best friend, but she was as mercenary as any other dame of the *ton*. At least one good thing resulted from their family's indigence. As much as she liked Freddie, Aurelia could not imagine spending the rest of her life with him.

Sinking down upon a chaise opposite of him, she accepted a proffered drink from a tray that appeared before her. "Thank you, Cecily," Aurelia murmured, lifting the cup to her lips.

Cecily winked. Only a year older than herself, the servant was like family. When they were forced to reduce the staff by half, Cecily had remained. Not only did she act in the capacity of her and Mama's maid, she helped in the kitchens and lent a hand when entertaining guests. She did whatever was required with no complaints.

Cecily gave a slight nod at something beyond Aurelia's shoulder and released a dreamy sigh. "Lord Camden is looking very fine tonight," she whispered.

Sipping her punch, Aurelia frowned and resisted looking. She didn't need to. She need only close her eyes and she could envision him perfectly standing naked in the middle of Sodom.

"Aurelia!" Rosalie cried, making her way across the drawing room with Violet at her side. "I did not see you arrive. You're quiet as a church mouse tonight."

Aurelia rose to her feet and returned Rosalie's embrace. "I did not want anyone to notice that I was the last to arrive."

"You? Not want to draw attention to yourself?" Rosalie leaned in close to whisper. "This coming from the female who challenged me to don a domino and sneak into Sodom?"

"Well, that was a year ago." Heat crept over her face at the memory of their late night visit to Sodom. With a tight smile, Aurelia looked away.

Her gaze drifted over the room—and collided with Max's gaze.

Their gazes locked. She wondered how long he had been staring at her. His gray-blue eyes were brilliant and piercing even across the distance. Set deeply beneath the slash of brows a shade darker than his chestnut hair, those eyes of his looked her up and down. He was probably hoping she stayed far from him. They tread warily around each other these days. Ever since the night at Sodom things had been tense. Even more than before.

To everyone else in the world, Camden was all charm. Not a serious bone in his body as he stood flirting with Freddie's sister. Aurelia considered the brunette. Henrietta was comely enough, and yet not to his precise taste. She knew he was fond of petite, golden-haired beauties.

Aurelia was neither dainty nor golden-haired.

She squeezed her eyes in a tight blink, reprimanding herself for caring how he might perceive her. Every once in a while it shocked her to remember that they had been friends. So many years had passed with each making war on the other.

She opened her eyes and took a deep breath. Perhaps it would have been easier if he was not such a handsome package. His good looks had not lessened over the years. His hair had not thinned. Nor had his chin begun to disappear into his neck.

Rosalie and Violet laughed then. Aurelia turned and joined in, feigning awareness of their discourse.

Out of the corner of her eye, she watched as Lady Agatha called Henrietta over to her side, beckoning her with sausagelike fingers. Max was momentarily alone. He cocked a dark eyebrow at Aurelia in silent challenge and executed an abbreviated bow that only seemed to show off his great height and strong physique. He was unlike other gentlemen of the *ton* who padded the shoulders of their jackets to distract from the bulge of their bellies.

Deciding to behave in a mature manner tonight, she squared her shoulders and strolled across the room toward him, her hem lightly brushing the Aubusson rug—an item she had overheard her brother mentioning must be sold.

She pushed aside thoughts of her family's insolvency and stopped before Max. *We will not quarrel tonight. I will don a smile and be all that is cordial and courteous.*

"My lord, how good of you to come," she greeted.

She rocked lightly on her slippered heels, hands folded demurely before her as she gazed up into his too handsome face. Unfortunately, even unsmiling he was bone-melting attractive.

"*Lady* Aurelia." He inclined his head, eyeing her cagily. The way he stressed the word Lady emphasized precisely how unladylike he deemed her. "I would not miss an invitation to dine with the Merlton tribe. You should know as much . . . you are always remarking upon my *excessive* presence at your family's gatherings."

She held her smile, determined not to rise to his baiting. She had no wish for Mama or Will to spy her across the room and fuss at her for squabbling with Max. They disapproved of the rancor between them. Mama found it ill-mannered of her. Not Max. Mama doted on him like a son and blamed Aurelia for their discord. Will simply thought their sniping was annoying and something they should have outgrown by now.

With her smile pasted firmly in place, she cocked her head as though considering his words. "You do tend be underfoot a good deal, do you not?" She lifted one shoulder in a half shrug and attempted an innocent expression.

Something sparked in his eyes. "A trial for you, I know. You prefer me six feet under, do you not? Then you might not have to tolerate my mien."

She sighed. It didn't matter if she tried to be nice. He was determined to keep things hostile between them. "I merely thought a *gentleman* such as yourself would have far more *fascinating* pursuits. Certainly we are beyond dull compared to your usual nighttime entertainments." She held his gaze. So much for not rising to his baiting.

He shook his head. "You would know something of those nighttime pursuits, yes, my lady?"

The wretch would have to fling Sodom at her. She didn't know what got into her that night. She had no plans to enter into that wager when she sat down at the table. He simply provoked her with his cocked eyebrow and sneering voice. Before she knew it, she had wagered her virtue.

A small, sardonic smile played about his lips as he surveyed her coldly. For a moment she thought his gaze lingered a trifle long on the demure display of her décolletage, but when his gaze returned to her face, there was nothing there. Her generous bosom, she had learned, proved a point of fascination for many gentlemen, and yet the only thing she read in his expression was his usual dispassion. When he looked at her, there was only ever impassivity.

"Much could be applied to your person, Lady Aurelia . . . but dull would not be an apt description. The words I would choose to describe you would not do to be uttered aloud in polite society."

"Ah, you flatter," she murmured, well aware that he did not mean to compliment her. Indeed not. She shoved aside the sting of his words and forced a bright smile on her face, knowing that her good cheer in the face of his jibes always irritated him, and irritating him was the only way she could hope to affect him. The only way at all.

Chapter 3

Flattery was not in his intention. Indeed not. Whenever Max spotted Aurelia, the skin at the back of his neck pulled tight and prickled as though crawling with ants. Ever since Sodom when she had divested him of his clothes, things felt decidedly unfinished between them. They danced about each other, striking and swiping. Engaging in brief skirmishes and then retreating. It all felt as though it were leading to something.

He was rather accustomed to females chasing

him. He usually let himself be caught. He'd made an occupation of it actually. After all, who was he to deny a lady?

And yet this was not the same game. Aurelia was different. She did not chase him. Ever. She wasn't after a romp between the sheets. He grimaced. The notion of that was too appalling to even consider. She could not abide him and he could not abide her. He wanted to provoke her. Needle her. Antagonize her. Shake her up so that she didn't bestow one of her cold, unaffected smiles on him.

He gestured at her. "What could possibly be more fascinating than an evening in your scintillating company?"

Her brown eyes glinted with suppressed emotion. Those eyes had not changed since she was a child. The same could not be said for the rest of her though. Gone was the blushing, awkward girl. In her place was a bold chit with curves abundant. Some might even assert she was on the plump side. The confection of ruffles and ribbons she wore did nothing to improve her form. Indeed, her ruffled and beribboned gowns made it difficult to detect if she even possessed a waist. Except he knew she did. He'd seen it for himself a year ago at Sodom. It was something he had tried forgetting. The image of her in that scandalous gown with her breasts practically spilling out of the bodice. Her small waist and generous hips and deliciously rounded bottom had all been on display.

"Oh, I'm certain there is a lady somewhere in this Town enticing enough to lure you from my company," she countered.

He blinked and smiled slowly. "You underestimate yourself."

She eyed him warily. "Are you trying to provoke me?"

"Why? Am I succeeding?"

"Of course not. You give yourself far too much credit, I fear."

Meaning he did not deserve a reaction. He felt a flash of anger.

Her gaze darted across the room. "Please. Cease scowling."

He crossed his arms over his chest. "Why?"

"Please smile. At least for appearance's sake. I prefer no lecture from Mama this evening because we did not rub along well together."

"My apologies. I don't feel like pretense this evening." He lifted his glass to her in mock salute before taking a slow drink. "I've had quite enough of it these many years."

She shook her head and started to move away, but then stopped. Her chest heaved slightly and he knew he had affected her. He felt a rush of triumph as she glared at him with gleaming eyes. "I've explained to Mama that you're a big boy now. You feed yourself and everything. But for some reason, she thinks you cannot handle yourself and require coddling and protection from me." She smirked. "We know that's not true, don't we?"

"I've a tough hide," he agreed tightly, shoving aside the memory of when she had eviscerated him with a simple drawing. He avoided her gaze and scanned the room, tension tightening his jaw. What was it about her that made him feel as though he were about to come out of his skin? The sensation had only worsened since the incident at Sodom.

"Indeed," she murmured, her false smile fixed in place for the sake of her onlooking Mama.

"This is an intimate gathering tonight," he remarked, adjusting his stance. At the idleness of his tone, she shifted on her feet and moistened her lips, her brown eyes watching him warily. "No swains of your own to include in the group?" he added with a tsk of his tongue. "Usually your mother makes certain you have a few prospects in attendance. Whatever is the matter, Aurelia? Scare them all away?"

She hissed out a slow breath, as if battling for control. "Some of us have discriminating tastes."

" 'Some' of us," he rejoined, lowering his mouth to the rim of his glass, "are about as appealing as a rabid monkey." Her eyes flared and then narrowed at the bold insult. He continued, knowing he was close. She was about to snap. "Have you considered hanging a rope of garlic about your neck? That might improve your allure."

Her smile finally, at last, fled. Hot color suffused her cheeks. Her arms dropped stiffly to her sides, hands curling into fists. "Unlike you, my self-worth does not revolve around how many conquests I can make."

He chuckled, feeling very much like he had just won a skirmish. "The last I heard, you have no conquests. Pity." He leaned down close to her ear as though to impart something of great importance. His warm breath fanned her neck and he did not miss the small shiver that rolled through her. Nor did he miss the faint waft of bergamot that seemed to rise up off her skin. *Would she taste of bergamot, too*? The thought only flared his ire. He did not care what the hellion tasted like. "Might I suggest you cease being such a brat? That might improve your chances." He stepped closer. Perhaps unseemly so. He did not care. "Perhaps you should cease your inappropriate pursuits."

"I don't know your meaning."

"Leaving artwork all over Town that pokes fun at the echelons of Society?"

"Oh. That." Her lashes fluttered over her eyes.

"Yes." He nodded. "*That* inappropriate pursuit. You've become quite notorious. Did you think I would not know it was you?"

She shrugged in an attempt to look unaffected, but the color still rode high in her cheeks. "Why have you not said anything, then? To anyone? You know it's me. You could ruin me. That would give you some satisfaction, would it not?"

"Why have I not outed you? Denounced you?" He snorted and rubbed a finger against his bottom lip, considering her. "For the same reason that I did not reveal your identity at Sodom. I care for my friends. Your brother and cousin. Your mother. They needn't know what you really are."

"And what am I?"

"Don't make me say it."

"You've never held back before."

"You're a brat, Aurelia. Spoiled, shallow. And what's worse? You think you're so very clever."

She looked away quickly, her throat working

as she swallowed. The only outward sign that his words even affected her. Such a cold one. "Of course."

He nodded. "But you will be discovered."

"I haven't been yet." That chin of hers went up a notch.

"But you will be. You must stop."

"You don't understand." She shook her head.

"You're correct. I don't understand. I don't understand risking your reputation . . . your family's good name, all because you can't stop drawing your silly pictures and spreading them all about Town. Have you no care for your family?"

His words clearly struck a nerve. Fresh color splashed her apple-round cheeks, and she looked as though she wanted to strike him with one of her balled-up hands, but a quick glance across the room at her mother stayed her.

Aurelia inhaled a deep breath and forced a smile back in place. It looked downright menacing on her face as she snapped her gaze back and addressed him with a good amount of chill in her voice. "I understand you're courting the Widow Knotgrass."

And just like that she seized the advantage. Changing the topic and flinging the fact that he was—once again—the subject of gossip.

"Reading the scandal rags, Lady Aurelia?" he sneered.

He didn't like *her* nosing about his personal affairs. She meddled. If the opportunity presented itself to thwart him, she took it. Just like that night at Sodom. It had started before then, really. It had commenced when she drew him with a minuscule cock. And countless little injuries since then. Mud in his boots. Salt to his soup. And his porridge. And his pudding.

"It passes the time." She shrugged. "And news of Lord Camden courting is not mere gossip." She clucked her tongue and shook her head. "Oh, no, no. That's information of countrywide import," she mocked. "Tell me, do you have journalists camped out on your stoop?"

"Oh, is this when I should laugh at your shrewd wit? Hilarious. Again, it's no wonder you have not snared some fine, upstanding gentleman with an appreciation for being flayed alive. I've heard there are those sorts. Men who enjoy suffering at the hands of a woman. I can investigate the matter and make some recommendations."

"You're insufferable."

"And yet here you stand . . . riveted."

"I hear they are placing bets as to whether you will finally settle down with the Widow Knotgrass."

"Indeed?" He revealed nothing. Not a hint of reaction. He'd shared an opera box with the widow a week ago and already there was speculation that he would wed her? Ridiculous. He would marry no one. Ever.

Not that his intentions toward the Widow Knotgrass were platonic. He was certain their relationship would follow the natural course of things and end with him in her bed. The widow's hand fondling his crotch during the second act signified how amenable she was to that prospect.

"Mama is ever hopeful."

He snorted.

"I know. Laughable, is it not?" She sighed. "Mama fails to understand you as I do."

He narrowed his gaze on her. "You think you understand me?"

She leveled her brown eyes on him so steadily it unnerved him. He drained his glass and then looked about, in dire need of a refill. "For the record, the widow and I are not courting—"

"Bedding, then?" She gazed up at him in all seriousness, this dark-haired virago uttering things no gently bred lady should ever say. It was troubling. It played tricks with his mind. Made him momentarily forget she was a lady. It filled his head with dirty images of skirts hiked up around her thighs. *Bloody hell.* Such thoughts had to end. This was Aurelia.

"If your brother had any notion of the things you say—"

"But you're not going to tell him," she pertly reminded.

He scowled and glanced over at Will. A part of Max longed to inform him of her unseemly behavior. And yet he would refrain. A true friend did not alert one to the fact that his sister was less than innocent. And for whatever else he was, he liked to think he was a good friend to Will.

"I should," he grumbled. "Before you get yourself into trouble."

She smiled, evidently remembering the night she had divested him of his clothing—and a good amount of his dignity. "I was at no risk that night."

He shook his head and looked out at the room, feeling a quick stab of anger as he recalled her in the dress again. "I disagree. You cannot even fathom the risk you placed yourself in that night."

"You're not my father, Camden. Or my brother. And you certainly lack the moral integrity to sit in judgment of me. I do as I please." She whirled away in a swish of yellow skirts.

He watched as she crossed the room, marveling that he had intentionally provoked her when it was now he that felt unsettled. Muttering a curse, he turned in search of a fresh drink.

Chapter 4

Dinner proceeded in a much less diverting fashion.

Aurelia's ire at the nerve of Camden lecturing *her* on risky behavior had cooled considerably by the time she took her seat beside Freddie. Camden sat beside Henrietta, and Aurelia avoided looking in his direction throughout dinner lest she become annoyed all over again.

Toward the end of the meal, Will rose from his seat and took a position beside his wife's chair. He rested a hand on Violet's shoulder. A secret look passed between them as she smiled up at him, covering his hand with hers.

Something pinched in Aurelia's chest at the sight of the small, intimate look. The evidence of their love. She quickly pushed it away.

Will cleared his throat. Gradually, conversation faded as all attention shifted to her brother.

"We'd like to thank you all for gathering here with us. Family, friends . . ." He smiled as his gaze scanned the room. "We have much to celebrate tonight."

Aurelia drank in the sight of her brother, her heart lifting. Perhaps he had received news that his investments had finally reaped profits. Then she and Mama would no longer need to live underfoot anymore. They could give Will and Violet their space and take up residence elsewhere. A happy smile curved her lips and she leaned forward in her chair expectantly.

Will looked down at Violet, his blue eyes so like Mama's . . . bright and full of something she had never seen before. Not that she hadn't seen him happy before, especially since he met Violet. But this was a different sort of happiness . . . there was something soft and tender in his eyes.

His chest lifted on a breath as he announced, "Violet and I are expecting a child."

The room erupted. Mrs. Howard fairly screeched as she surged up from her chair, sending it toppling back with no regard for decorum. Rosalie soon followed with her exclamations, as did others. It was a blur of movement and activity as Will and Violet were beset with well wishes and hugs.

Aurelia did not move for some moments. She remained in her chair, processing this bit of information. She was not immediately filled with elation and could not fathom her reaction. Of course, she knew her brother would likely have children. She wanted that for him and Violet. She enjoyed children. She wanted to be an aunt. And yet she had thought this would be later down the road. When she was not living with her brother and his wife and a burden to them both. When the Merlton finances were more in order.

The enormity of the situation dawned on her then.

Dear heavens. She and Mama would be living with her brother and his wife as they raised their children. She winced, imagining Mama behaving as a second mother to Will's children. Well-meaning as she was, Mama would not be able to stop herself from interfering. It was embedded in her blood. She had been the matriarch of their family far too long. Aurelia could envision it. Violet growing resentful, and as a result, Will too. They would look at Mama—and her—as an old family painting no one wanted around any longer but couldn't do away with because of obligation.

Aurelia felt dazed as she uttered the proper congratulations and well-wishes. Even as she followed everyone into the drawing room for a celebratory toast. Amid all the chatter, amid Henrietta playing at the pianoforte, she felt as though her world had dramatically shifted.

"You do not look pleased," a deep voice said near her ear.

She blinked at Max standing so very close.

"Whatever do you mean?" Heat rushed over her face at his nearness. "Of course I am thrilled."

"Mmm," he murmured, looking unconvinced.

She fidgeted under this blue-eyed scrutiny. "You think you can read me so well?"

He stared at her for a long moment before announcing quietly, "You perceive me an idiot, do you?" He chuckled lightly but the sound held no mirth. Indeed, it made her shift uneasily on her feet. "Well, I know you," he quickly added. "Spoiled, selfish . . ."

She bristled, hating that his words stung. He did not have the power to hurt her. Not anymore.

"Perhaps," he continued, his voice silky now, "you are jealous."

"Jealous?" Her hand fluttered to her throat. "Of my brother and Violet having a baby?"

He nodded. "It happens among females. Your brother finding happiness, moving on, starting a family. Leaving you behind."

She sucked in a breath at the cruel jab of his words and blinked fiercely. He was wrong. She did *not* resent her brother's happiness. Even if she did wish for a slice of similar happiness for herself, she did not begrudge him his own.

"And what of you?" she demanded, leaning closer and pasting a smile on her face lest anyone glance their way and see her scowling. "The lone wolf standing? Are you not jealous? Do you not miss your companions? Who do you carouse with these days?"

He smiled that insufferable grin again. "I'm never alone for long. I've no difficulty finding companions."

She rolled her eyes and looked away, still fuming over his accusation.

Kendrick, the butler, entered the room then. He glanced around, appearing quite harried, his commonly splotchy expression even more flushed than usual. Spotting Max, he quickly made his way across the floor to where they stood together.

With a polite nod at Aurelia, he cleared his throat before leaning in to whisper for Max's ears alone. She edged closer, trying to decipher whatever he was imparting.

A frown marred Max's features for a heartbeat—then he was smiling again as though nothing was untoward. Rising, he murmured to Aurelia, "If you'll excuse me. I need a bit of fresh air."

With a meaningful nod at Kendrick, he exited the drawing room through the balcony doors.

Something was afoot. She was certain of it.

Aurelia tracked Kendrick's movements as he made his way across the room to her brother's side. In much the same surreptitious manner that he had whispered to Camden, he whispered into Will's ear. Curious indeed.

She was debating whether to approach her brother and demand an explanation or to follow Camden outside when the door to the drawing room, left slightly ajar, was flung open. It struck the wall with an unceremonious crack. A gentleman strode in, glancing wildly around.

Everyone stopped talking at his bold entrance. His cravat hung askew, as though he had been in the process of removing it not very long ago and then forgot he had set about the task.

She had to applaud her brother. He failed to look the least shocked as he turned to face the intruder. "Lord Arlington. This is an unexpected surprise."

Ah. Arlington. Aurelia vaguely recognized the gentleman now.

"Merlton." The man nodded once at Will, his gaze hardly touching on him. He was too busy scanning the room, his gaze skipping over each person, clearly searching for someone.

Obviously dissatisfied with his findings, he grunted and swung his gaze back to her brother. "Where is he?"

"He? Who?" Will blinked innocently.

Arlington expelled a great breath, as if mustering patience. "I just left his town house where I was told he was dining here this evening."

"My apologies, Lord Arlington, I haven't the foggiest notion who you're talking about. As you can see, our entire party is assembled here." Will gestured about the room, the lie tripping easily off his tongue.

Arlington returned his gaze and surveyed the room again, as if he had somehow been mistaken in his first inspection.

Declan moved to stand beside her brother. "Who is it you seek, Arlington?"

"You bloody well—" He stopped himself abruptly, his cheeks reddening as he assessed the ladies present. He nodded at each of them in a semblance of apology. Leveling his voice, he addressed Declan again. "You know of whom I speak. You three have been thick as thieves all your lives," he accused. Again he looked as though he wished to add more but the presence of the women in the drawing room cut him short.

"Do you mean Camden?" Will exchanged a searching look with Dec. "I've not seen him since . . . er, Wednesday. No Tuesday, I believe."

Her brother should have been on stage. Who knew he could lie so well?

She crossed her arms. Why were they protecting him? Max was a big boy. He'd obviously offended Lord Arlington in some way. Let him answer for his transgressions. And yet she held her tongue.

"Yes, it's been a few days," Will said. "He is not here."

Aurelia narrowed her gaze on the flushed-face gentleman, quickly appraising him. From the way his hands clenched at his sides, he wanted to see Max. Badly. And it wasn't to chat about the weather. No. He was here for a pound of flesh.

"You speak of Camden?" Freddie called out across the room.

She cringed, already knowing what was coming. Dear Freddie was not the sharpest lad.

"Of course he's here, Will. You must have forgotten." Grinning, Freddie nodded as though glad to be of service. "I just saw him step out into the gardens for some fresh air."

Will and Dec both glared at dear Freddie, and his smile faltered in confusion.

With a fulminating look at Will and Declan, Arlington stormed past her and charged out the balcony doors.

"Really, Freddie?" Will snapped.

Freddie glanced around the room. Even Mama looked aggrieved. Feeling sorry for him, Aurelia moved to Freddie's side and patted his shoulder, trying to assure him he had not done something wrong. "It's not his fault," she defended. He was not to blame for Max having men hunting him down. Perhaps Camden should act in a manner that did not send angry men after him.

Without a reply, her brother was out the door, fast on the heels of Arlington. Dec followed.

The room was silent in their sudden absence.

Aurelia lifted her gaze to find everyone staring at each other, the question avid in all their gazes. Unable to stand the silent stares a moment longer, and overcome with curiosity as to what was occurring in the garden, she quickly turned to follow the men outside.

"Aurelia, where are you—"

She looked over her shoulder. "I'll be back in a moment, Mama."

"Aurelia," Violet called after her. "Are you certain you should go out—"

"I'll only be a moment."

Once outside, she followed the voices to the balcony that wrapped around the house.

"Damn you to hell, Camden!"

She gawked as Arlington charged across the balcony with a roar and barreled into Max, knocking them both over the balustrade and into the garden.

She gasped and hurried to the railing, hoping Max wasn't seriously hurt. Heart pounding, she peered over the side. The pair had landed in the bushes in a tangle of thrashing legs and swinging fists. Her brother and cousin raced down the steps. She flinched at the sound of fist meeting flesh.

Thankfully, the spectacle did not last long. Will

and Dec peeled Max and his attacker apart. Her heart raced as she eyed Max's mussed appearance. His too long hair was in disarray, his face flushed. A trickle of blood marred the corner of his lip. He looked savage and her heart gave a treacherous little flip.

Will held Arlington tightly around the chest. The man struggled to break free, shouting, "You bloody bastard, Camden! Stay away from my wife!"

Aurelia crossed her arms. He was dallying with another man's wife. Not such a surprise, that, and yet a small thread of disappointment ribboned through her. Apparently Max had spoken the truth. He had not yet bedded the Widow Knotgrass. Or he was dallying with both the widow and Arlington's wife simultaneously.

"Come now, Arlington!" Will interjected. "This is poorly done of you, man."

Suddenly Aurelia wasn't the only one on the balcony. Unable to stay away, her mother and the rest of the guests crowded around her, gasping at the tableau below.

"Poorly done of *me,* is it?" Arlington demanded.

"Yes, you cannot barge unannounced into my home—invade a dinner party, no less, with my family and friends in attendance—"

"How can you call that man a friend and bring him around your family?" Lord Arlington jabbed a finger in Max's direction and attempted another lunge for him.

Will pulled harder at the furious man, briefly lifting him up off his feet.

"Arlington," Dec tried to reason, but the man was hearing none of it.

"You dare address me as though I am in error when it is your friend there having a go at my wife like she's some street tart? Is that not poorly done of him?"

"Arlington," Dec said sharply. "I'll remind you there are ladies present." Her cousin flicked a glance to where she stood with everyone else on the balcony.

Will followed his gaze and scowled. "Everyone . . . please make haste inside," he pleaded.

"Come now, I believe we have some of Cook's iced biscuits," Violet said, ushering everyone back inside.

Aurelia remained.

"Ari," Will called. "Go inside."

"And miss this spectacle? Not a chance. I've not seen so riveting a performance at Covent Garden."

With a scornful shake of his head, and an ominous look that told her she would hear more of this later, Will returned his attention to the irate Lord Arlington, who was now on his feet and facing her brother.

Aurelia recalled everything she could remember of Arlington and his wife. Lady Ophelia was much like the Widow Knotgrass—another darling of the *ton* in her day. A little porcelain doll with enormous blue eyes, a pink bow mouth, and golden hair Aphrodite herself would envy. Of course, Max would be drawn to her. And she to him. She was beautiful, and vain enough to be lulled by his handsome visage.

Arlington was once again shouting at Max. "I should call you out right here—"

"But you shan't, so get the fool idea out of your head," Will calmly interjected, hauling the nobleman from the garden and up the balcony steps. "For one, it's a crime. For two, it would bring shame on your wife . . . on *you*. Now you're going to go home and tend to yourself and your wife. Rest assured Camden will not trouble her again."

"Me? Trouble *her*?" Max laughed, wiping at his lip and smearing the blood at the corner of his mouth. He looked like a pirate. Or a Viking. Tall and muscular and unaffected at the violence directed at him. "I did nothing she did not ask me to do."

Aurelia gasped. Heat washed through her.

Lord Arlington broke free of Will and started running down the steps again, his intent to attack Camden abundantly clear. Will caught up with him and hauled him back. This time the man collapsed, the fight gone from him. Her brother wrapped an arm around his waist and practically carried him from the garden.

The garden was silent for a long moment then, save for the thud of Max's boots. Aurelia narrowed her eyes on him as he made his way back up to the balcony. He laughed lightly, looking bemused as he straightened his rumpled jacket, coming abreast of her.

"You laugh? You're repellent," she whispered.

His blue-gray eyes settled on her, and the frost there chilled her. "Ah, high praise from you," Max mocked. "Am I not worse? Perhaps rat droppings?"

She squared her shoulders. "Oh, I just assumed that comparison tacit."

"Ari," Declan chided, obviously hearing their exchange as he joined them.

"Don't 'Ari' me." She looked swiftly to her cousin before looking back at Max. "You have your pick of women and yet you choose to dally with a married lady."

"Haven't you something else to do besides stick your nose in my life?"

"Perhaps you should stop dragging your life into the middle of my drawing room," she bit back.

"Enough," Dec snapped. "I grow tired of you two bickering. Is it not enough that we had to break up a brawl at a dinner party where Will and Violet just announced their happy news? That shall be a memory for them to cherish, won't it?"

Max looked suitably reprimanded. His lips flattened into a hard line.

"If you'll excuse me," Aurelia murmured. It was not her intention to add to the evening's unpleasantness by quarreling with Max.

She avoided the drawing room where everyone was assembled and exited the balcony through the salon, slipping unnoticed upstairs without making her farewells. She knew the breach in etiquette would be addressed later. Mama would not let such a thing pass, but at the moment she did not care. She simply craved the solitude of her room.

Cecily soon joined her and helped her unpin her hair for the night. Reading her mood, her friend did not ask too many questions.

Aurelia stared pensively at her reflection in the

mirror as her hair fell in dark waves around her shoulders.

Will and Violet were having a baby. She would be an aunt.

A brief smiled crossed her face in the reflection of the mirror until the memory of her own bent-back, doddering spinster Aunt Daphne flashed across her mind. Daphne collected pillows and cited scripture about the evils of man whenever one was in her presence.

No. She wouldn't be an aunt like that. She was still young. She had years ahead of her. Years to live and experience life. To taste a kiss other than the one Archibald Lewis had forced on her behind the vicarage when she was sixteen. She would know a kiss that didn't taste of fish and soured milk.

Her mother chose that moment to enter her bedchamber.

Aurelia bit back a groan and pushed to her feet, knowing very well what was to come. "Mama," she began. "I know you're here to lecture me, but you needn't. I know I should have made my farewells to everyone. My apology for that . . ." She ducked her head, permitting Cecily to pull her gown over her head. "I'm sorry, Mama. It was badly done of me."

Mama waved a hand. "No. I'm not here about that." Cecily's eyes met hers in silent question. Mama did not mean to reprimand her? Something must have happened to distract her from Aurelia's social gaffe of the night. Something grave indeed.

Her mother sank down at Aurelia's dressing table bench. She stared at her hands in her lap for several moments before speaking. "Have you given thought to your future, Aurelia?"

Aurelia started, blinking several times, questioning whether her ears had deceived her. Mama often spoke on the subject of her future, but she never inquired as to what she wanted . . . or thought . . . or planned. No, she only ever talked *at* her. Telling her what *she* expected her to do. Who she expected her to wed. For marriage to a suitable gentleman was the only option Mama ever presented.

Mama lifted her gaze. She considered Aurelia for a long moment before looking away, glancing at Cecily. "Leave us for a moment, dear, would you?"

Cecily nodded. Gathering up Aurelia's discarded garments, she left the room after shooting a meaningful look at Aurelia. Her friend would expect a full report later. Aurelia gave her a slight nod of affirmation and then turned to her mother as the door clicked shut behind Cecily. She looked at her expectantly, waiting for what she was certain would be a momentous conversation. It had begun in such an uncharacteristic manner, after all.

"This is splendid news, is it not?" Mama said. "Will and Violet are to have a child." She paused, a soft smile lifting her lips as she stared at something beyond Aurelia's shoulder. "It's a boy, you know. I feel it. I'm always right about these things."

Aurelia smiled, nodding indulgently. "Every time?"

"I was right about Will and you and Dec. About Agatha's children. All my friends. You can outfit the nursery based upon my predictions." Her expression grew faraway. "It seems so long ago that I was expecting my first child." Her smile grew wistful. "Your father was so very proud. Oh, I know he had his faults, but he loved me. And each of you."

"Mama." Aurelia sank down on the bench beside her mother, not about to argue the point. She had never felt as though her father cared for her one way or another. "Are you . . . sad? You're worrying me." Her mother was usually so cheerful. Aurelia could never recall a time where she had waxed nostalgic like this.

Mama took her hand in both of hers. "Those were good years. Your father . . . Will and you. Declan. He was like another son to me. His mother would have been happy to know he became a part of our family when his father denounced him. She can be at peace, knowing he's happy after how abysmally that man treated him."

Aurelia nodded.

"That's important for a mother. To see her children content . . . happy and settled."

For some reason these words made Aurelia uneasy. She was not discontent. She had her drawings. Not that she felt free to explain that to Mama, but they gave her purpose. And yet she could still not truthfully profess to be happily settled. There was something missing. She had become more aware of that since her brother's and Dec's marriages. Love was missing. The kind they shared with their wives.

"Even that scamp, Maxim. He's been like another son."

Aurelia's smile turned brittle at that remark, but she held it in place.

Mama focused her attention on her. "I'm satisfied that the boys will be fine . . . but I worry for you, Aurelia. I've done my best to lead you. To help you find a good husband." She sighed and looked tired then. Every bit of her years. "It has been for naught. My efforts have produced no results—"

"Mama—"

She hushed Aurelia with fingers to her lips. "So, now I shall cease my efforts. I'm finished. I'm not telling you this out of anger or to make you feel badly, my dear." With a final pat, she released her hands. "It's your turn to decide what you want in life. And whatever you decide, it's up to you to make it happen."

Aurelia stared, not even recognizing the woman before her as her mother . . . or the words that were coming from her mouth as anything her mother would ever say.

Mama squared her shoulders. "I'm leaving at the end of the Season."

"L-Leaving?" Aurelia stammered.

"For Scotland." She took a deep breath, as though the action somehow fortified her. "I'm going to live with Aunt Daphne. I will not force you to join me, but the alternative . . ."

The alternative was as plain as the nose on her face. If she did not accompany her mother, she would remain here, a yoke about Will's neck. No, Mama would not force her, but she knew Aurelia would accompany her rather than be a burden.

Aurelia could say nothing for long moments.

Mama's words rolled through her, penetrating gradually like rocks settling into silt. She suddenly felt . . . alone. More alone than she had ever felt before. Mama had made this decision without her.

Her mouth worked, searching for speech. They had always jested about living with Aunt Daphne some day, but she had never thought Mama serious. Her mother loved London too much. Her friends, Society and all its amusements. Even when they retired to Merlton Hall during the winter months, there was much Society in the country—a good deal more than they would find in the small corner of Scotland where Aunt Daphne resided. Surely Mama realized that?

Aurelia shook her head slowly, determined that Mama did understand it. "Aunt Daphne lives in the middle of nowhere . . ."

"There is Society there . . . in a manner. Thurso will be a quieter pace, to be certain, but enough for me. It's time. I can't stay here. It's not right. I need to let Will and Violet have their turn. It's only right that they start their family without me underfoot."

Or me.

She didn't say it, but Mama thought it. She felt it. As did Aurelia. She had been feeling it before, but now with Will and Violet's good news, it was only more evident. The three of them were a family. Will, Violet, and the baby. It was time for *both* Mama and her to go.

Her mother moved for the door. "I shall leave at the end of the Season." Her words rang with a finality that left no doubt in Aurelia's mind she had decided.

She slipped from the room with a whisper of muslin. Aurelia uttered not a word, her mind spinning, thinking of her fate. She should leave with Mama. That much was clear. It was the right thing to do. The kindest thing for Will and Violet.

Another sudden realization jarred her. She would not be able to continue her drawing. At least not in the same way. Life in Town provided endless inspiration. There was endless material to be gleaned from members of the *ton*. She would not find such inspiration in Thurso. And even if she did, there would be no opportunities to share her caricatures. No more leaving them all about to be discovered. Thurso was but a small hamlet. She would be discovered if she even attempted it once.

An ache started at the center of her chest.

She had convinced herself she was making a difference. Perhaps it was arrogant of her to think she held such influence, but she thought she was giving a voice to the voiceless. With the exception of her first caricature, she used her skill, attempting to shed light on the transgressions that occurred every day throughout Society. An earl being overly free with his hands. An old dame spreading ugly rumors. A groom publicly mistreated by his employer. All of that she would lose if she left with Mama.

Unless she came up with a plan. Another way to remove herself from her brother's house that did not require moving to Thurso.

A small knock preceded Cecily's return to her chamber. "Aurelia?" she said as she came up behind her and began brushing her hair. "Is everything . . . well?"

She nodded numbly. Everything would be fine. She fixed a wobbly smile to her lips. She merely had to adjust her objectives and accept a husband. It wasn't as though she was opposed to marriage. She just had never been very welcoming to prospective suitors. She simply had hoped for . . . more. Perhaps too much. Marriage to a man whose kiss did not make her want to wipe her mouth off afterward. She had admired her fair share of gentlemen. But all from afar. No one even potentially desirable had ever paid court to her. Her lack of dowry and rumors of her caustic wit ostensibly did not help in that endeavor.

Cecily gave up pressing her further for information and helped ready her for bed, casting her concerned looks.

"We'll talk tomorrow," Aurelia promised, feeling suddenly weary. "Good night."

Nodding, Cecily dimmed the light and slipped from the chamber.

Alone again, Aurelia slid beneath the cool sheets of her bed and tucked her hands behind her head, staring into the shadowy recesses of the room, her mind backtracking over all the gentlemen who had approached her over the last few seasons—regrettably, a short list—and wondering if she should have given them more encouragement. She now wondered if any one of them might have suited. She was no grand prize, to be certain, but perhaps one of them could have made her happy. And she him.

Perhaps it wasn't too late to try.

Chapter 5

Max had not made it two steps from the drawing room before Will and Declan waylaid him. With a clap on his shoulder, Will motioned in the direction of his office. "Come. Let us have a word."

He hesitated only a moment. His friends no longer kept late hours. They were thoroughly domesticated. Gone were the days when they stayed out all night and returned home at dawn. A late night for them consisted of dinner before retiring to bed with their wives. Besotted. The both of them.

His parents had been that way. His father had often chased his mother into their bedchamber, their laughter ringing down the corridor for all to hear. At the time, such love seemed a beautiful thing, if not slightly embarrassing. For the most part, though . . . it had been beautiful. Those were happy times. He and his sister felt lucky having parents so happy and in love. Life had been good. Rich and full of color. Until the accident, and then that love became dangerous. Killing the weak. Robbing his world of color and painting it in strokes of gray.

Max learned from his father's mistake. Love made one weak. It was a serpent in the grass, ready to strike when one was vulnerable. He would not be like his father and give himself so wholly to a woman. That path led to destruction. And why should he change his ways? He was perfectly content with things as they were now. There was simplicity in his existence. Freedom. No responsibility. No duty to anyone except himself.

Will's office was unchanged since his marriage. It was still masculine, with dark tones and rich colors. Max felt the most comfortable in this room. His entire town house was outfitted in much the same manner. Dark woods. Dark drapes. Functional.

"What is this, boys?" Max demanded lightly, falling back on the leather sofa. "Your wives have no need of you tonight?"

It was a jab, to be certain, and he didn't know why he'd said it. He supported his friends. He wanted them happy. He was fond of their wives and wished them only well. He'd even been instrumental in Will and Violet's union.

"At the moment, our most pressing concern is you," Declan answered evenly, crossing his arms over his chest.

"Is it? That's kind of you, but I'll be fine." He worked his jaw gingerly and tested the tender flesh of his lips with his fingertips. "Nothing that won't heal." He might very well bruise. Who knew Arlington had it in him? The nobleman spent more time at the gaming hells than in the company of his young bride. A sore point for Lady Opheila—and one she had complained about frequently. Not just to Max, but to anyone within her sphere.

Max did not often dally with married ladies. There were plenty of other willing females. Widows, maids, independent females that did not bow to Society's rules. But Lady Arlington had been lovely and ripe for the picking . . . and most insistent that she be picked.

He smiled, and winced at the motion. Lightly prodding his aching face, he crossed his booted ankles and stretched his legs out before him. His friends gazed at him like a morose pair of monks. "You're staring at me like I'm the recalcitrant child and you both the stern parents."

"Then I suggest you heed us as you would a set of parents. It's time for you to grow up, Max."

He blinked at Will's clipped words. He resisted the urge to reply that he was quite grown up. That he had been grown up ever since he was eleven years old and his mother and sister died. Ever since his father, crazed with grief, put a bullet in his head. The loss of his mother and sister had been tragedy enough, but walking into his father's bedchamber and finding him in a pool of blood and brain matter, his pistol still smoking next to him, had effectively killed what remained of his childhood.

He said nothing, however. He never spoke of that time—that day. Not even to his closet friends. It was enough that they knew his father took his life. All of the *ton* knew that, and looked at him as though he were somehow tainted. Those who had known his father saw him every time they looked at him. Max knew he was the mirror image of the man. Everyone saw Lord Kenneth Camden when they looked at him, and they wondered if he was equally fragile, if he would one day cave and surrender to weakness, crumble in the face of loss and adversity.

Max saw that question in their eyes—even now, when he worked so hard to distance himself from the specter of his father and to live a life as differently as possible.

He maintained his relaxed pose, but responded with an edge to his voice. "Grow up, hm? And I suppose marriage is the way to accomplish that? What? You've both gotten yourselves leg-shackled and now you expect me to as well?"

Will and Dec exchanged looks. "We can't have incidents like tonight occurring—"

Max laughed and held up a hand in supplication. "Come now. It was a little amusing, was it not?"

They stared back at him, their expressions stone-faced.

His own smile slipped and he sighed. "You would have found it so once. Marriage has rid you both of your humor."

"Someone could have been hurt, Max. What if Arlington came here with a pistol? Have you considered that?" Dec demanded. "Ladies were present. My wife was here—"

"As was mine," Will interjected, his face flushed. "And she's with child."

Max dragged a hand through his hair, feeling like the veriest wretch right then. "Of course. They should not have been subjected to such . . . barbarism." Not Rosalie or Violet. Not Lady Peregrine—she had been like a mother to him since his own died. Not even Aurelia—for all that she probably enjoyed witnessing him getting struck in the face. "Perhaps I should keep my distance?" he asked. "I'll see you both at our clubs or—"

"That's not what we're saying, you idiot," Dec snapped. "We don't want to cast you out of our lives. We simply want you to stop your philandering ways and—"

"I'll not marry—"

"We bloody well understand that. Take a mistress, then. Cease dallying with married women . . . cease flitting from woman to woman like you require a new flavor every day of the week."

"Max," Will said earnestly. "I've never known you to be with the same woman more than once."

"That's not true. There was . . ." He paused, thinking. " . . . Margaret." He stopped. "Wait, no." Their trysts had totaled two times. It had just taken a little longer to woo the actress into his bed.

"See there," Will announced.

"I cannot help it that I bore easily." He wasn't about to confess that he refused to get attached to any single female. He knew love existed. He'd been witness to it. He'd been a part of it. And then he'd stood by as it was lost. As it destroyed everything in his life. He simply took precautions against letting it happen to him.

"We're simply asking that you behave more responsibly."

They were asking for more than that. Perhaps they didn't realize it, but he did. They were asking him to change. He didn't have the heart to tell them that he couldn't. That he wouldn't.

Staring at his friends, he realized this was the beginning of the end. The three of them had been together all these years, but they would never be the way they used to be. Will and Dec loved nothing more than their wives. Will was going to be a father. Dec would soon follow in his footsteps. His friends were moving in another direction.

He was on his own now.

Max departed the office half an hour after Will and Dec left him there. He saw no sense in letting good brandy go to waste, so he remained, finishing his drink and having another one before rising to leave. He supposed this would be his lot now. Ending his nights alone, drinking in the shadows of a fire-lit room.

Stepping out into the corridor, he cursed the near darkness. Apparently the household had retired for the night, forgetting that he lingered in its expanding silence. Or perhaps they were so exasperated with his behavior and the spectacle he had created this evening that no one cared if he stumbled about in the dark and made it home to his bed or not. That sounded about right. Friends with their own lives to attend. No wife. No mistress. No one to give a damn.

He made his way down the long corridor, seeing a faint glimmer of light at the end, where the hallway opened up to the stairs that wound down into the foyer. Before Will or Dec married, they would have just been getting a start at this hour. Domesticated bliss. He snorted. They could have it. Perhaps he should make a visit to Sodom. The night would just be getting started there.

Rounding the corner, he collided with another body, smaller than his own. His chin struck something hard and he cursed, pain rocketing along his already tender jaw. He instinctively reached out to steady the body. A female, he knew at once. His hands slid around her back, bringing her closer. Even in a dimly lit corridor, he identified the softness of her form, the flowery fragrance of hair, the sweet catch of her breath.

Perhaps it was his mood. The nip of loneliness chasing him after being reprimanded by his friends. He flexed his fingers against her back. The thin cotton of a nightgown filled his palms. Womanly hips nestled against his hardness and his cock stirred.

He narrowed his gaze, peering through the gloom, sweeping over the fall of unbound hair, darkly rich and long. Neither Rosalie nor Violet possessed hair so dark. Instantly assured of that, he permitted his hands to travel slowly up her back.

"My apologies," he murmured, his fingers playing along the line of her spine. A servant girl not abed, then. Perhaps she would be amenable to his company.

"Max?"

He froze, recognition slicing through him. *No . . .*

He closed a hand on her arm and dragged her toward the top of the stairs where the light bled brighter from a nearby sconce.

"Aurelia." He breathed her name like an epithet and quickly dropped his hand from her as though burned.

A quick survey confirmed she was indeed

only wearing a night rail. The loose garment concealed her from neck to ankle, but he was acutely aware that only a thin veil of lawn covered her curves.

Swallowing a curse, he jerked his gaze back to her face, wishing he could unsee her body. Unfeel it. "Why are you not abed?" he demanded.

He glanced left and right as though expecting her brother to materialize from the woodwork. Rubbing a hand at the back of his neck, he tried to shut off his awareness of her standing before him in only a thin layer of fabric.

"Me? This is my h-home." She stammered a bit at this last word, as though it stuck in her throat. "Why are you still here?"

"Merely took a moment to lick my wounds after a set-down from your brother and cousin."

"Oh."

"'Oh'? Is that all you have to say? I thought you would relish that. No applause, brat? No words of smug satisfaction? I know how much you enjoy knocking me down a peg."

She shook her head, and the light from the sconce caught in her hair, gilding it to fire in certain spots.

Against his will, his gaze skimmed her body again. Heat flamed his face as he noted the swell of her breasts against the fabric of her nightgown. Even after his brain shouted at him to look away, his eyes made out the dusky shadow of her nipples.

Heat scored him. This was Aurelia. Will's vexing little sister.

Only not so little anymore.

He could not pretend otherwise. He'd first noticed that when he faced her amid her mother's garden party years ago. But it was too late then.

And it was much too late now.

"Do you always make it a habit to stroll the house at night in your bedclothes?" he snapped.

Hot color flooded her face. "Should I not? I've no one to fear in my brother's home. At least that was my assumption."

"Not everyone in this house is kin to you. There are servants, are there not? And the occasional guest."

She snorted. "Such as yourself? Is it fair to call you a guest? You're constantly underfoot."

"Well, you have made it your mission to remind me that I'm not a part of your family, so what else am I if not a guest?"

"Your unsavory reputation withstanding, I have nothing to fear from you."

"No? You're awfully confident in me." He advanced a step. "How uncharacteristic for you to have faith in my ability to behave as a gentleman."

She snorted. "I know very well I'm not the sort of woman to interest you."

"True," he agreed, forcing himself not to let his gaze rove over her again and disprove his words.

Her nostrils flared and he knew he'd offended her. Which was preferable to her knowing that he actually did find her appealing.

"And yet," he added, "I imagine another man might not feel as I do."

"Oh, indeed? A man 'might' exist to perceive me—wretched cow that I am—in a favorable light? Are you certain about that?" She made a sound of disgust and then stormed around him.

He grabbed her arm and forced her back to face him. "Don't presume to know what I think."

"I know your opinion of me." He backed her up until she bumped the wall. She could not escape without touching him—a fact of which she was clearly aware. She pressed herself as far back as possible, her gaze skimming the breadth of his shoulders and chest before snapping back to his face.

"You know very well the effect you have on men. You had a table of men panting for you at

Sodom. You took their clothes, their dignity. They gave it gladly. All for the chance to have a taste of you. I haven't forgotten that."

Her eyes widened. He'd flustered her by flinging that at her—by speaking of that night. *Good.*

He took a step closer, until the wall of his chest brushed hers. His attention fixed on her mouth. That plump bottom lip jutted out and the insane urge to take it between his teeth seized him. It still aggravated him. That she had turned into this—a temptation he had not seen coming.

"Can it be?" he taunted. "Aurelia at a loss for words? Impossible. Let us mark this day."

She opened her mouth, gaping like a little fish. It was tempting to step closer. To feel those breasts against his chest, the nipples pressing into him like scorching points.

"You're soused," she accused, her nostrils flaring as she smelled the liquor on him.

"I've had a brandy or two." Or five.

"Clearly, you've had one too many or you wouldn't corner me here like this. I'm not one of your giggling tarts—"

"Of that I am painfully aware, *Lady* Aurelia. They know what to do with their mouths, and it isn't talk."

Bloody hell. Even in the dim glow of the corridor, he did not mistake the rush of color to her cheeks and throat. He blinked once, hard, as he considered that blush, wondering how far it extended beneath her night rail. Would it reach her breasts? Her belly? The dip of her navel? The insides of her thighs? He ground his cock into the soft slope of her stomach. Her breath caught in a sound that resembled a moan. A shudder racked him.

"But then you aren't so innocent, are you? You've been to Sodom."

She shook her head, but he couldn't stop. With her, he could never stop. Never back down.

"Did you go upstairs? Did you see anything you liked? Did you do anything in one of those rooms? Let someone put his hands on this very ripe body of yours? Would you like that? To be touched, stroked? Your breasts were made to be caressed, tasted—"

"N-No," she choked.

He blinked.

Bloody, bloody hell. He stepped back quickly and dragged a hand through his hair. Perhaps he had imbibed too freely tonight. That, or Arlington's fist to his face had done more damage than he originally thought and shook his brain loose.

She blinked those wide doe eyes up at him. They looked almost black in the near-dark, glowing with an emotion he had never seen from her.

He opened his mouth to say something. An apology for acting like a rutting beast. Nothing seemed adequate. He'd just spoken to Will's little sister as though she were some vulgar minx he met at a sordid pub. To say nothing of his actions. He'd just ground his cock against her like she was a seasoned whore. This on the heels of Will and Max telling him he needed to behave more circumspectly. He really was a bastard.

Without a word, he turned and fled, descending the stairs with his cock throbbing. When he reached the bottom floor, he was tempted to look up, to see if she watched him, as he felt she did, or if that notion was just in his head.

He resisted. Keeping his eyes trained straight ahead, he opened the door and stepped out into the night.

Aurelia leaned over the railing and watched Max depart the house as if the hounds of hell were after him. She had done that. To him. She had sent the rogue running for once . . . and it was not because of her barbed tongue. It was because of *her*. He had left because of what swelled between them. The heat . . . the desire that even now still pumped between her legs.

For a moment there, pressed against the wall, she had thought he might kiss her. Finally, she would have a kiss other than the one Archibald Lewis forced upon her. She would know a kiss that did not taste of fish. She would be kissed properly. If nothing else could be said of Max, she felt certain it was this. He would know how to go about pleasing a woman.

She returned dazedly to her bedchamber, not recalling precisely how she got there. Somehow her feet moved, one step after another, until she was tucked back beneath her sheets, her hand pressed to the curve of her breast where her heart pounded like an incessant hammer.

The night had been eventful. Her hand slid to her throat where her pulse hiccupped a mad staccato as she recalled Max's body so close to hers. What would he have done if she closed that space? If *she* had kissed *him*? She'd witnessed all manner of illicit activity in the private rooms at Sodom. She had seen kissing and more. Her cheeks caught fire. Much more.

She was no ignorant girl. Images of those people coupling had stayed with her, filling her mind with fantasies when she was alone in her bed at night and aching. Her imaginary partner had always been a phantom man. Vague and face-less. But in this moment, tonight, he possessed a face. He was Max. A breath shuddered out of her.

She had no misconceptions of what Max was. She wasn't romanticizing him. She'd seen him in the greenhouse, trysting with the maid. She knew of his innumerable exploits after she, however inadvertently, christened him Cockless Camden.

They know what to do with their mouths . . .

A breath shuddered past her lips. He was a rogue who lived for pleasure. And his body had felt so good against her. Hard and strong. Her hand swept over her breast, fondled it, finding the nipple and giving it a squeeze, imagining it was Max's fingers. A small whimper escaped her.

And then reality crashed down around her. This was Camden. He would never cross that line with her. No, not with Will's little sister.

Sighing, she rolled onto her side. She had made up her mind tonight to find a husband and save herself from a lifetime of obscurity in Scotland with Aunt Daphne and her horde of pillows every shape, size, and color.

She best forget about Max and formulate a plan. Her gaze drifted to where her armoire stood. The room was too dark for her to see its hulking shape, but she knew precisely where it was, and she knew what resided within it. Countless gowns all handpicked by Mama. None were suited for her shape or coloring. She'd always known this and yet had never cared enough to oppose Mama on the matter. That would have to change. Starting tomorrow, she would need new gowns. She would begin there. A small and yet necessary change if she wanted to secure a proposal this Season.

She had two months before Mama left for Aunt Daphne's. And yet lying in the dark, the idea of marrying someone so that she could remain here only filled her with an aching bleakness. For the first time in years her drawings and the purpose they fed her soul didn't seem enough. Perhaps it was greedy of her, but she wanted more.

A shaky breath slipped past her lips as her mind touched on Max's face, his voice, the sensation of his bigger body so close to her own tonight. She'd felt him all over . . . against her, around her. Everywhere, right down to her toes. And he had not even laid a finger on her. How would it be, how would it feel, if he did?

Snuggling deeper under the covers, she slipped her hand between her thighs and touched herself, gently at first and then with growing pressure. Closing her eyes, she increased the friction and arched her back, envisioning it was someone else's hand on her, someone's body. Someone she wanted, someone she craved as desperately as her next breath.

As she brought herself to release, it was Max she saw in her mind.

Chapter 6

Max was not certain what he was doing in the crowded ballroom of Lady Chatham's house. Perhaps it was to prove to his friends that he could walk the line of respectability and they needn't fear having him around their families like some manner of infectious ailment. Even so, he hugged the shadows, sticking close to the potted ferns, where he could avoid being coerced into dancing with one of the several eligible young ladies in attendance.

"Come, Max, you did not attend simply to skulk

in shadows, did you?" Someone queried behind him.

He turned and forced a smile for Declan's wife, Rosalie. She eyed him with a twinkle in her eye. "I am quite certain there is at least one young lady to tempt you."

"Oh, there are lovely ladies aplenty, to be certain, but none so lovely as you, Rosalie." He pressed a hand over his heart. "I prefer to stand here and pine for the one that I let slip through my fingers."

She rolled her eyes. "Poppycock. As though I would have tempted you from your steadfast bachelor status."

He chuckled, rubbing a hand over his nape. "Well. No woman is capable of that, I fear."

"Oh, I do not believe that for an instant. There is someone for everyone."

What was it about those happily wed that made them hell-bent for everyone around them to wed as well? He held up both hands in mock surrender. "I would never be so disagreeable as to argue with a lady."

She laughed. "And yet you argue with Aurelia. Incessantly."

"Ah, yes. Aurelia. Well. We have a special relationship." There was a gentle euphemism.

"Hm," she murmured, lifting her drink to her lips and giving him a sly look. "We are in accord on that. Quite *special*, I think."

He frowned, not liking the suggestive lilt to her voice. Especially after last week, when he had backed Aurelia into that wall, pushed his hips against her as though she were an eager tavern maid and addressed her so crudely. He had avoided her since then but had not forgotten the look on her face, the sound of her tiny gasp . . . or her tempting shape beneath that filmy night rail. It was not his custom to deny himself. Any other woman he would not have hesitated to touch. To kiss. If she had been anyone else, he would have had that night rail up around her hips in two seconds flat. The very notion was starting to make him hard with lust.

Even more problematic was that he'd decided to forgo Sodom that night and instead returned directly home. He had stroked himself to satisfaction, all the while envisioning her face. A decided first and a new low. Much could be said of him, but it was not his practice to debauch untried girls. Especially when they were the sister of his best friend. If he ever had a doubt, he no longer did. He was going to hell.

"We thrive on discord," he said now, as though

Rosalie needed to understand what he meant by special. He wasn't going to explain their complicated history, but he'd been around enough matchmaking mamas to recognize a conniving mind, and he didn't want her to get any ideas when it came to Aurelia and himself. Now that would be a disastrous match. They would likely kill each other within the first week.

"You know what they say of enemies and lovers . . ." she said, looking at him archly . . . almost as though she could read his mind. "It's a fine line between the two," she elaborated.

"Your romantic nature is running away with you."

"Ah, speaking of Aurelia. There she is." Rosalie nodded toward the ballroom floor. "She's looking exceptionally fine tonight, is she not?"

A familiar tightness lined his shoulders as he braced himself, preparing for the sight of her . . . the moment their eyes would meet and she would give him that cool, dispassionate look. The empty smile. As though he were nothing. Simply a subject to be sketched in her pad, torn down, and reduced to something of ridicule.

He followed Rosalie's gaze to Aurelia. She did indeed look exceptionally well. He swallowed past a sudden tightness in his throat. Like a Mediterranean princess. A sultry red rose in a sea of pale English primrose.

Her hair was swept up in a mahogany mass atop her head. A single long ringlet draped over the smooth expanse of her naked shoulder. She wasn't wearing the usual ruffles and flounces. No, she was garbed in a sleek amber gown with simple lines that fit her torso tightly before flaring out at the waist. Her gaze was trained on the gentleman waltzing her about the floor—a man who seemed equally attentive to her as well. *Bastard.*

"What's she wearing?" he muttered beneath his breath. Her partner's hand rested not on her dress but on the bare skin of her back above the dress. He glared at the man's pudgy hand on that smooth, olive-toned back, wanting nothing more than to wrench it free of her. He told himself this was because she was Will's sister, that he felt protective of her for Will's sake. Nothing more. That flash of desire he'd had for her last week was an aberration. An anomaly. Thrust him alone with a half-dressed woman and tell him she was off-limits and he would react the same.

"Isn't the dress stunning? Much more flattering than her usual gowns."

"What was wrong with her usual gowns?" he grumbled.

"They weren't precisely memorable."

This dress was memorable. Or rather, Aurelia *in* this dress was memorable. The waltz came to an end and another gentleman was already there, waiting for the next dance.

"Aurelia is memorable no matter what she's wearing," he murmured, watching her closely as she drifted into the arms of her new partner.

"That's kind of you to say," Rosalie said, sounding surprised. "You should tell her that."

No he shouldn't. And he wasn't trying to be kind. Her saucy mouth made her impossible to ignore. That was all he meant. Presently, he simply did not care for the looks she was getting in her gown. Her display of cleavage did not go unnoticed.

Rosalie continued, "I think Aurelia was hoping to attract a little more attention for herself tonight."

"Why?" He frowned. For some reason, he didn't like the notion of Aurelia attracting suitors. He'd gotten accustomed to her role as Will's unwed sister. He'd assumed she would remain just that. A fixture in Will's household for the years to come, there to quarrel with him whenever he visited.

Rosalie ducked her head evasively. "I should

not speak on her behalf. Perhaps you should ask her yourself."

He returned his gaze to the ballroom floor, stiffening the moment he spotted Mackenzie cutting a direct line for Aurelia. What the hell was he doing here? He'd seen the man around Town, and he knew his reputation. The Scot was ruthless. He was also big. Muscular like a dockworker. He owned several gaming hells and other questionable establishments in Edinburgh and Glasgow and had recently begun expanding into England after he won a popular hell in the rookery.

There was much scandal attached to his acquisition of Rapture. Rumors that he cheated abounded. He had heard the former owner was deep in his cups at the time of the card game, and several people questioned Mackenzie's right to claim Rapture through such spurious means. Of course, no one challenged him directly. It was said the man carried the vouchers of too many noblemen.

It was also rumored that the Scot's ruthlessness extended to the bedroom. He was purported to enjoy bed sport of the rough variety. Max's hands clenched as he thought of Aurelia beneath the burly Scotsman.

And aside from all that, he recalled hearing

something about Mackenzie being on the hunt for a blue-blooded bride to give him an added stamp of legitimacy among the *ton*. He watched grimly as the Scot cut a path for Aurelia, thinking only one thought. *Hell no.*

Mackenzie stopped before her and bowed over her hand. Surely she would not think him an appropriate suitor. There was a brief exchange between the two and then she was suddenly swept up in the Scot's arms and waltzing around the room. *Senseless chit.* He glanced around, searching for Will or Dec, determined that they put a stop to this at once. Only they were nowhere in sight.

"Oh, see there. He's a handsome gentleman, is he not?" Rosalie commented. "They make a fine couple. She with her dark looks, and he a fair Viking." He glared briefly at Rosalie. She stood on tiptoes to whisper up at him, "They would make such beautiful babies, do you not think?"

She had lost her bloody mind. Until that moment, he had quite liked Dec's wife. Now he could toss her out the nearby French doors. If she thought Aurelia and Mackenzie would be making babies together, she was sorely mistaken.

He returned his attention to the dancing couple. At that particular moment, Aurelia tossed her head back and laughed at something Mackenzie said. Clearly she did not know the manner of man with whom she danced. Nor the way that action pulled the bodice of her gown lower, revealing more of her delectable décolletage. Of course, Mackenzie noticed. With her head thrown back, every man in the room feasted on the sight of those impressive breasts.

Max growled low in his throat, wondering at the surge of aggression he felt.

He suddenly lost sight of them among the couples and had to step to the side, searching for them among the whirl of bodies. His tension eased only marginally when he identified Mackenzie again. Fortunately, the Scot stood taller than most of the other dancers, so he was able to spot the man's dark blond head.

"He's not eligible," Max muttered.

"No? What's wrong with him?"

Was Rosalie still here? He had forgotten about her. He looked down at her, still irked with her earlier comment. She watched him keenly, waiting his explanation. "Everything."

Rosalie frowned. "You dislike him that much? If he's truly ineligible, then perhaps I should fetch Will to—"

"No need. I'll take care of it." Max started off

through the crowd, cutting across the ballroom floor, ignoring the people staring after him, who doubtlessly were marveling that Lord Camden had not only graced the ball of a very proper dame of the *ton*, but was actually on the dance floor.

He dodged a lady that reached for his arm in an attempt to drag him into conversation—or perhaps a dance. He walked with single-minded purpose toward Aurelia, ready to save her from herself.

No, he was not going to wait for Will to put an end to her flirtation with the likes of Mackenzie.

He was going to end it himself.

Aurelia exhaled in relief when the waltz came to an end. Of all the gentlemen who had danced with her tonight—and there had been a record high number, thanks to her new gown—Mr. Mackenzie was the only one whose stare made her decidedly uncomfortable.

His green eyes were as sharp and cutting as glass, peering into her as though he were trying to evaluate her and decide her worth. Those all-seeing eyes made her feel naked. She almost thought he knew the changes that she had wrought within herself over the last week.

She had taken control of her wardrobe. A long

overdue duty perhaps. Gone were the pastels and flounces and ribbons that did nothing for her shape. A necessary change to avoid a fate of spinsterhood. She needed gentlemen to forget everything they had ever heard of her and want to court her.

As the waltz came to an end, Mr. Mackenzie stepped back very properly and performed a quick bow. "Thank you for the dance, my lady." His Scottish burr rolled over her, and she had to admit that it was rather attractive. Truthfully, the man himself was attractive . . . if not a little overwhelming. He was nearly as tall as Max, but burly, not lean. Unlike Max, he looked as though he had spent half his life plowing a field.

Her thoughts came to a screeching halt. *Must she compare every man to Max?*

"You're welcome, Mr. Mackenzie."

"Perhaps I might call on you?"

Aurelia considered him for a moment. Here was a man who could probably rescue her from her fate—the move to Thurso, the loss of her drawings. Marriage to him could solve everything. And yet she hesitated at the notion. She recalled the feel of his hand at her back. So big it had felt like a giant's paw.

"I should like that very much," she said, telling

herself she simply had to grow accustomed to the idea. She had to be open to it . . . to *him*.

He inclined his head, the barest of smiles touching his lips. "Very good, then. Until we meet again."

She watched as he departed, slipping seamlessly through the crowd. He was handsome. Wealthy. He spoke with an enticing accent. She should be thrilled.

"You do realize Mackenzie is highly unsuitable."

She stiffened at the sound of Max's voice. She looked over her shoulder at him and sucked in a small breath. He looked startlingly handsome in his dark evening attire. His too long hair was brushed back from his forehead, but she knew it would not take much to ruin the effect. The first moment she exasperated him, he would drag a hand through the rich brown locks and send it feathering back down over his brow in an artful mess.

Blast, why must she notice things like that? She had known him all her life. His good looks were merely a shell.

Without bothering with a greeting—he had not, after all—she answered, "He cannot be that unsuitable. He was invited here this evening. Lady

Chatham would never allow someone unsuitable through the doors."

"The man has deep pockets. Deep enough to gain him entry to any ballroom."

"So that makes him unsuitable? He's rich?" She flicked him a glance of disdain before looking back out at the dance floor as if vastly interested in the view. If he was rich, then all the better. He might be able to help save her family from its impending ruin. So what if he was as big as an ox? She would not let that intimidate her.

Fortunately, at that moment she recognized a familiar face. Young Buckston was heading her way, the gangly youth's Adam's apple bobbing almost in rhythm with the music. He was one of the rare few to always beg a dance of her over the years. Even without encouragement, she knew she could rely on him. She smiled, confidant she was about to be rescued from Max's company.

"I'm certain a conversation with your brother will save you from any future association with Mackenzie," he said, the threat unmistakable. "He would not approve after I tell him what I know of the man."

She whipped her gaze back to him and pasted a smile on her face. "Do not meddle in my affairs, Camden."

"If I see you engaging in reckless behavior, it's my duty to intervene."

She resisted the urge to stomp her foot. He would not thwart her. Not when she had finally come up with a plan for her future.

Buckston was closing in, ready to claim his dance. She breathed her relief and shifted position to greet him, feeling quite smug as she turned her back on Camden. The vexing man could be left staring after her in the middle of a dance floor for all she cared. She refused to allow him to stick his nose into her life. She already had a brother and cousin to look out for her. She didn't need him, too.

Buckston gestured to the dance floor in invitation, that ridiculously large Adam's apple of his bobbing as he opened his mouth to request his turn with her.

She inclined her head with a smile and extended her hand, ready to place it in his waiting palm, reminding herself to be amenable. Buckston was no longer a kindly dance partner, he was a prospect she must consider.

Suddenly, she was whirled around and pulled into Max's arms. He swept her past a scowling Buckston and whisked her out onto the dance floor.

Aghast, she stared up at his smug face in astonishment. "What are you doing?" she demanded.

"Waltzing with you."

"You don't dance. With anyone. Ever."

He frowned momentarily, as though realizing the truth of this reminder. Then he shrugged. "Clearly, I do."

Furious heat crept over her face, and she tried to pull away.

He tightened his grip on her hand and pressed her closer to his chest. "Stop pulling away from me. People are staring."

"Because of you," she hissed. "*You* are dancing." She cast a look about the room, her gaze stopping on Rosalie and Violet. They both wore curious expressions as they watched her and Max. Even they knew that Max did not dance.

"You're Will's sister. He's my best friend. No one will think anything of it as long as you stop wiggling to get away. And rid yourself of that sucking-lemon expression while you're at it."

"Oh!" She forced herself to relax in his arms. Smiling was a harder feat to accomplish.

He pulled her even closer. "Much better," he praised.

Her breasts brushed his chest. Her face flamed hot as she remembered the night in the corridor, an encounter that she had been trying so very hard to forget. "You're a cad. I promised this dance to Buckston."

"Buckston's a peacock."

"He's a gentleman."

"Don't waste your time on him," he advised.

The man drove her mad. "Mackenzie is unseemly. Buckston a peacock. Is there anyone on this earth good enough for me?"

He didn't reply, and she risked a look up at him to find him staring down at her. His stormy eyes gazed at her in an unfathomable way that made her chest tighten to the point of discomfort.

She looked away, glad that he did not answer that question . . . but also wondering why he did not.

Chapter 7

Her eyes gleamed like topaz. Max cursed the fanciful thought as her question echoed through his head. *Is there anyone on this earth good enough for me?*

His internal response was immediate: *No.*

And then he wondered what he was thinking. He should pity the man that took her to wife.

He told himself it was because he had grown up with this girl. He had known her since she was a child. Since they were both children. No matter what had happened between them, no matter how deep the rift, no one would ever be good enough for Aurelia. He was certain that her brother and cousin would agree with him. Why did it feel so very troubling then for him to have a similar reaction?

Her question hovered between them. Answering it truthfully was out of the question, so he simply danced with her. Neither spoke for some moments. He couldn't help thinking they fit well in each other's arms. She was graceful, trusting in his ability to lead. He glanced down at her the precise moment she risked another glance up at him. The warm gold of her gown brought out the fire in her eyes, and he was hard pressed not to lose himself in that gaze.

"Very well," she said with a relenting sigh, breaking their silence. "Why is Mr. Mackenzie so very unsuitable?"

"I've heard many unsavory a tale of the man. He is far beneath you."

She turned wide eyes on him, clucking her tongue. The act brought his attention to her mouth. Had she applied some manner of gloss there? They seemed plumper, a shade deeper . . . like she had been sipping from a glass of claret.

"You're not the type to give credit to rumors, Camden."

With difficulty, he brought his gaze back to her eyes. "It's a fact. He owns a string of gaming hells from here to Edinburgh."

"That hardly makes him disreputable. Don't tell me you're one of those stodgy noblemen who actually looks down his nose at anyone who has to work for a living."

He frowned. "It's not that." He himself worked, in a manner, spending a goodly amount of his time managing investments and researching new prospects. Gone were the days where any man could rest on his laurels and expect everything in life to be handed to him. He'd seen what such thinking had done to Will's father. It had stripped him of nearly everything and left Will scrambling for ways to support his family. No, he respected any man who worked. Only Mackenzie was dangerous. He wasn't certain everything he did could qualify as law-abiding.

"He's trying to buy a bride and everyone knows it," he said, confident that would put the nail in Mackenzie's coffin as far as Aurelia was concerned. One thing he knew for certain was that she was a prideful creature. Her principles wouldn't allow her to condone a man so mercenary in his pursuit of a bride.

To his shock, she shrugged. "How is that different from any other gentleman in the market for a bride? At least he's not hunting for heiresses."

He stared hard at her for a moment. "You like him," he accused.

She shrugged. "I don't know him. Yet."

"Yet?"

She looked at him in exasperation. "He's one of the few gentlemen not dissuaded by my lack of dowry. He's handsome, and as you pointed out to me recently, I don't exactly have a legion of eligible men beating a path to my door. Why wouldn't I consider him?"

He bit back a curse, feeling like an utter ass. He had said something to that effect to her. "I thought you had no wish to marry," he reminded her.

"Have I ever said that to you or was that simply the assumption?" She angled her head, considering. "Hm. Whatever the case, I have had a change of heart. I will be engaged before the Season is out."

Stunned, he stared down at her. The dance ended and he escorted her to the edge of the ballroom floor. He looked down at her enticing display of cleavage. "Is this why you're dressed as . . . as—"

"As what?" she demanded, a sharp edge to her voice. "A woman?" An angry flush stained her face. "I simply took charge of my wardrobe from Mama."

About bloody time. And then he retracted that thought. Perhaps if she were still wearing one of her pastel, frilly concoctions she would never have caught the notice of a man like Mackenzie.

"And what brought about this sudden urgency to wed?" he asked numbly.

"Mama is leaving at the end of the Season. She's going to live with my Aunt Daphne in Scotland. Permanently."

"Permanently?" His mind raced, concluding that Aurelia would likely be compelled to go with her. That is what unwed daughters did. They remained with their mothers. Only in this case, he had not imagined Lady Peregrine ever leaving the comforts of Town.

"Well, there will be the occasional visits, I'm sure." Her voice thinned into something small. Even she did not sound too convinced. "Well. Not too often. Thurso is a great distance."

The very ends of the earth. "It's the most northerly town in the mainland, is it not? And you intend to live there?" He stared at her, troubled at the idea of her isolated in faraway Scotland. "The weather can be quite inclement that far north." Was he actually using the climate as a reason for her not to go?

"If I should go, I can withstand a bit of cold. However, it's a few months until the Season ends. A very great deal could change before then."

He studied the resolute set of her jaw, the firm press of her lips, as she stared out at the ballroom, gradually coming to understand her sudden interest in gaining suitors. He followed her gaze, scowling when he found it resting on Mackenzie.

"He's not for you," he heard himself saying in a hard voice.

She snapped her gaze back to him, color spotting her apple cheeks. Her chest lifted on a deep breath. "Stay out of my affairs, Camden." A thread of emotion shook in her voice, and that was entirely different from her usual blithe repartee.

It sank in for him then. She was utterly serious about this suitor business. She was on a mission to find a husband. Aurelia not only wanted to marry, she was hell-bent on it.

Chapter 8

The ladies' retiring room offered much needed solace following her dance with Max. Aurelia chose a couch angled in the corner, where she could sit with her back to the row of dressing tables. At the moment a pair of middle-aged ladies powdered their noses and discussed their fractious daughter-in-laws. Thankfully, she was of no interest to them. She pressed a hand to her heated cheeks.

What on earth was wrong with Max, daring to insert himself into the matter of whom she chose as a suitor? She shook her head and dropped her hands from her face. He was a distraction she didn't need. The gall of him interrupting her dance with Buckston. Indignation crawled over her skin like a swarm of angry ants.

Sighing, she smoothed a hand down her bodice and froze when she heard the crinkle of paper. Goodness! She'd almost forgotten the drawing of Lord Eddington that she had rolled up and slid inside her corset. Blast Max for throwing her off-task. Not only from her quest to find a husband but also from keeping her from her work tonight. He was muddying her head.

She slipped a tip of finger inside her bodice, feeling the sharp edge of the parchment she had rolled into a tight scroll.

She had intended to leave it at the ball this evening when the opportunity presented itself. She glanced over her shoulder at the women sitting at the dressing tables. One of them caught her eye in the mirror and Aurelia forced a bright smile, slipping her hand from the edge of her bodice. Obviously now was not that opportunity.

"Aurelia?"

She looked up as Rosalie entered the room. Her sister-in-law sank down on the couch beside her and covered her hand with her own. "Are you well? You left the dance floor rather suddenly."

She nodded. "I'm fine."

"You were dancing with Camden." Rosalie searched her face, apparently waiting for her to contribute something on that topic.

Aurelia winced. "Yes, well, he asked me—" She stopped with a deep, bracing breath. He hadn't precisely asked her. He simply snatched her up and hauled her onto the dance floor—and that was only so that she couldn't dance with Buckston. She winced at that reminder. The man lived to thwart her. There could be no other reason for his behavior.

"You parted his company rather hurriedly. Did he say something to offend you?" Rosalie's reddish brows furrowed tightly. "Did you two have another quarrel?"

She shook her head, although she supposed they had quarreled. When did they not? "He took exception with Mr. Mackenzie." Familiar anger nipped at her as she replayed his words in her mind. "He thinks he's unsuitable."

Rosalie leaned back and lifted both eyebrows. "Indeed?" A beat of silence followed as she studied Aurelia's face. "Interesting . . ."

"How is that interesting?" She knotted her hands in her lap.

"Well, that he should care is interesting. Is it not?"

She snorted. "I'm certain it's pure contrariness. Or some misguided sense of brotherly obligation."

Rosalie tossed her head back and laughed loudly.

Aurelia frowned at her and sent a self-conscious glance to the other two ladies, who were now openly staring.

"Oh, I'm sorry. Forgive me, Aurelia." Rosalie forced down her laughter, dabbing at her eyes. Inhaling a sobering breath, she leveled a steady gaze on Aurelia. "That man is *not* like a brother to you."

A flash of him closing in and pressing against her made her flush and shift her weight on the couch. There had been nothing brotherly about him in that moment, true. "Perhaps," she allowed, and then shrugged.

"Not in the least." Rosalie nodded decisively.

"My brother is far kinder," she agreed. "As is Dec." There was by far too much hostility between Max and her. Although sabotaging her attempts to make a match seemed malicious even for him. Why should he care what she did with her life?

Rosalie reached up and smoothed the tension lines in Aurelia's forehead with gentle fingertips. "Come now. Don't scowl so. You look ravishing this evening. I'm sure all the lads are missing you. Let's go back out there, so that you can dance with them."

Rolling her eyes, she permitted Rosalie to lead her from the room, not bothering to contradict her. They wove through the crowded ballroom once again. Aurelia kept an eye out for Buckston, fully intending to honor her promise to dance with him.

"Ah, look. Speak of the devil. It's Camden."

Even as a part of her willed herself not to look, she felt herself turning. Felt her gaze tracking across the crowded room until she spotted him.

He moved with purposeful strides across the ballroom, weaving between dancing couples. She and Rosalie weren't the only ones watching him. He cut a fine figure. People stared after him. Women and men alike. He was that handsome, that tall and virile in his dark evening attire. The consummate rake, he was a rare sight in ballrooms of the *ton*.

At that thought, she angled her head. Why was he here? Polite Society functions were not his forte. Aside from her family's gatherings, he eschewed the balls and routs that occupied so many of her nights. Places such as these, events such as this, they were not for him. Sodom was for him.

Curiosity piqued, she continued to watch him. He slipped from view for a moment and she stepped to the side, craning her neck and gaining sight of him once again as he stopped before a woman pressed against the far wall. The girl shrank into the wallpaper as though she were part of the pattern.

He bowed before the lady. Aurelia assessed her—the pale brown hair pinned demurely atop her head, the length of her nondescript gown. The woman was no older than herself and vaguely familiar. Aurelia felt fairly certain they had shared the same wall before on at least one other occasion.

"Oh, he's asking Miss Bell to dance." Rosalie clapped her hands lightly, pleasure writ all over her face. "How kind of him. I don't think I've ever seen Miss Bell take to the dance floor before."

Miss Bell. She searched her memory, finally recalling her. Yes. Miss Samantha Bell. She was the late Duke of Faircloth's stepdaughter. Miss Bell's half sister, Lady Mariah, was the toast of the Season. Miss Bell was her constant companion and shadow.

Gazing across the ballroom at her, Aurelia noted the girl's stunned expression as she gazed up at Camden. She was clearly not the one accustomed to handsome swains begging a dance. Unfair, she supposed. Miss Bell was not unattractive, but existing aside of her younger, prettier half sister? Who happened to be the daughter of a duke, whilst she was merely a gentleman's daughter? It must not lend many opportunities for dance partners. Nor suitors, for that matter. Aurelia could relate to such a situation.

She angled her head, watching as he led the still startled-looking Miss Bell onto the dance floor. They watched in rapt fascination—as did many others. Camden seemed unaware of the stares his action was eliciting. Either that or he was indifferent. He looked straight ahead, unaffected as he led Miss Bell to the center of the ballroom floor.

"Isn't that kind of him?" Rosalie nodded approvingly.

"Yes. Indeed." It was *kind* of him. Which was not a word she had ever applied to him before, and yet here he was doing something generous and wholly unexpected.

Riveted, she continued watching as he swept Miss Bell in a graceful circle. Camden didn't dance. Ever. Well, with her, yes, but that had only been to torment her. Dancing with Miss Bell was not driven out of his need to torment. Something had motivated him to walk across a crowded room and beg a dance from a girl who clung to the shadows. Could it simply be compassion? Had he seen her between the potted ferns and decided to take pity? He said something then that cracked Miss Bell's timid shell and made her smile, and Aurelia suspected it was just that. He was being charitable.

"Good for Miss Bell," Rosalie said. "I imagine this raises her in the estimation of most gentlemen in this room." She plucked a glass from a passing tray and took a sip. "A sad state of affairs, but no less true."

"There you are, wife." Dec slid close beside Rosalie. "I've been looking for you."

A besotted grin instantly curved her lips. A grin that turned downright dazed as Dec leaned in and whispered something in her ear. She pressed fingertips to her lips but that did little to stifle her giggle.

"Cousin." Dec winked at her. "Would you mind if I stole my wife away for a dance?"

"Of course not. I might even let you have her for two dances."

"So kind," he murmured, lifting Rosalie's drink

from her hand and passing it to Aurelia. With a lingering kiss to his wife's palm, he swept her onto the dance floor.

Aurelia found a place to deposit the glass and then meandered along the edge of the room, glancing around to confirm that no one seemed particularly attentive to her movements. With a final glance around, she slipped from the ballroom. Lifting her skirts, she hurried down the main corridor, smiling as she passed a pair of ladies.

With a quick glance over her shoulder, she turned down a narrow hall. The sounds from the ballroom were distant and muffled now. She opened one door and peered within. A salon. The room did not feel very used. Her drawing might not even be detected for some time in here. She needed a room that met more traffic.

Shutting the door, she continued down the corridor, opening several others until she came to a set of double doors that led to the library. The vast space smelled of rich wood and leather. Several sconces lit the room and a fire crackled in the hearth. The room appeared to be well lived in. A book sat open on the couch where the reader had left it. There also appeared to be a chess game still in play at a table. A plump tabby cat that might outweigh Mama's fat cat by a good half stone lifted its head from where it rested on the sofa and let out a plaintive meow.

With a final glance over her shoulder to make certain she was still alone, she slipped the scroll from her bodice. She moved to the chessboard, already envisioning placing it there for later discovery. Stopping before the board, her hand hovered over the center.

"What's this?" A deep voice sounded in her ear. An arm stretched over her shoulder, reaching for the drawing. Her heart jumped to her throat. She whirled around with a yelp just as her palm shot out and smacked Max in the face.

"Ow!" He covered his cheek with one hand. "What was that for?"

"You shouldn't sneak up on people. You startled me!"

He lifted both eyebrows and then lowered them, drawing them tightly over his blue gray eyes. "What do you have there, Aurelia?"

She shook her head. "Nothing."

He smiled, but it was deceptive. There was no humor in the curve of those well-shaped lips. "Let's see it." He reached for the rolled up drawing in her hand.

Gasping, she tucked it behind her back and

shuffled away, stopping when her thighs bumped the chess table.

His eyes narrowed and he stepped closer. "I can't believe you. You're doing it again, you bloody fool."

"Don't call me that!"

"Don't *be* that!" His gaze devoured her, eyeing her overheated face. "Give it to me."

"No."

He shook his head. "Have you any notion what would happen if it wasn't me standing here right now? If someone else caught you? This little hobby of yours is as reckless as your trip to Sodom. With you it's one stupid decision after another."

"Oh, you arrogant, overbearing—" She swallowed back the rest of her words and inhaled a burning breath. "My actions are none of your business."

"I can assure you your quest for a husband would be at an end. No one would have you then."

"I'm sure you care so very much about that," she scoffed.

A muscle in his jaw ticked. "Indeed I don't. But I care about Will and Dec and their wives. I care about your mother. So stop being a selfish brat and end this."

Anger and hurt welled up in her chest. She suddenly felt tired. Tired of his insults. Tired of his interference. Tired that he made her feel guilty for doing the one thing that gave her fulfillment. She would not be caught, but even if she were, the consequences would be on her. Not her family. They'd weather it. The risk was on her, and it was worth it.

She blinked stinging eyes. "I despise you."

He smiled then, clearly indifferent, and she despised him all the more for that. She loathed that he could be so cold and unaffected in the face of her animosity. She especially despised that despite her best arguments with herself, he could make her feel ashamed.

"Give me the drawing."

Her chin went up. "No."

"Fine," he bit out. Tension feathered along his square jaw and something knotted low in her belly. "Then I'll take it from you."

Max felt as feral as a predator as he watched her shake her head and send the dark coil of hair bouncing over her shoulder. Angling his head, he followed the trail of it. The tip curled enticingly between her breasts. He inhaled at the view. He wanted to wrap his fist around that hair and haul her closer. Lick and kiss that saucy mouth of hers into submission.

She arched away and forced her arm deeper behind her back. The action only caused her breasts to rise even higher within her bodice.

"Stay away from me." Her voice shook a little, and he smiled down at her, enjoying that he was so obviously affecting her.

He closed in, wrapping his arms around her, bringing her flush against his chest. He fought to ignore the sensation of her pressed against his body as his hands slid down the length of her arms. Her eyes gleamed amber fire in her face, widening as his fingers reached her wrists.

She scanned his features as though she had never seen him before. Indeed, he, too, felt as though he was seeing her anew. He could actually count the tiny flecks of gold in her eyes. He noted the freckle beside her right eyebrow that was darker and larger than the rest of her freckles.

The two of them weren't standing in a ballroom or the drawing room of her brother's house. No one stood nearby ready to step in and put a stop to their quarreling should it become too much. This wasn't Sodom with countless eyes on them, watching their every move, staying his hand from doing anything he should not.

They were alone. Anything could happen. Especially things that shouldn't happen.

Her stare dropped to his mouth before snapping back up to his eyes. A telltale flush stained her cheeks.

His hands folded over hers, clenched so tightly together. Her fingers were long and slim. He tested their shape and length. An artist's hands. He felt the parchment through the cracks in her fingers.

"You don't understand," she whispered.

"No, you don't," he growled. "You can ruin people's lives."

Her gaze bored into him. "It's all I have. There's nothing else. I need this."

"Find another hobby," he said, refusing to let her thaw his ire. She risked too much. On this, he wasn't wrong. Her drawings could wreak havoc. He knew that firsthand. He pried her fingers apart and snatched hold of the drawing, holding it away from her with no care for crinkling the parchment.

But she cared. She cried out and tried to grab it back. He backed away, moving out of range. He glanced to the hearth. She followed his gaze and her eyes widened in horror.

"No! Don't!" She lunged at him. He placed a hand on her shoulder, holding her at bay. She pushed against him, trying to reclaim the scroll.

He turned and faced the fire, ignoring her hopping and surging against his back, beating him with balled-up fists.

He had a moment's hesitation as she choked out behind him, "Camden, please! Don't!"

Pushing aside the stab of doubt, he tossed the scroll into the fire, watching grimly as it went up in an angry nest of red and orange flame.

With a strangled cry, she surged around him as though she would dive for it, heedless of burning herself. He hauled her back by the waist, and she turned in his arms, raining her fists on his chest in a violent fury.

"Enough! Have you lost your mind?" He wrapped her in his arms, but she still struggled and writhed as though he had just tossed a living thing into the fire and not a simple drawing.

"How could you?" Her brown eyes blazed at him and he muttered a curse at the sheen of tears there.

The doubt he had felt earlier came roaring back now.

"Satisfied?" she demanded, her voice flat, dull. Her gaze drifted to the fire where the parchment was naught but blackened ash. "You must have enjoyed that."

"It was for your own good—"

"Spare me your altruism." She struggled to break free and he let her go this time. She backed away, her steps hard little jarring drops on her heels. Her gaze seared him, raking him with such burning contempt. "This is about punishing me and nothing else."

Was it? Perhaps it was. For years that had been his sole function around her. He couldn't even remember what it was like to be anything else with her. This was just what they were.

She rubbed the heel of a palm against her eyes. *Ah. Bloody hell.* She was on the verge of tears. He'd never seen her cry before. He didn't think Aurelia the sort of female to succumb to tears.

"No more." She shook her head, inching back farther and jabbing a finger at him. "Stay away from me." She turned and fled the room as if the hounds of hell were after her. He stared after her until she was gone.

He should feel triumphant. He had done nothing wrong. Her almost-tears should not matter. Whether he had crossed a line and hurt her feelings should not matter. And yet it did.

Chapter 9

Sketch pad balanced on her lap, Aurelia lifted her gaze to study the park, studying the serene scene. She had just finished sketching a nanny being dragged by a set of raucous twin boys. Aurelia had given the boys the bodies of monkeys—tails and all—but kept their features virtually the same.

She was giggling by the time she finished and flipped the page. It wasn't her usual material, but it amused her and it felt good to laugh. For days she had mourned the loss of the caricature Max destroyed. Picking up her sketch pad again felt like a return to herself even if she wasn't creating anything of satirical meaning. It also served as good practice until she decided on her next subject.

Because she wasn't quitting. Max might have destroyed her drawing and crushed her in that moment, but she was not beaten.

She scanned the landscape. People dotted the picturesque view. Nannies pushing prams and guiding their young charges. Couples sharing curricles. A few people cast their lines off the small bridge stretched out over the pond. It was just the kind of scene to take her mind off Max.

She scowled. Only apparently not. There she went again, thinking of him and his cruel manner.

Squaring her shoulders, she renewed her search for a new subject to draw, determined to push him from her thoughts. A feat that was destined for failure. Her stomach dipped and twisted when she spotted him.

He sat in a boat in the middle of the pond with none other than the Widow Knotgrass. He leaned across the small space of the boat and brushed something off her face. Apparently the rumors were true and they were lovers—or soon to be. Max would not be in her company otherwise. He did not waste his time on proper courtships. This rankled her. Who was he to criticize Mr. Mackenzie? At least Mr. Mackenzie's intentions were honorable.

Max was wrong about him. Struan Mackenzie had called on her this morning and behaved only as a gentleman should. It was clear the Scotsman's intention was to court her honorably. Max merely wanted to aggravate her. Impede her quest to find a husband out of pure contrariness. Because that's what he did. He thwarted her attempt to dance with suitors and he burned her caricatures.

Fury burned in her blood as she started feverishly sketching Max, giving him a pair of horns, drooling fangs, and a large salivating tongue as he sat beside the Widow Knotgrass. The widow was not to be spared either. Indeed not. In her sketch, the angelic lady sat upon a pile of squirming debutantes. Aurelia did not stop there. She gave the widow several spiders' legs. The wiry black limbs crept out beneath her fashionable striped muslin gown, assisting in pinning down the struggling debutantes.

To say she possessed fond memories of the lady would be a lie. Before she became a widow, the young woman had taken her first curtsy with Aurelia. Whenever Aurelia spoke to her, she had stared at her as though she were repugnant before whisking past, her retinue fast on her heels, leaving Aurelia among the titters of onlookers.

Despite all that, when her betrothal to old Knotgrass was announced, Aurelia had felt only pity for her. True, the man was wealthy beyond reason, but he was ancient and bound to a wheelchair. No one seemed to acknowledge the wrongness of a girl of eighteen marrying a man in his nineties.

Ever since his death a year ago, the Widow Knotgrass had been seen about Town with all manner of handsome, unattached gentlemen. It stood to reason she would eventually turn her eye to Max.

Aurelia finished her sketch with a few angry flourishes and then sat back—still fuming. She sat there for some moments, waiting. The anticipated euphoria never came. As good as it felt in those moments to create her image of Max and the widow, she had not totally exorcised her demons. Deciding her day at the park had been ruined, she stuffed her sketch pad into her satchel and rose to her feet, ready to return home.

She took the most direct path, the route that edged the pond. She couldn't, however, stop her gaze from straying to where Camden rowed the boat serenely back toward shore. She bit her lip and paused, realizing that if she kept her course she would come abreast of them as they came ashore. Unless she broke into a run. She winced, considering her options. Or she could turn around and lurk somewhere, waiting until they disembarked and left the park. Her chin shot up as she considered that undignified image of herself.

Rubbish. This was a public park. She had every right to be here. She had nothing to be ashamed of. She certainly wasn't afraid of them. She would not hide or skulk away.

Moments later her brave thoughts didn't seem so wise. Max spotted her as the nose of the boat bumped shore. Holding her spine straight, Aurelia readjusted her satchel and continued a steady pace, watching as he hopped into the water, submerging his fine Hessian boots ankle deep as he worked to pull the boat fully ashore so his lady could disembark without wetting her slippers. Aurelia snorted, trying not to notice the way his back flexed and moved beneath his jacket. Such a gentleman. When the purpose served him.

There was no saving her, however. As she suspected, they would come face-to-face. Max assisted the widow onto solid ground almost the precise moment Aurelia came abreast of them.

"Hello, there," she greeted with a nod. "Mrs. Knotgrass. Lord Camden."

Max executed a quick bow, keeping his eyes fixed on her face. They had not seen each other since the Chatham ball. Since he sent her fleeing from the room, very close to tears. Thankfully, she had kept those tears at bay until she was alone.

He watched her face closely now. She stiffened her spine. What? Did he think she would break down at the sight of him? Did he think her that fragile? "My lady. Fine day for a stroll."

She hugged her satchel closer to her side. "Indeed." She fanned her fingers over the supple leather. "A lovely day to sketch by the water."

His eyes narrowed. Her message had been received. Now he knew he had not broken her. She would not stop drawing her caricatures no matter how much he tried to bully her.

The widow looked her over, a pouty frown tugging at her mouth. "Do I know you?"

Aurelia sighed, suddenly feeling like it was her first Season all over again. Invisible. "We made our first curtsies together," she reminded. Only she didn't know why she bothered. Either the widow didn't recall her or was feigning lack of memory. Either possibility rendered her dreadful.

"Ah, yes. Arielle, isn't it?"

"Aurelia," she corrected.

"That's right." She released a tinkling laugh as she sidled closer to Max, curling her hand around his elbow. "I should have recognized you." She looked down at Aurelia's muddied hem. "Still a mess, I see."

Aurelia stood there, trying not to feel so small. She could sense Max staring at her. She couldn't look at him. Not while his soon-to-be paramour was treating her to such thinly veiled insults. Or perhaps they already were lovers. She inhaled a stinging breath. She didn't want to see the pity in his eyes. Or worse, that he approved of Mrs. Knotgrass's remarks.

The widow looked back and forth between the two of them. "And how is it the two of you know each other?" she asked. When her gaze settled on Aurelia her top lip curled faintly. Aurelia knew she found it hard to believe a female like her could be within Max's sphere of acquaintances. If not for Will and Dec, she certainly would not be.

"My brother and Lord Camden—"

"Ah, of course. Lord Merlton is your brother." She glanced at Max. "He's your dear friend, yes?"

Max nodded.

Still smiling that smile that did not reach her

eyes, she returned her attention to Aurelia. "It's been a good many years. Still unwed, are you?"

Aurelia inhaled at the not so subtle slight. "Yes, I'm still unwed."

"Well, take heart. Not everyone can have success their first Season out. Or second . . . or, well who's counting?" She shrugged and smiled brightly, readjusting her grip around Max's arm. They really did make a handsome couple. He with his chestnut hair and she with her golden beauty.

Aurelia's pride nosed to the surface. Perhaps it was because Max stood there and she was always in a combative mood around him, but she didn't feel like enduring the abuses in mute indignation as she had years before. "Yes, well, some of us have high standards."

Twin flags of color stained Mrs. Knotgrass's cheeks. "Oh, is that your excuse?" She nodded her head slowly. "Well, one must believe what they will to get through their days." She leaned forward slightly, offering, "You know what they call women with 'high' standards, don't you?"

"I'm certain you're going to tell me," Aurelia said wryly, bracing herself, waiting for the inevitable *spinster* to ring out. It wouldn't be a new designation. It wouldn't even hurt.

"Pathetic."

Aurelia started. The word dripped from the woman's mouth with cruel relish. That one was new.

And it hurt.

Silence stretched between the three of them. Mrs. Knotgrass preened, all smug satisfaction.

"Marriage," Max inserted, "is not for everyone."

Aurelia's gaze flipped to him, grateful for the break in the awkward silence and heartened that she had some support against Mrs. Knotgrass's barbs. She waited for Max to remind the little viper that *he* had never been married either. Certainly that was what he meant by his remark.

Instead, he added, "Have compassion, Mrs. Knotgrass. Not everyone can be so charming as you." His eyes warmed over the widow before sliding back to Aurelia. "Lady Aurelia is a lost cause, I'm afraid."

She couldn't breathe. Her lungs constricted inside her aching chest. Her treacherous eyes stung. Vanity she didn't know she possessed just took a crying leap off a cliff. He'd insulted her before. God knew she had done the same to him. This shouldn't be any different. It shouldn't hurt so much.

But it did.

She gazed up at him standing there, his eyes

full of mockery. Beside him, the widow's feral little eyes gleamed with deep satisfaction. Perhaps it hurt so much because he said it in front of Knotgrass. The devil's own mercenary. And to think a moment ago she thought he might defend her.

She supposed she should not have been so caught off guard. And yet she felt betrayed. Flayed and exposed. His words rooted deep, bruising her to the bone.

"You . . ." A thousand fractured thoughts flashed through her mind as she gazed at his smug face. None proper. All ugly. But the one she landed on, the one she seized with greedy hands and launched at him, was perhaps the worst of all. "You . . . Cockless Camden."

Shock rippled across his features. His mouth pulled tight, the corners edging white. Mrs. Knotgrass gasped and slapped a hand over her mouth to muffle a burst of laughter.

Belatedly, Aurelia realized this moment must echo the first time that moniker was uttered. There was laughter then, too.

"Aurelia," Camden growled.

"What?" Aurelia blinked. "Did I say something amiss?"

The widow recovered enough to mutter, "With

that ill-mannered tongue, it's no wonder she can't catch a man."

Max looked very capable of inflicting bodily harm. Rationally, she knew he wouldn't, of course, but when he took a step toward her she simply reacted.

Her palms came up and shoved. Hard.

It all happened in an instant, though for her time slowed to a crawl. Max's eyes flared wide as he fell back, his arms flailing in wide circles, seeking balance, but he only succeeded in colliding into Mrs. Knotgrass as he went down. She yelped, her own arms flapping as she followed him into the pond.

Oh. Dear, God. Aurelia's hand flew to her mouth as Mrs. Knotgrass screamed loud enough to gain the attention of every bystander within miles. She stood, frozen, rooted to the spot, watching the scene unfold with macabre fascination. Several others crowded along the shore, gawking at the spectacle as well.

The woman continued to shriek as though she was injured, her arms flailing wildly while Max attempted to help her from the pond to the shore. Her lovely white and lavender striped gown was a muddied beige color now, with bits of sludge and indescribable matter sticking to it in various spots. When she looked down at herself, another long wail escaped her. She hopped several times, flapping her hands, which made her lose her footing again. Her hand shot out and snatched hold of Max, bringing them both back down into the water. Again.

As horrified as Aurelia was, a small trickle of satisfaction ribboned through her. She told herself it would be no less than Max deserved.

She clamped a hand over her mouth to stifle a sound that was part giggle and part groan. Max's frustration was clearly writ upon his face as he struggled to his feet, hefting the widow back up with him.

The gathered crowd watched the ongoing spectacle in fascination.

Even though it was an accident, Aurelia swallowed back a twinge of guilt as the widow started sobbing, plucking at the soaking wet snarls of her hair. A chorus of gasps rippled through the crowd as one large snarl came loose in her hand.

The widow's sobs became ear-shattering then.

"Egads! Her hair is falling out!" a man to the right of Aurelia exclaimed.

"No, no . . . it's not her real hair," the woman

beside him explained. "Some women do that, you know. To make their own hair appear thicker."

So much for all her gold tresses.

Everyone, including Aurelia, backed away as the two of them slogged to shore. By then Mrs. Knotgrass's maid had arrived—no doubt hearing the commotion—and Max turned the thoroughly wrecked woman over to her waiting servant. He then turned to face Aurelia, his gaze finding her in the crowd.

Her stomach knotted. He looked severe—frightening—as he pointed a finger at her and curled it, beckoning her closer.

She shook her head, her stomach coiling sickly. *It was an accident,* she mouthed at him, pleading with her eyes.

His eyes narrowed on her. She felt the chill of them across the short distance. She had never seen him look like this before. Not even when they quarreled and she irked him. He took a step toward her and then stopped when the widow started wailing for him, motioning for him to return to her. With one last look at Aurelia that promised retribution, he turned his back on her.

A relieved breath shuddered from her. She never thought she would feel gratitude toward Mrs. Knotgrass for anything, but in that moment she could have hugged her. It would be short-lived, she knew. She had seen Max's face. He wasn't finished with her.

Swinging her satchel across her shoulder, she started for home with no thought to dignity.

She ran.

Chapter 10

He would throttle her.

It was Max's sole thought as he trudged up the hill, his feet squishing in his soaked boots as he escorted the widow across the park to her waiting curricle.

She wept the entire way. And no small, delicate feminine weeping either. She wailed like a lowing cow, exclaiming over the state of her appearance, drawing all eyes their way. He resisted the impulse to shush her. She was embarrassed over what had transpired, to be certain, but her howling only attracted more attention.

He told himself he should not be so surprised. He knew Aurelia was capable of outrageous behavior. It was clear that she wanted him to think it was an accident. *Ha!* She wanted to punish him for burning her drawing. Even without that discord between them, she would go to any lengths to annoy and pester him. He could almost excuse her for this—he was accustomed to their skirmishes, after all—but the Widow Knotgrass had been innocent in their little war.

Innocent? She had not exactly kept her claws in check with Aurelia. He winced as he cast her a glance. She was murdering his ears with all her caterwauling. His perception of her as an enticing, soft-spoken lady was now shattered.

The maid trotted behind them, holding the widow's discarded parasol and pieces of her lost hair. Max tried not to look at the mangled chunks of hair that resembled slaughtered rodents, but he couldn't help his lip from curling. Again his thoughts returned to Aurelia and the ear-blistering he would give her when he caught up to her. It was bad enough she was the reason he had sought out the widow in the first place. He'd thought a good tupping might take his mind off Aurelia and her stupid quest for a husband. He thought it might help him forget the devastated look on her face when he flung that scroll into the fire. At the very least he would exorcise his lusts so he would stop getting so inconveniently aroused in Aurelia's company. At least that had been his reasoning.

"My lord, you're hurting me," Widow Knotgrass complained, tugging on her arm.

"My apologies." He quickly loosened his grip.

She sniffed, looking mollified. "And you're walking much too fast. I cannot keep up."

He sucked in a breath, reaching deep inside himself for patience as he slowed his pace to a crawl. Aurelia was likely fleeing for home already. From the one glimpse he'd had of her face—her wide eyes and sagging mouth—he knew she was afraid of him. And rightly so. His jaw clenched. He was not finished with her. Not by any means. He merely needed to free himself of the weeping woman at his side so that he could track down his quarry before she locked herself in her bedchamber and hid from him for the remainder of the Season.

She'd have to come out eventually, he assured himself. She was intent on winning a husband, after all. For some reason, this only made his mood darker. His free hand flexed at his side in anticipation of unleashing his ire on her.

"She should be horsewhipped," the widow complained between gulping sobs, stepping high and holding out her soggy skirts. "She deserves no less. You should call on her brother and see that she is punished."

He stared straight ahead, struggling to slow his stride for her dragging pace. A prickly feeling swept over his chest as he listened to this woman disparage Aurelia. "It was an accident," he heard himself say, defending her.

"She's a menace. That one should be kept on a tight leash," the widow complained. "Her family should put her in a sanitarium."

He released a long suffering breath. "Come now. That's a trifle extreme, don't you think?"

She blinked at him. "I am serious. It's done, you know. For women of her mercurial temperament."

He shook his head. The chit was abhorrent. He could not hide from that reality any longer. He'd prefer sharing a bed with a diseased monkey. He wanted nothing more than to deposit her in her curricle and be rid of her for good. She tempted him no more. He supposed he could thank Aurelia for giving him the opportunity to see her true colors . . . but he rather resented the fact that she had provided him with that insight.

Max enjoyed his bed sport. He didn't need great insight into the character of the females he enjoyed. He took his pleasure, gave it in return, and then moved on. Aurelia had made that impossible in this instance and he entirely blamed her.

"Camden," the widow whined. "You're still walking much too quickly."

He slowed his pace yet again, convinced that if he went any slower he would be standing still.

His gaze scoured the far edges of the park, searching for a glimpse of Aurelia in the rolling green. He knew she was fleeing for home not a far distance from where they were. She enjoyed her walks. She would not have made use of a carriage or mount on so short a length. He would overtake her on horseback.

He dragged a bracing breath deep into his lungs. No more of her pranks. This had gone far enough. No more of her sharp tongue. It would end this day. Once and for all.

Reaching the curricle, he assisted the widow up into it and closed the door after her. He had tied his horse to the back of the conveyance earlier so that they could ride together, but his only goal right now was to reclaim his mount and go after Aurelia. His blood pumped harder at the thought of delivering her a much deserved set-down.

"Lord Camden! Where are you going?" Mrs. Knotgrass demanded from where she sat, her hair hanging in wet tangles around her. For some reason he had a flash of Aurelia's hair . . . the dark mahogany flowing freely over her shoulders. He blinked, banishing the mental comparison and focused on the woman before him. There was not a man who would turn from the invitation in the widow's eyes. And yet he did not want her. *Bloody hell.*

He bowed smartly. "It's been a pleasure."

Her face reddened. "We did not even yet have our picnic . . ."

He motioned to his person. "I am hardly in a fit state." It would be ungentlemanly to point out that she was not either.

She moistened her chattering lips and pouted. "But we had been having such a lovely time."

Had they? He recalled their interaction before they happened on Aurelia. He'd been going through the motions . . . flirting, praising her beauty, entertaining her with empty conversation. And he had never been more bored. Not that he was one to share anything of himself with his paramours—but she had not asked a single thing about him.

She reached out and covered his hand with her own. "No need for it to end so soon. We can retire to my house. My servants can see to your clothes . . . while we make ourselves more comfortable in my rooms . . ."

There was no mistaking her meaning. It was what he thought he wanted from her. He slipped his hand free and moved to untether his mount from the back of her carriage. She watched him, her eyes narrowing in clear affront.

"I appreciate the kind offer, but I could not impose on you. Recently widowed . . . you're too vulnerable. And I must think to your reputation." He lifted her hand and pressed a kiss to the back of it.

From her bewildered expression, she did not believe he cared one whit for her reputation. "This opportunity, my lord," she said tightly, "will never come again."

He shrugged lightly, still smiling. "I will suffer the regret."

Her lips compressed into a hard line. She leaned back in her carriage and called for her driver to move.

Max did not linger. As far as he was concerned, he had already dallied too long. He mounted in one smooth motion and turned in the direction of the Merlton town house. Digging his heels in, he set off at a gallop across the park.

Chapter 11

Aurelia knew there was a good chance he would come after her.

She felt hunted. The gate clanged behind her, reverberating on the afternoon air. Her lungs burned with labored breath as she hurried down the path, just short of a run. Dignity held her in check . . . as well as sheer stubbornness. She'd done nothing wrong. It was an accident. Only the guilty ran.

Heat flushed her face at the half-truth. Very well, she had been somewhat in error. She had, in fact, pushed him. But that was only after he insulted her. And her intention had never been for the Widow Knotgrass to fall into the pond. That part was purely accidental—no matter how satisfying it had been. A snort escaped her that bordered on laughter. She had, admittedly, for one fraction of a moment, enjoyed seeing Widow Knotgrass emerge looking like a drowned cat. She sobered, forcing her amusement down. There would be time enough for laughter when this day's events were well and fully behind her. Only from the glimpse she'd had of Max's face, it would not be for another five years.

She shook her head lightly at the exaggeration. Max's wrath would cool. In time. Just as it had when she divested him of his garments in that card game at Sodom. His ire had cooled over that He'd eventually get over this, too.

She sidestepped a maid walking down the path, nodding a greeting and hoping she didn't look as frazzled as she felt. She need only escape to the sanctuary of her bedchamber.

The back entrance of the house appeared and she bypassed it, deciding to ignore it in favor of the servants' door a little farther around the back. That entrance saw less traffic, and she wouldn't risk bumping into Mama or Violet. They would only want to chatter and delay any escape into her room.

She knew she was being silly. It's not as though he would give chase straightaway. He still had Widow Knotgrass to escort. And yet, the fierce look in his eyes had made her shiver.

She took comfort in the knowledge that he would arrive via the front door, and then her comfort dissolved. How would he explain his very wet and disheveled person? That would invite questions. Questions like how did he get wet . . .

Dear God. What if he told Mama? Or Will?

She shook her head. No. He wouldn't. If he wouldn't divulge her night activities at Sodom or that she was the artist responsible for the caricatures popping up all around London, he wouldn't report on her now. At least, she prayed he wouldn't.

Aurelia forced in a calming breath. By the time Max called she would be safe in her bedchamber. Cecily will have been coached by then, armed with excuses as to why she was unavailable. He'd know the excuses were lies, of course, but she didn't care.

War called for different rules.

Spotting the ivy-covered back of the house, tension eased from her shoulders. Her pounding heart slowed. She had made it. Even with all the traffic coming in and out of the servants' door, the lush ivy threatened to swallow it. She closed her hand over the latch, ready to pull it open, when a hard hand clamped down on her shoulder and whirled her around.

She jumped, and quickly swallowed her startled cry as she came face-to-face with a wet, disheveled, very angry Camden.

He was not quite dripping wet, but he was indisputably soaked. Thanks to her. Heat crawled up her face.

He'd rid himself of his jacket and unbuttoned his vest to reveal the fine linen of his shirt. The white fabric was so wet it was rendered translucent. She stepped back, her gaze raking over him, stopping at the tan gold of his skin visible through the material. The flat expanse of his chest, the sharp contours of his pectoral muscles with their dusky brown nipples, so flat and dark and very different from her own, made her flush and feel all shades of awkward. Her gaze dipped lower, identifying the cut lines of his abdomen. Her mouth dried. She'd seen him shirtless before. The memory of him at Sodom was etched permanently in her mind. It wasn't right that one man should be so blessed.

Swallowing in an attempt to gain moisture in her mouth, she donned a look of calm innocence. "Lord Camden, what a surprise."

"A surprise? Oh, you didn't just see me in the park?" He advanced on her, bringing to mind a stealthy jungle cat. She could not stop herself from retreating, backing away as he spoke in that dangerously gravely voice. "You didn't just push me into the pond, then?"

"Oh," she stammered, eyeing his towering form warily. "That . . ."

"Yes. *That,*" he growled, settling his hands against the ivy-layered wall on either side of her head. For all his dampness, his body radiated enough heat that she felt singed.

She gulped, and then felt certain he had heard the sound. He had never talked to her so menacingly. He pressed his body against hers as he had once before. It was heaven. No, it was hell.

She struggled for bravado, refusing to let him know how intimidating she found him. "You're being a brute, Camden. Let me go."

"And you're a brat," he countered. "So we're well-matched."

A small shiver coursed through her. She was not certain how to manage him like this. She met his gaze, clashing with eyes that were now more gray than blue. The coldness in those smoky depths chilled her. She pushed lightly at his shoulder in an attempt to get him to let her pass, but he wouldn't budge.

"What do you want from me?" She fell back against the brick wall, and he only pressed closer. Her breasts ached where they mashed into him, her nipples hardening, and it was mortifying to think he probably felt her reaction to him—knew of her arousal.

She closed her eyes tightly, and in the darkness behind her lids, the long-ago image of him with Ingrid in the greenhouse flashed into her mind. The physicality of him as he worked himself over the maid made her flush hotter. Desperation shot through her. She would *not* be one of the countless women to fall at his feet. She had to break away before she revealed herself to be just as vulnerable to him as they were. Her pride could not withstand that embarrassment. Being demoralized once by him was all her ego would allow.

"Let me go," she demanded as she opened her eyes, hating that it sounded like she was pleading.

"You're not going anywhere until we're finished." He inched in, bending his arms so he could thrust his face close. So close that she could see the dark ring of blue surrounding his irises. "And we're not even close to being done."

Max knew he should release her. Trapping her against the wall of the house, where anyone could happen upon them, was a bad idea. This was Aurelia. No matter how angry she had made him, he shouldn't be touching her . . . much less manhandling her. Especially considering the inappropriate thoughts he had been harboring for her lately.

Lately?

If he were honest, he would admit he'd lusted after her for a long time. Ever since he first turned around at that garden party and saw her standing there. It was a dangerous realization—knowing he had wanted her for so long and being this close to her now, without an inch even separating their bodies.

He eased back, but then that obstinate chin of hers went up and she actually had the gall to look affronted. As though *she* were the victim and not the perpetrator of this day's deeds. "It was an accident, Camden. Unhand me."

"Was it? You pushed me—"

"You were being a wretch!"

"Enough," he bit out, closing in again on her. It was as though his body had a mind of its own. "Aren't you tired of it? The quarreling. The pranks? I know I am. You're a child . . . you have to stop acting like a spoiled little girl."

Her eyes widened. "And it's all me? You have no part in any of it? How dare you! You're not my father! Or my brother!"

He glanced down. Standing this close together, he couldn't see much of her body, but he felt every inch of it. The press of her breasts against his chest. The soft splay of her stomach against his hardening groin. As much as he wanted to throttle her, he could not stop his body's response. With a pained breath, he inserted some much-needed space between them while still keeping his hands anchored to the wall on either side of her head. "Oh, I'm well aware of that fact."

"And I'm not a child either."

"You do whatever you want—say whatever you want with no thought." Then, before he could consider his next words, he flung out, "No wonder no man wants to marry you."

The color drained from her face.

Cold washed through him as he took in her stricken look. He was a bastard through and through. A slap to the face could not have wounded her more. He recognized this at once.

"Aurelia . . ." he started, but her stricken expression fled at the sound of his voice. A shutter slammed over her eyes and her expression turned to steel. That should have given him warning.

"Go to the devil, Camden!" Her fist landed squarely in his stomach, knocking the wind from him in a whoosh. He bent over, catching his breath. Stunned, he lifted his face, his eyes locking with her equally shocked stare.

She'd hit him.

The air hummed around them, electric and alive.

She covered her mouth with her hands, in shock or horror. Then she fired into action, trying to dodge past him.

Something primal took over. There was only one thing to do. Only one recourse.

He didn't think. Simply hauled her back against the ivy-thick wall and covered her mouth with his own.

Chapter 12

The moment his lips crashed over hers, she felt as though she was swept up into a dream. None of it was real. Not the firm pressure of lips that felt surprisingly soft against her own. Not the slant of his mouth or the placement of his thumb on her chin, urging her jaw to loosen.

And if it wasn't real, then she could indulge herself in the delicious fantasy. Embracing that delusion, she parted her mouth for him on a sigh of surrender. His tongue slid inside and she moaned at the taste of him.

He shoved her deeper into the wall and it might have been uncomfortable if not for the cushion of ivy at her back and the delicious press of his body sinking against hers.

His hands gripped her shoulders, powerful fingers digging into her skin through her gown. She relished the sensation. The feel of him everywhere, the man, the body she had fantasized over since her gaze feasted on him at Sodom—and this with layers of clothes between them. She couldn't fathom what it might feel like skin-to-skin. The very possibility made her light-headed.

His mouth scorched hers, his tongue colliding with hers, licking and stroking until a hungry fire burned in her belly. She whimpered as he tore his mouth off hers. His gray eyes glittered brightly down at her.

His hands eased where they gripped her shoulders. "Did I—" His voice sounded dark and strained. "—hurt you?"

"Don't stop," she growled, pulling him back with one hand around his neck, letting that suffice for her response.

The kiss burned hotter, feverish and hard. Teeth clanged, but she didn't care. She had waited too long for this. He feasted on her lips, slanting his mouth one way and then the next. She caught on fast, mimicking his movements and quickly forgetting all about the kiss she had suffered long ago at the mercy of Archibald Lewis.

Lust sizzled through her veins. It wasn't enough. Her palm glided across his chest, sliding inside the open V of his shirt so that she could touch and feel his warm, firm skin. So much softer than she imagined he would feel. And yet hard. Muscle, sinew, and bone beneath taut skin.

Still not enough.

He returned the favor, his palm finding her breast. Stabbing pleasure shot straight to her core from the contact and she moaned anew. He drank in the sound, squeezing her breast, his fingers unerringly finding her nipple through the fabric of her bodice and pinching down. A needle of pleasure so sharp it bordered pain grayed the edges of her vision.

She cried out into his kiss, but thankfully his mouth swallowed that sound, too. Ripples of pleasure eddied over her. Her legs shook. If not for the pressure of him at her front and the wall at her back, she would have slid to the ground in a quivering mass. The tension coiled tighter and tighter in her belly.

His fingers gentled, rolling her nipple softly, teasing until she was gasping again, shaking in his arms, desperate and throbbing. She surged against his hand, wanting more, dying for a firmer touch again, for the release to the building pressure.

He positioned his hardness where she most ached and ground down against her, one hand cupping her bottom to lift her higher for him. Her eyes flew wide. He felt huge. Even through layers of clothing, she felt the enormous ridge of his manhood. Tortured little sounds escaped her mouth and nose as he rubbed himself against her, building and stoking that pressure until she felt ready to explode.

And he never stopped kissing her. His mouth and tongue continued tasting her, fierce and consuming, ravaging her lips.

Her fingers smarted where she clutched his shoulders, pulling and tugging him closer. It was madness, but she didn't want it to stop. He could take her right against the wall of overgrown ivy and nary a protest would pass her lips.

She lifted her mouth from his. "Please," she begged, needing an end to the ache.

She'd brought herself to release before. She knew she was close. She knew it would not take much more from him. He looked down at her with cobalt-dark eyes . . . a stranger, as new to her as this experience was. He watched her intently, his jaw locked and hard, his eyes penetrating and dark as he thrust his manhood once more against her and then pinched down sharply on her nipple.

She shattered in his arms, her body jerking against his. He claimed her mouth again, swallowing her cry. Her hands drifted from his shoulders, her arms sliding around him so she didn't melt into a puddle at his feet.

"That . . ." she gasped, her chest heaving as though she had just run a great distance.

That had been nothing like the pleasure she gave herself in the darkness of her bedchamber.

And she had not even removed her garments. Her mind reeled, thinking about what it might be like to truly *be* with him. The two of them with all the time in the world and not a stitch of clothing between them.

She dropped her head back against the wall, ignoring a pointy twig of ivy poking her in the temple. Max stared at her, his expression unreadable but no less penetrating, no less thorough. He stared at her long and hard, as though seeing her for the first time.

She moistened her lips, trying to think of something to say. What did one say after sharing such intimacy? His breathing was nearly as labored as her own. His gaze stark and searching.

The door suddenly opened beside them, and Max flattened against her, pressing them both back to the wall again. Hopefully the ivy obscured them. Aurelia watched over Max's shoulder as a maid left the house and departed down the path, humming softly under her breath.

They held still for a moment, Max's body aligned with hers, his heart beating against her rib cage in rhythm with her own.

"She's gone," she whispered, her fingers lightly fluttering against his shoulder.

He glanced behind him and then stepped back several healthy steps. Fortunately, she didn't slide to the ground. She smoothed a shaking hand over her dress and stepped away from the house.

She studied him then, waiting for him to say something, anything. Certainly, they needed to discuss what just happened. Acknowledge it in some way?

He held her gaze, his stare unflinching. Her heart beat faster. The undeniable wish stirred inside her that he would declare himself in some manner. That after their kiss, he would not be able to *not* kiss her again. That it had been special for him, too. Perhaps . . . that *she* was.

It was an absurd and fanciful notion, but he had said he was tired of the quarreling. Did he mean that? Could they move on from the bickering and be friends again? Could they have this now? The *more* she had always hoped for. Had she found it with Max, of all people?

He edged back a step, putting more distance between them. She frowned, beginning to realize he wasn't going to say any of those things. Indeed not. He would not say anything at all. He was leaving.

With one final look at her, he spun on his heel and quickly disappeared down the path without a word to her or a backward glance.

She stared after him for some moments, her lips still burning, her body still humming in the aftermath of the shattering release he had given her. He was running away from her.

Feeling slightly dazed, she brought her hand to her mouth, lightly fingering the kiss-bruised flesh. A slow smile took hold of her lips. A kiss like that . . . it wasn't ordinary. She didn't need vast experience to know there were sparks between them. Chemistry that couldn't be found just anywhere or with just anyone.

He'd be back.

He didn't come back.

A week. A blasted week had passed with no

sight of Max. Perhaps that kiss hadn't been so shattering for him, after all.

She busied herself, working on a new sketch and even taking calls from Mr. Mackenzie and Lord Buckston. Even if her heart wasn't invested, she accepted their courtship. Contrary to what Max said, they were suitable and her pickings were slim. Time was slipping through her fingers like water escaping a sieve. Her mother had begun packing for Thurso, and Aurelia knew that unless she wanted to go with her, she needed to concentrate more on finding a husband and less on Max.

She sighed. Easier said than done. She had possessed only vague notions of what a proper kiss *should* be. She'd witnessed Rosalie's and Violet's starry-eyed expressions and secret smiles when they were with their husbands. She knew there had to be something behind it all. Some thrill. She had been certain a kiss should not taste of fish and sour milk, as had the kiss she endured from Archibald Lewis, but until Max she had no notion of what a proper kiss could be. How it could make her forget everything else in the world. Everything except the sensation of lips and skin and sweetly warm breath.

That kiss had changed everything—ignited a deep craving in her.

She set her sketch pad aside and rose from the chaise beside her balcony. "He's avoiding me," she declared, pacing a hard line between her bed and dressing table.

Cecily glanced at her with an arched eyebrow from where she was airing out Aurelia's dress for the evening. They were dining with Declan and Rosalie. Unfortunately, Max would not be there. She knew that much. She had already inquired. He had declined the invitation.

"A prior engagement," she snorted, throwing her arms out wide at her sides. "What prior engagement could he possibly have to keep him from a simple dinner? He has to eat, does he not? And he never declines Will or Dec invitations! No, this is because of me." She pressed a hand to her chest, nodding, certain of it.

Was he avoiding her because of her brother? Naturally, dallying with his best friend's sister was a line he would be reluctant to cross. And yet he had.

Cecily shrugged as she selected a pair of brocade slippers that had seen better days from the bottom of the armoire. "Perhaps he's preoccupied making amends to the Widow Knotgrass."

Aurelia's shoulders tensed. That was a possibility she had not considered. She ran her hand over her long plait of hair, tugging lightly on the loose end. Had he left her with her lips bruised and aching for more and raced off to the Widow Knotgrass, the woman he *really* wanted to be with before she had wrecked his assignation? Perhaps he found Aurelia a poor substitute for the lovely and far more experienced widow? Had he spent the day in the widow's bed with Aurelia a pale memory?

She sank down at the end of her bed, clutching the bedpost with both hands as though it were a lifeline. Glancing up, she caught sight of her face in her dressing table mirror, bright flags of color riding high in her olive complexion. "That is a certain possibility," she finally admitted.

Cecily clucked her tongue and dropped down beside her on the bed, giving her shoulder a comforting squeeze. "Come. This isn't like you."

Pining for Max? It most certainly was not like her. Not in a good many years, at least. But then he had never kissed her before. And there was that other side of him she had seen at Lady Chatham's ball. When he had asked poor Miss Samantha Bell to dance. That was hardly the actions of a shallow, arrogant man.

She closed her eyes in a pained blink. A kiss from Max shouldn't have changed anything, but it had.

Perhaps it shouldn't have been such a surprise that Max had been the one to deliver her from tedium. Max was made for pleasure, after all.

She had to believe that the chemistry between them was unique. Surely it was not like that for him every time he kissed a woman? She refused to believe it. It had been special. He felt it, too. Hadn't he?

She glanced up at Cecily. As though reading her thoughts, her friend shook her head in sympathy. "There are plenty of men like him. My sister fell prey to the sweet words whispered by a handsome man. I was just a girl but I remember it well. My father shouting. My mother's tears. This man . . . he ruined her. Took Marjorie's innocence and left her reputation in tatters." She looked away for a moment, inhaling deeply. "My father tossed her out. She moved to the city, tried to find work. I lost track of her, but I like to think she's . . ." Her words faded and she blinked quickly, as if clearing the memories from her mind.

"Cecily." Aurelia closed a hand over hers. "You never told me."

"There's nothing to tell." She smiled a shaky grin. "Nothing to do about it now. No way to change it. I know you're not Marjorie, but I just . . . I just don't want you hurt, Aurelia."

The image of the Widow Knotgrass materialized in her mind's eye. She imagined Max kissing her . . . pressing the widow down on a bed and having his way with her with the same fervor he had displayed when he kissed her. Only with the widow, he did not stop. He was too overcome with desire. He was unable to tear himself away as he had with her.

Oh, she was a blasted fool. Of course he had not felt anything special for her.

Aurelia sucked a breath into her lungs. It was a hard truth. She had been so busy reveling in how that kiss felt that she had just assumed it was momentous for him, too. She had forgotten the cold contempt with which he'd treated her to all these years. She remembered now.

Cecily was correct. She needed to be careful. She needed to remember that Max was a rogue who didn't care whose bed he shared.

"You're right, Cecily." She nodded, feeling at rights again. If she continued fixating on Max, she was bound for disappointment. The Season would be over, and she'd be in a carriage on the way to Scotland before she knew it. "I think I will have Will invite Mr. Mackenzie to dine with us."

Cecily arched an eyebrow. "Indeed."

"Yes." Feeling better with her decision, Aurelia

nodded and returned to the chaise. Picking her sketch pad back up, she made a few strokes on the parchment before stopping. Her concentration continued to stray.

She felt Cecily's stare on her. "Something amiss?"

Aurelia lifted a shoulder in a half shrug. The possibility that she might not wed in time . . . that she might not receive an offer of marriage, nagged at her. The matter wasn't entirely in her control, after all . . . even if she made herself utterly amenable. And she hated that . . . the sense of not having control.

Seized with a sudden impulse, she rose from the chaise again and moved toward her small desk. She rifled through the drawer until she located the stationery.

"What are you doing now?" Cecily asked as Aurelia sank down on the chair and started scribbling on the parchment. Finished, she folded the missive, stuffed it inside the envelope and stood again.

"Here. Would you please deliver this for me?" She extended the envelope. "Now?"

Cecily stepped forward and took it from her hand. She looked from Aurelia to the missive, her eyes widening as she read the name on the outside of the envelope. Her fingers stroked over the clean lines of script that proclaimed Mrs. Bancroft's name on the outside of the envelope. The proprietress of Sodom. "Are you certain?" Cecily asked.

Naturally, her friend knew of her exploits to that club with Rosalie a year ago.

Aurelia nodded. "Yes." Part of the reason she had not revisited Sodom was that Rosalie couldn't accompany her. The rest of the reason might have to do with what happened with Max. The events of that night could have been too scandalous even for her.

Cecily nodded slowly, still looking unconvinced. "If you are certain . . ."

"I am." She moistened her lips. "Cecily, what if no one proposes—"

"Someone is going to propose to you. I wouldn't be surprised if they both ask you within the next fortnight." Cecily shook her head, smiling as though Aurelia was out of her mind.

Aurelia grinned ruefully. "Of course you would say that, but what *if* they don't? I want my last few months here to be memorable." Max had given her a taste of passion. Who knew what other adventures waited for her? With a fortifying breath, she continued, "There is a side door at Mrs. Bancroft's. A doorman is there at all times and will take the missive from you."

"Very well," Cecily said. "I don't think you have anything to worry about, but I will go." At the door, her friend paused and smiled ruefully. "I haven't your adventurous spirit." That said, she slipped from the room, leaving Aurelia alone.

Aurelia stared at the unmoving door for some moments before murmuring to no one, "Lucky you."

Her life would be so much simpler if she didn't want more. If she didn't crave it with an intensity that had only grown since Max pushed her up against the back wall of the house. He'd doomed her.

There was no going back now.

Chapter 13

Max stared into the dying flames flickering low within the great hearth of his study. He held his third drink of the night loosely in his hand, his legs stretched out before him. He scratched at the bristly growth of hair on his jaw. He had not shaved in days, and he felt in no particular rush to do so.

For the fifth night in a row he stayed in. It was a record.

The first two nights following that shattering kiss with Aurelia, he had gone out to all his usual haunts. He'd rubbed elbows with acquaintances, friends, strangers. He'd laughed, consumed copious amounts of liquor, and flirted with women. Rather *desperately* he had flirted with the fairer sex, trying hard to banish the memory of how perfect Aurelia had fit against him. How she had tasted of bergamot and mint. How she had shuddered and come apart in his arms.

Bloody hell. He lifted his glass and drank deep.

He had contemplated taking another woman to bed, but whenever he leaned in close to kiss one, he found himself pulling back. He could only see amber-brown eyes and olive skin. Every. Bloody. Time.

With a hissed breath, he rose and refilled his glass and then dropped heavily back into his armchair with a muttered curse.

He needed to forget her. Forget that kiss. Her smell. Her taste. Her wild responsiveness. He wasn't about to ruin a lifelong friendship because he had an itch to taste what was beneath Aurelia's skirts. Even he possessed a code. There wasn't much he wouldn't do, but virgins and best friends' sisters were off limits.

He'd reached a decision. It was the reasonable thing to do. The responsible thing. Come morning, he would depart for the country. He hardly ever left Town during the Season, but given the circumstances, a visit to his family estate seemed the only recourse.

He would absent himself from Town for a few months. By the time he returned, Aurelia would either be gone for Scotland or engaged. He took another deep gulp from his glass and pushed the thought of Aurelia married to someone else from his mind. He refused to think of her unleashing her uninhibited passions on some other man. With a groan, he brought his hand to his cock and readjusted the growing bulge in his trousers. Clearly, his attempts to not think about her weren't working. He eyed the decanter across the room, debating getting well and thoroughly soused.

A tentative knock sounded at his door. His staff was well aware of his black mood for the last week.

"Go away!" he bellowed.

A long moment followed before another knock came, a fraction louder this time.

He glared at his glass, contemplating tossing it at the door. "I said go away!"

The door creaked open and his butler stuck his head into the room like a turtle poking his head out of his shell. "M'lord?"

"Go away, Barton."

"You've a caller—"

"I don't want to see anyone tonight."

"She says it's an emergency."

She? He straightened in his chair, his mind racing.

She wouldn't dare . . . nor would he want her to. Of course, he would turn her away after a severe tongue-lashing. And immediately his thoughts took a dive into the gutter over what manner of tongue-lashing he would subject her to. *Bloody hell.*

"Send her in."

She must have been waiting outside the door. Barton scarcely withdrew back out into the hall before she entered.

Disappointment stabbed him in the chest. It wasn't Aurelia.

The fact that he had hoped it might be Aurelia indicated he was far from putting her out of his mind. The eagerness that tripped through him at even the possibility of seeing her again was wrong on every level. Aurelia visiting his bachelor residence this hour of night? It would ruin her. Of course, he didn't want that. He would be forced to marry her in that event.

He relaxed and fell back into the chair, eyeing the female before him as the door clicked shut behind Barton. He recognized her, but it took him a moment to place her. When he recalled that she was Aurelia's maid, he immediately tensed.

"What are you doing here?" Even a servant had a reputation to protect, and he suspected this girl was more than a servant to Aurelia. He'd often spotted them with their heads bent close together, whispering like schoolgirls.

She squared her shoulders. "I'm not going anywhere until I've said what I've come here to say."

He eyed the slim length of her. She was thin, but wiry. As though she had spent a good portion of her life hard at labor. "What's your name?"

"Cecily Calloway," she replied. "And I'm here at my own peril, to be certain. If Aurelia finds out I've come to see you, she'll horsewhip me." She inhaled a sharp breath, narrowing her brown gaze on him. "And if you're half the man I suspect you are, she will find out."

He arched an eyebrow, not certain whether to be complimented or not. "Indeed? And why is that?"

She nodded. "She'll know . . . because you will be going after her."

He sat up slowly. "Explain yourself. Why are you here?"

"She might be in trouble. It's just a feeling I have. Call it intuition."

With Aurelia, that was a very real possibility.

Cecily continued, "I told her not to go . . ."

Concern shot through him. Suddenly avoiding her over the last week seemed stupid. She was always one for rash words and behavior. Who knew what manner of trouble she had gotten herself into?

He stood, braced for what was to come, resolved to go after Aurelia no matter how risky it was to be around her. No matter that he only wanted to take her to his bed. Someone needed to protect her from herself.

"Where is she?"

"It's been a long time," Mrs. Bancroft said as she guided Aurelia down the corridor.

For the proprietress of an illicit underground club, Mrs. Bancroft was attired modestly in an understated gown of dark blue. It fit her snugly from throat to hem, but was still somehow provocative for the lack of flesh revealed. The most elaborate thing about her happened to be the black-feathered domino covering most of her face. Aurelia's domino covered nearly as much but was not nearly as opulent.

"Yes, it has been," Aurelia agreed rather lamely. She had not been this nervous the first time she visited Sodom.

That time you were not reeling in the aftermath of Max's blistering kiss.

She shook her head. That should not matter. If anything, it should only motivate her to extend her education in all things of a wanton nature.

"Truthfully, I did not know if you would remember me, Mrs. Bancroft," Aurelia said as they made their way up the stairs to the second level of Sodom.

"Of course I remember you. Aside from the fact that I make it my business to remember the names and faces of everyone to pass through the doors of Sodom, this establishment doesn't see too many inexperienced doves." Mrs. Bancroft assessed her slyly. "I take it you are a maid still? You've not married yet, I presume?"

Heat crept over her cheeks but she nodded. "Yes, I am."

"And how is your friend with the lovely red hair? I hazard to say she is a maid no longer."

"No, she is married now. Happily so."

"Well, good for her. I suspect she will never frequent Sodom again."

"Ah, that is unlikely," she hedged, in reference to Rosalie. Her friend would certainly never be returning. She didn't have the need for such adventures anymore. She was in raptures over her marriage. "I think one visit to Sodom was enough for her."

Mrs. Bancroft smiled vaguely. "Hm. Indeed. But once was not enough for *you*. You made quite an impression on your last visit here. Your card game was talked about for months. A few of the gentlemen that you played cards with have inquired about you."

Before she could respond—perhaps she wasn't expected to—the proprietress turned down the corridor, motioning at the doors on the left and right. "Do you have any notion of what you're looking for tonight in the way of entertainment? You may recall that various amusements can be found in specific chambers. Perhaps you prefer to observe in one of our voyeur rooms again?"

Recalling the eyeful she had gotten the last time she was here, heat crawled up her face. She had learned much. Those images had haunted her over the last year.

"Er, no. Perhaps I could mingle about the main room again. Are there still games downstairs?"

"Indeed, yes. Let us see what games we have tonight. Perhaps you will be lucky at cards again."

The memory of soundly trouncing Max made her grin. Until she recalled that he could possibly be here tonight. Which only made her scowl.

If he was here, it could be only for one reason. It would be so he could enjoy other women. Kiss them and fondle them as he had done with her. Take them to his bed as he had *not* done with her.

She knew it was contrary of her. She was here for the similar purpose of seeking her own pleasure . . . and yet it signified very little when her heart constricted painfully in her chest. She did not relish the idea of him with another woman.

Shaking her head, she vowed that she would exorcise the man from her thoughts. What happened between them had not affected him. So she wouldn't let it affect her either. She would indulge herself tonight, and tomorrow she would continue her husband hunt.

Dinner had gone well with Mr. Mackenzie and her family, and Buckston was taking her for a ride in his new phaeton tomorrow. Mackenzie was attractive if not a little intimidating. With young Buckston, there would be little risk—and Mama adored him. There was that.

Aurelia followed Mrs. Bancroft down to the main floor, trying not to feel uncomfortable at the eyes cast her way. She told herself that much of the attention was directed at the mysterious Mrs. Bancroft. Several gentlemen nodded and waved at the masked lady, hoping to gain her attention. All for naught. The proprietress's gaze did not linger overly long on any one individual, and yet there was no doubt that she took everything in, missing nothing that was occurring amid the walls of her establishment.

"Would you like me to find a spot for you at one of the tables?" She motioned to the room with an elegant sweep of her hand.

"Um, I think I should like to watch for a bit before deciding." She flashed a reassuring smile. "Don't let me keep you from your duties."

"If you're certain." Mrs. Bancroft considered her for a long moment, hesitating before leaving Aurelia alone. "Is there not something specific you're seeking that I could help you with? You seem different from your last visit . . . troubled perhaps?" She folded her slim hands in front of her with an air of patience. As though it were her custom to listen to the woes of her patrons. And it likely was, Aurelia realized.

Troubled? She winced at the apt description. She mulled over the well-meaning question. Was she seeking something specific? She supposed she was. Only the same mind-numbing passion she had felt in Max's arms. Not too much to ask. She swallowed back a derisive laugh, accepting that it might not be something she could likely replicate.

She scanned the large room. Conversation and laughter buzzed in the crowded space. "I should have no difficulty finding what I need, thank you."

Her stomach grew queasy as she assessed the various men. Several who now looked her over with speculation . . . as though she was a piece of horseflesh to be appraised. None of them enticed her in the slightest, and it occurred to her that she might have a slight problem even permitting anyone to touch her.

"Very well, then. Send for me if you need anything. The staff can locate me at a moment's notice."

"Thank you." She forced a smile for Mrs. Bancroft.

"It's simply good to have you back." With an elegant bob of her head, the proprietress turned and made her way back up the stairs.

Alone, Aurelia stared out at the room. Loud laughter in one corner snared her attention. She looked that way and gasped. A woman sat on a man's lap, halfheartedly batting his hands away as he tugged her bodice down to reveal one ripe breast. She squealed as he lowered his head to suckle her.

Mortification burned through Aurelia and she

suddenly became self-conscious of her breasts in her low-cut gown.

She knew she shouldn't be shocked. It was not her first time here, but she recognized several faces among the room's occupants. The Earl of Hedderfeld, an old friend of her father's, sat at one of the tables with a girl who couldn't be older than herself snuggled up beside him. Aurelia's skin crawled as she watched him feed her grapes like she was some kind of pet. Hm. Perhaps she should keep him in mind for a future sketch.

She continued to scan the room, pressing a hand over the stomach of her tight bodice. Any time she made eye contact with anyone, she quickly looked away as though she were staring down the barrel of a rifle. Her stomach knotted and she glanced behind her toward the door. Perhaps this had been a bad idea. It did not seem nearly as enticing without Rosalie for company. Last time, the experience had been adventurous. Now it just felt . . . tawdry and uncomfortable. Max's face flashed through her mind. She could only envision him across a table from her in this very room, stripping his clothes off to the titillation of onlookers. Her flesh warmed at the memory of his body, all long lines and hard angles

A tray passed her and she lifted a glass of champagne off it and downed it in one fortifying gulp, hoping it would supply her with some courage. The last thing she wanted to do was return home right now and endure Cecily's well-meaning I-told-you-so stare.

Someone suddenly stepped beside her. She looked sideways and then quickly stared straight ahead again, her pulse hammering in her neck. She pressed her hand against her throat, pushing her fingertips to her warm flesh there in an attempt to still the flutter. *Don't look at him. Don't look at him.* She knew the man.

Struan Mackenzie. The very man who had sat beside her this evening at her family's dining table now stood here beside her. Her heart pounded so hard it hurt inside her rib cage.

Please don't recognize me. Please don't recognize me.

"Hello, there," he murmured in his deep brogue.

She didn't dare glance at him. Relieved for the protection of her domino, she fixed her gaze on Lord Hedderfeld's balding head. When her eyes started to sting, she realized she hadn't blinked for several moments. With a small shake of her head, she blinked several times. *Behave normally,* she told herself. *Say nothing. Not a word. Give him no encouragement and he would move on.*

His brogue came at her again, heavy and deep with a ring of satisfaction. Or perhaps that was just her own doom she heard in his words. "I said hello there."

"Hello," she finally returned, her voice a shaky whisper.

"Ah, she speaks. I knew it."

She inhaled thinly. Did he not recognize her, then? Perhaps he simply toyed with her. If she continued to treat him with aloofness, he would go away and she could somehow escape this night without being utterly ruined. At least she hoped so.

He plucked her hand up and placed a kiss to the inside of her wrist. Panic jolted her at his touch.

"You know what else I know?"

She shook her head fiercely, processing the sensation of his mouth on her skin. A warm little flutter sifted through her. It wasn't *unpleasant* precisely.

"I know ye . . . my lady . . ."

He looked up, his moss green eyes holding her gaze in a knowing manner that made her stomach knot.

"You must be mistaken," she whispered.

A slow smile curved his lips as he lowered his head to kiss the inside of her wrist again, this time lingering and letting his teeth scrape the sensitive flesh there.

She sucked in a sharp breath. "You are too bold, sir." She attempted to tug her hand free, but he held fast.

He lifted his head, gazing at her as if he could see her face clearly . . . as though a domino was not covering half of it. His stare moved, roaming over her in her gown. She flushed, aware more than ever that it was a size too small and the bodice indecently low-cut. It might be pink, but it was not demure by any stretch of the imagination. Suddenly, she wished she was somewhere else. Wearing something else.

He leaned in closer. "Is this place not for the bold? *Lady Aurelia?*"

All hope died. She gulped at the very deliberate use of her name. There was no doubt now. He knew it was she beneath the mask.

"I had hoped we would grow better acquainted." His voice whispered for her ears alone. "I simply did not imagine it happening here. What a curious little minx you've turned out to be."

She considered insisting he was mistaken, that she was not who he thought, but that would be pointless. He could rip off her domino if need be. Or he could follow her home. There were any number of ways to verify her identity. "How did you know it was me?"

"Not many English girls have yer coloring . . . or impressive . . ." His voice faded, but she could guess his meaning.

The heat was back, flooding fire to her face. "You're *too* bold, sir."

"Am I? I would not think anything too bold for a girl who frequents Sodom."

She clashed eyes with him. "Rest assured, this is not customary for me."

He nodded. "I surmised as much. I would have remembered ye here."

"So you often frequent this establishment, then," she shot back. She supposed she should mind if a suitor spent so much of his free time at Sodom. If she cared for that suitor even a fraction, she *should* care.

She gazed at the Scotsman looming over her with fresh eyes. He was certainly handsome . . . and yet she didn't feel anything for him. *Blast!* It would be exceedingly convenient if she did.

"It's all professional, I assure ye. I like to keep an eye on the competition."

She shrugged. "It is none of my business."

"No? Well, I confess I'm surprised to find ye here tonight, Aurelia. What else might I learn of ye?" He trailed a fingertip against her collarbone.

She met his gaze directly. "What are you going to do with this knowledge, Mr. Mackenzie—"

"Struan," he corrected, his deep brogue practically purring the sound. *Strewan*. "I believe we can use each other's Christian names at this point."

"Struan," she amended. "Will you inform my family?"

He angled his head thoughtfully. "I dinna think I need to do anything so hasty, lass. I can be discreet." He dragged his fingers from her neck over her shoulder and down her arm. "Especially when it concerns a friend."

She echoed numbly. "A friend?"

He inclined his head and the motion caused the chandelier light to gild the gold-brown strands. "We're friends, are we not? Although I confess I'm interested in something more than friendship from ye . . ."

"Take your hand off her."

Chapter 14

Aurelia whirled around, her mouth parting to find Max standing there. He was hardly attired fittingly. His hair was wild and untamed around his head. He wore no vest beneath his jacket and his shirt was rumpled and open at the throat, minus a cravat. And his face. *Good heavens.* He looked like a pirate. Clearly he had not seen a razor in a week. All that said, he should not have been so achingly handsome.

It wasn't fair . . .

It wasn't fair that she had a big, strapping Scotsman flirting with her and she felt nothing. And yet the moment her eyes clapped on a wickedly disheveled Max, all her feminine parts stood up in salute. In a flash, everything she had felt squeezed between Max's body and that ivy-covered wall came back to her in a rush of heat.

"What are you doing here?" she demanded, and then felt like a prime idiot. Did she think because they'd shared one kiss he would stop coming to Sodom? He was likely here to do what he always did—take his pleasure with any random woman to catch his eye.

"That is a question I think best directed at you." His gaze raked her, making her acutely conscious of the indecent amount of flesh on display. Her hand drifted to her chest. Perhaps an ill-planned move. His gaze followed the action. The flesh near his eye ticked and his gaze darkened a shade.

She dropped her hand and squared her shoulders. An action that only brought her chest into greater focus. His bloodshot eyes fixed unerringly on that expanse of flesh. His mouth hardened into a thin line as a dull flush of color crept up his cheeks. She thought she had seen him at his angriest in the park, but no. This was the angriest she had ever seen him.

"I don't see why my presence here is any concern of yours."

"Indeed? Don't you?"

"I think I should point out that we are drawing more attention than perhaps desired," Struan interjected drolly.

A quick glance around the room confirmed that several interested gazes had settled on them.

With a stinging curse, Max took hold of her arm and pulled her from the room.

"Let go of me," she said between clenched teeth as they stepped out into the empty foyer.

"I'm taking you home," he snapped.

"Perhaps it is I who should escort the lady home," Struan Mackenzie announced from behind them, following them at a casual stroll.

Max stiffened and turned slowly, dragging Aurelia behind him. "Over my dead body."

Mackenzie looked him up and down assessingly, as though that were a fine prospect to him. The two men stared at each other in charged silence, a silent exchange passing between them.

"The lady and I are courting. Perhaps we should ask her what she prefers," Mackenzie declared at last.

"Her preference does not signify." The twin

lines bracketing Max's mouth whitened. "Rest assured, her brother would prefer I escort her—"

"Oh, enough of this!" She pushed herself between the two of them, waving her hands. She wasn't about to have bloodshed over such a trivial matter as who escorted her home—since, apparently, she would be going home.

In truth, she didn't have the stomach to remain at Sodom. A fact she rested solely at Max's feet. The inclination for such sport, it seemed, had left her.

She stabbed a finger in Max's chest. "You may escort me home." She swung her gaze to Mr. Mackenzie. "Lord Camden is a family friend. I will be fine."

His unreadable gaze drilled into her. It was difficult to tell whether he objected or not. Not that it mattered one whit to her. The decision was hers whether he was a prospective husband or not.

Without waiting to hear whether the Scotsman agreed, Max grabbed her hand and pulled her after him through the house, his stride so swift she practically tripped.

"Slow down," she hissed.

"Would you rather I carry you?" he growled.

With a huff of affront, her legs worked faster to keep up with his longer strides. He dragged her out a side door she'd never noticed before, attesting to his knowledge of the establishment. For some reason, that only incited her anger further.

His carriage was waiting in the dark alleyway. She realized that he must have communicated their destination beforehand, so confident he would retrieve her, because they ascended into the carriage without a word to the driver. Once the door shut behind them, they were off.

She chose the far corner of one seat, her back facing the front of the carriage, relieved when Max took the opposite side. The more distance between them, the better. She had struck him before in a fit of pique, and although she felt like doing it again, she curled her hands under her thighs, determined to resist succumbing to violence.

The carriage started down the alley with a gentle roll. His eyes glittered across from her in the dark interior of the carriage.

"What can you have been thinking?" he demanded.

"I don't owe you an explanation for my actions."

"You owe your brother, do you not? Your mother? Would they not be influenced by your utter ruin?"

"I'm not ruined."

"You know that for fact? Mackenzie saw you. You think he can be trusted?"

"He said he would not tell—"

"Oh, and you know him to be trustworthy. What happens when you anger or slight him?"

"What makes you think I would anger him?"

"Because that's what you do. You're infuriating . . ."

She crossed her arms. "He's been very attentive in his courtship. I think he quite likes me."

He growled, "I'm sure he does. What happens, though, when he learns that he cannot have you? That might anger him."

"I don't know," she replied with deliberate casualness. "I'm not so sure he can't have me. I am looking to get married."

A deadly stillness came over him. The back of her neck prickled with unease. She looked toward the curtained window, but eventually turned back to look at his shadowy features, compelled by the sensation of his stare crawling all over her face—as tangible as a touch.

He finally spoke, and his voice was as rough as sand against her skin. "You've settled on Mackenzie, then?"

"He has been calling on me ever since Lady Chatham's ball. It's him or Buckston." *Or obscurity with Aunt Daphne. No, thank you.*

Staring at Max's shadowy shape, she almost

hoped he would say something. That he would have a better idea. Very well. If she was completely honest with herself, a part of her wanted him to say she couldn't marry Mackenzie or Buckston because their kiss had meant something to him, too. She wanted him to tell her that he didn't want her to marry anyone. *Except him.*

Irrational laughter bubbled up inside her chest. *Blast it.* That kiss again. She couldn't shake it. It had addled her thoughts. Returning to Sodom had been a disappointment . . . and a revelation. Now she knew she wouldn't be able to find what she felt with Max so easily with anyone else.

When he spoke, his voice was even. Reasonable. "You don't think you might not be rushing into this?"

"I'm three and twenty . . . the oldest debutante in London. At least that's what the other debutantes call me." Among other things. Dark-complexioned opinionated girls did not win many friends in the *ton*. "I've had several years to find someone—"

"So you'll rush into it now?"

"I'm finally being responsible. I'm doing what girls—" She caught herself and amended her remark. "—what women do. What my family expects me to do."

"Since when do you care what's expected of you?"

"Yes, well, maybe I should. Why should it be a question? Maybe you should, too."

"What's that supposed to mean?"

She gestured at him. "Do you intend to live this way forever? I mean . . . since Will and Dec married, what do you have, Max? I know they don't spend nearly that much time with you anymore. So what do you have? What's left?"

"What's wrong with the way I live? I enjoy my life."

"You use women, Max. You flit from one to another. You're the last in your line. What of an heir?"

"I have a distant cousin in Wales. The title will pass to him."

"That's *your* brilliant plan? How is that better than mine?"

"We're not talking about me."

"And why is that? Why is it we never seem to talk about you?" At his silence, she pressed on. "Let's talk about this grand plan of yours. Your determination to never wed. How will you have children? I'm sure your parents are looking down on you now and thinking—"

"Don't." The single word struck her like a

slap. "I'm not discussing my parents with you or anyone." His raspy voice reverberated into the silence of the carriage.

If she hadn't already known how little she signified to him, there was no denying it now. There was no part of himself he was willing to share with her, and she felt foolish for thinking there might be a chance of that otherwise. She moistened her lips, on the brink of apologizing, "Max, I—"

"No." His voice rang with such finality, and she felt the chasm yawn between them. She felt his gaze more than she could see it glittering across the darkness at her. She wiggled her bared shoulders, regretting her choice of gown, sensing the crawl of his eyes over her. "It's none of your business, Aurelia."

She sucked in a silent breath, suddenly glad for the near darkness. Glad that he could not see the splash of color heating her face.

She stared blindly at the curtains, stiffening her spine where she sat. Had she really been on the verge of apologizing to him? For what? Trying to scratch beneath the surface for a glimpse of what he kept hidden from the world.

The carriage rolled to a stop and the driver knocked, signaling their arrival. Her hand flew to the latch, but Max's hard voice stopped her.

"If you're so resolved to marry . . . Mackenzie or someone else, then what were you doing at Sodom?"

Good question, and a little too mortifying to answer with any semblance of truth. How could she reveal that she worried no one would ask her before the Season ended? That she was, perhaps foolishly, trying to make a memory?

"Aurelia." His hand circled her wrist, exerting the barest pressure, demanding an answer and keeping her from leaving, even though they sat parked not far from her home.

"I just wanted . . . a good time."

"A good time?" He inched closer, his knees bumping hers. "Is that what you were having when I showed up? A good time?"

"A little." She tossed her head, sliding a loose curl off her shoulder and down her back. "I had barely arrived when you showed up. You interrupted me before I could even get started."

"Pardon me for ruining your fun, then." His voice rang with anger, and she knew he believed her. There was that at least. He didn't know that she was having an abysmal time and on the verge of leaving. She didn't want him to even suspect that he had ruined Sodom for her.

He continued, "But I don't think your brother

would have approved of me leaving you to your own devices in Sodom just so you could have a good time." She heard the censure in his voice, which struck her as the height of absurdity.

"You're no one to cast stones. How often do *you* go there?" She shook her head. "Never mind. I don't want to know the sordid details of your life. I know enough already."

He answered her anyway. "You're not me."

"Clearly. Or I would be having a far more enjoyable time right now." She should just come out and tell him that she hadn't even been enjoying herself when he showed up, but she could not bring herself to say the words . . . to give him even the slightest satisfaction.

Instead, she heard the lie tripping off her lips, "I'll just have to keep going back until I'm fortunate enough to choose a night you aren't there."

He pulled her closer, until she was practically in his lap and their noses inches from touching. "You will not go back there."

"You have no authority over me."

"Damn it, Aurelia," he growled, his hand sliding to hold her face, fingers spearing through her hair. "You're leaving me with little choice."

Unease skittered across her already knotted shoulders. "What do you mean?"

A long moment passed. His mouth was so close she could almost taste it.

"I'm going to have to tell Will."

His words landed like a blow. She pulled away. His hand slid from her face. "Tell Will *what*?" she demanded, deliberately failing to grasp his meaning because he couldn't possibly mean he would tell her brother about her venturing out to Sodom.

"About tonight and the last time."

"You wouldn't dare!" she charged.

"I don't see any other way to stop you from hurting yourself."

Oh, the gall! She blew out an angry breath. "I'm sick unto death of men . . . *you* being able to live the life you want . . . and if I step even a fraction outside my mandatory box—"

"Sodom is only a fraction?" he cut in.

She ignored him. "If I want even a fraction of the freedom you enjoy, I'm bullied and threatened. By you more than anyone else! Go ahead. Do your worst. While you're at it, tell him about my caricatures, too. Tell him everything!" She pushed the door open and stepped down before he could stop her. Outside at the door, she turned to glare at him. "Do it." Her chin lifted. "I dare you . . ."

"Aurelia . . ." he said warningly, moving to climb down after her.

She didn't linger. She was too angry. Lifting her skirts, she started down the walk, opening the gate and passing through it, hastening when she heard him behind her. She didn't make it very far. His tread quickened, hard footfalls that matched the pounding of her heart. His hand clamped on her arm and whirled her around.

Her head fell back to look up at his shadowed features. She didn't give him time to say anything before charging ahead. "You think you shall remain unscathed in all this if you tell him? You forget you were there with me both times I went to Sodom. Each of those *ruinous* times. And you did not even tell him about the first time a year ago. How will he view you after that? You, his supposed closest friend?"

She was grasping at straws. She knew it. Will would be furious with Max, no doubt, but it would take something far greater to ruin their friendship.

"That's a risk I'll take," he said.

"I'll tell him," she vowed.

For a moment he said nothing. She tasted his breath so very close to her own, but she was not certain he heard her or understood her meaning until he said, "About us?"

She nodded. "Last week . . . behind the house."

"He . . ." His voice faded.

"Would be very upset," she finished. "A man's sister is off limits, no?"

His hand came around the back of her neck, hauling her up on her tiptoes. Nearly covering her mouth with his, he growled, "Are you trying to rope me into marriage, Aurelia? Is that what you want?"

His words struck a blow to her heart—and shook her to the core. "N-No! I—"

"Because that is what would happen if you did such a thing. And I promise you, marriage to me . . . you would regret it every day of your life."

A small shiver rolled through her at the threat. He meant it. The notion of being married to her was so very repellent to him that he would punish her if it came to pass. She swallowed against the lump in her throat. "I'm certain you would make sure of that."

"It would not be so difficult a feat. I'm not made for matrimony, Aurelia. Even if I find you tempting—" He stopped abruptly, as if he had said too much. More than he intended.

"You find me . . . tempting?"

A long beat of silence ensued before he ignored her question and said, "You must promise me not to go back to Sodom."

She narrowed her gaze, not liking his tone. "I must?"

"Yes. I forbid it."

"You forbid it?" She inhaled sharply, everything inside her tightening with affront. She stepped back, severing the contact of their bodies.

He clamped one hand on her wrist, stopping her from completely fleeing. "I will have that promise from you or—"

"Or what?" She thrust her face close to his.

His gaze flicked over her features. "You think I'm jesting? I *will* go to your brother."

She held his gaze a moment longer before demanding, "Why are you really doing this? It's not to protect me. You care nothing for me."

That seemed to silence him. She took his silence for agreement. He was certainly *not* denying her claim. She turned to glare out at the darkened garden. For some silly reason her eyes stung.

"Of course I care for you."

"Because of Will," Aurelia accused.

"Because I can't get you of my mind." He swore and flung his hands in the air before dragging them through his hair. "Your desirability is unquestionable," he allowed, his voice grudging. "But you know that."

She blinked. "Why would I know that?"

He peered at her through the gloom. "You've seen men look at you—"

She snorted. "Where? At Sodom? That's because they believed me a soiled dove. It doesn't count."

"You've seen the way *I* look at you."

"Like you want to strangle me? Yes." She snorted again and laughed awkwardly. "I've noticed that on occasion."

"True. Sometimes I look at you like that." Humor edged his voice as he circled her wrist with hard fingers and reeled her in. She dug in her heels. "But that's not the only way I look at you." His voice dropped to a husky murmur that made her skin ripple with heat.

She opened her mouth, but the words were wedged too deeply in her throat. He pressed her palm flat against his chest. She stared at her pale fingers, slim and long, splayed wide against the dark fabric of his vest. She could feel his heart pounding through the fine fabric.

His deep voice continued, vibrating against her hand, "Sometimes I look at you like I'm looking at you now."

She swallowed and forced the words up to her lips. They escaped in a tremulous whisper, "I can't see you well enough. It's too dark." Not entirely true. She saw the way his eyes gleamed in the night. As though lit from inside.

"Then perhaps you can *feel* how it is I'm looking at you."

Before she could ask him how it was possible to *feel* that, he took her hand and dragged it up to his mouth. He pressed a hot, open-mouthed kiss to her palm.

His lips grazed her as he talked, sending sparks through her body. "Can you feel this? It's how I'm looking at you. Like I want, no—need to kiss you." She gasped at the feel of his tongue against her sensitive skin. "Lick you, taste you. Here—" His mouth moved to the inside of her wrist. "And here." He trailed kisses up the inside of her arm.

Her chest tightened, aching. And then his lips were at her throat. His mouth closed over her pulse point. A jagged moan spilled from her lips and her knees gave out. His arm snaked around her waist, catching her against him.

His teeth scraped a trail up to her ear. He gently pulled the lobe between his lips, laving with his tongue and then biting down. A sharp stab of pleasure pounded to life between her legs and she groaned.

"Everywhere," he breathed into her ear.

"Stop. Please," she begged hoarsely, arching

her head to the side. "I don't require this manner of convincing from you to make myself feel better. We've spent years despising each other—"

"Convincing?" he growled into her ear, one hand finding its way into her hair, spearing through the heavy strands. "As though this isn't real? When have I ever pretended with you?"

Then his mouth found hers.

He swallowed her cry, crouching in one quick motion and lifting her off her slippered feet so that their fused mouths were the same level. It was exhilarating. No standing on tiptoes. Her hands framed his face, holding him as they kissed. No. More than kissed. His mouth ravaged hers in a collision of lips, tongue, and faintly scraping teeth.

She slid her hands from his face and wrapped both arms around his shoulders, hanging on for the tumultuous ride.

They were moving. Aurelia was faintly conscious of that. She didn't open her eyes to look. She was too lost, reveling in his tongue in her mouth, his fingers diving into her hair, scattering pins.

She gave the scarcest grunt when he backed her against the garden wall, his big hands firmly gripping her bottom. The sound didn't even give him pause. No. He didn't ease the pressure of his mouth on hers one tiny bit.

His kiss was hot and aggressive, punishing on her tingling lips. She felt him everywhere and this was only a kiss. *Good heavens.* What would it be like to have him? Fully? To come together as a man and woman?

"Is this what you wanted?" he growled against her lips. "Have I *convinced* you I'm not pretending?"

She whimpered against his mouth and adjusted her arms, practically crawling higher up his body, parting her legs for him to settle between her thighs. He pushed his hips into her and she moaned, shifting slightly so that the core of her met the hard thrust of him. All her womanly parts melted to warm butter.

She longed to feel him there without the barrier of clothing. He increased the pressure of his mouth on hers, his body rocking and grinding into her until she wanted to tear their garments off. It was that or die from this exquisite torture.

She kissed him desperately, out of breath and drowning. Coherent words were beyond her. She could only gasp his name as he sucked her bottom lip into his mouth. "Max."

He pulled back, and she chased his lips for a moment, gradually focusing on his eyes flashing with enough heat to incinerate her. "Well. There. Can you say you despise me now? A woman doesn't kiss a man like that if she hates him."

She giggled nervously and squeezed out between him and the gate wall, trying not to reveal how shaken she was. "Your arrogance knows no bounds."

"It's not arrogance. You kissed me—"

"I beg your pardon? *You* kissed me just now," she corrected him, shaking her head.

He shrugged. "Whoever moved in first—"

"You moved first." The distinction was important. She stabbed him in the chest with the tip of her finger. "You won't twist what happened to suit you . . . to cover your shame. You came after me. *You* kissed me."

A muscle feathered across his jaw. "Very well. I moved first."

She sniffed, mollified. And yet he didn't back away. She sucked in a breath. His proximity made her dizzy. It was tempting to grab him and continue where they had left off. His gaze dipped again, brushing over the low-cut bodice of her gown.

"And," he added, "there was no shame in that kiss." His voice deepened to a rumble. "I liked it." His gaze crawled over her face in the moonlit garden, missing nothing, inching over her eyebrows, down the slope of her nose, and stopping at her lips. "You liked it, too."

She moistened her lips, her heart stuttering as his eyes followed the movement of her tongue.

"We were once friends." He angled his head, his gaze drifting back up to her eyes. "Sometimes I forget that."

"Me, too," she whispered. A long moment passed as they stared at each other. Perhaps truly seeing one another for the first time.

"What happened, Aurelia?"

She shook her head. "Who can say? It just became so natural, you know?"

"What did?"

"Being enemies."

Nodding grimly, he exhaled as though her words had served as some sort of reminder. He took several steps back, holding himself stiffly. She breathed a little easier with the added space between them.

"It doesn't matter anymore, does it?" he finally asked. "We can't . . . perhaps it's for the best."

She frowned. "What do you mean?"

"We need to remember who we are."

If possible, her frown deepened. "And who are we?"

"You're Will's sister. And I'm a man not looking to get married."

Pain knifed inside her. "That works out exceedingly well." She lifted her chin, digging deep for her pride. "Because I'm not looking to marry *you*."

He opened his mouth as though he was going to say something more, but then he shook his head and instead said, "I need your word that you will never step foot in Sodom. I care for you. And I worry. As Will's sister—"

"Oh, rot!" He *worried* for her? A moment ago he couldn't stop kissing her, but now she was back to being Will's sister again.

She shoved at his chest, catching him off guard and finally getting around him. She held her skirt up with one fist, her slippered feet racing down the damp path. There was a certain degree of déjà vu. She running. Max in pursuit. At the door, she stopped and glanced back at the empty path. She gulped a breath. He wasn't coming this time. Of course. That would be foolhardy. The hour was late. The last thing he would want was to be discovered in her company. Especially with her attired in a gown like this. That would complicate matters.

As they had agreed, Cecily had left the door

unlocked. Aurelia hurried through the kitchen, still warm and smelling of the bread that Cook had baked for the following day.

She made her way up the back stairs and emerged onto the second floor, pausing when she thought she heard a sound. A creaking step on the servants' stairs.

Fearful that a servant had returned, she rushed down the corridor and plunged into her bedchamber.

Once inside her room, she locked her door. Her heart beat like a drum inside her too tight chest. She gulped for breaths, admitting to herself that she was half afraid he would follow her. And half hopeful.

Stupid. She knew better. He had wrecked her evening, told her he would never marry her, kissed her to an inch of her life and then told her she worried him. The man infuriated her.

She pushed off the door. He wouldn't come after her. He wouldn't dare do something so inappropriate. He would keep her firmly at arm's length from now on.

Moving to the foot of the bed, she started to struggle out of her gown. A difficult task without Cecily's help. It was wretchedly tight, and the buttons so tiny at her back, impossible to grasp. With a groan, she fell back on the bed, staring up at her canopy.

She felt trapped, and the restrictive gown was only partly to blame for the sensation. Her gaze flitted ahead unseeingly into the shadows. Her mind worked, searching, groping for something.

There would be no more sneaking out to Sodom. She winced. No regret there. No more kisses from Max. She winced again and ignored the stab of regret.

Finding a husband . . . Struan Mackenzie . . . was her only hope left.

Chapter 15

Max returned to Sodom only to learn that the Scotsman had left. A few carefully directed questions and he was able to ferret out the man's address. Shortly after that he was being escorted into Mackenzie's well-appointed office by a bleary-eyed butler.

The man looked up from his desk. Several ledgers were spread before him. Apparently after a night at Sodom, he preferred to work. "Camden. To what do I owe the pleasure?"

"We need to talk about Aurelia."

Mackenzie leaned back in his chair, crossing his arms over his broad chest. "Oh?"

"Stay away from her."

"Now why would I do that? My intentions are honorable . . . and I happen to know that Lady Aurelia is in the market for a husband."

Max stopped before the desk. "That husband won't be you."

"And you intend to marry her, is that it?" At Max's expression, he chuckled. "Oh, you should see your face."

"I'm not interested in marrying her."

He scratched his jaw. "Then I fail to understand what you are doing here."

"She's the sister of my best friend . . ."

"Then why is Lord Merlton not here?"

"He doesn't know—"

"I'd wager there are a good many things Lord Merlton doesn't know about his sister . . . and *you*."

The words hung in the air, threatening. Max did not mistake the implication.

"There are other eligible girls," Max said. "Move on to one of them."

Mackenzie sighed and cocked his head like he was contemplating the suggestion. "Ah, I'm going to say . . . *no*. I like Aurelia."

You can't have her.

"What do you want?" Max growled, his fists curling and uncurling. He would like nothing more than to feed his fist to the arrogant bastard's mouth.

Mackenzie settled his considerable bulk more fully into his chair and considered Max at length. "Unless you have a marriageable daughter or sister with appeal equal to Lady Aurelia, you have nothing I need, Lord Camden." He waved his arms wide, encompassing the opulence of his office. "I'm a wealthy man, as you can see. I need very little of a material nature."

"You have a price," Max proclaimed with certainty, his hands tightening at his sides.

Some of the mirth faded from Mackenzie's eyes. "I don't know if I should be offended, but let me be clear. There is only one thing I would like and that is a blue-blooded wife to secure my position in Society."

"And you've chosen Aurelia to be that wife?" He wondered what the man would think if he knew his prospective bride was the same person drawing satirical caricatures of the *ton* and leaving them all over Town. There were wagers in betting books as to the identity of the mystery artist. Aurelia was a breath from ruin at any given moment. Would Mackenzie be quite so certain she was the perfect blue-blooded wife if he knew?

"I like her well enough. So far."

Max's skin prickled with the conviction that Mackenzie would have a change of heart if he knew of Aurelia's hobby. "You'd be surprised . . . you don't know everything there is to know about Lady Aurelia."

Mackenzie lifted an arrogant brow. "Oh? Do tell."

He swallowed against the tightness in his throat. That would be one way to kill Mackenzie's pursuit of Aurelia. Except he remembered her devastated expression when he tossed her scroll into the fire, and he knew that, for her, this would be far worse. She'd feel utterly betrayed if he revealed her secret. He couldn't do it. *Bloody hell.* When had he started caring so much about her feelings?

Max didn't agree with the risk that she was taking, but somewhere amid their arguing he finally understood. It was more than a hobby to her. It was a part of her and a calling, and as long as the world didn't know she was behind the drawings she was utterly free to express herself with no fear of censure.

Except from me.

He had censured her, and suddenly he regretted that. He felt a little ill with the knowledge that he had destroyed something that was important to her.

He couldn't reveal her secret to Mackenzie even if it meant saving her from the man.

"I'm just saying you don't know each other very well." He shrugged, attempting to defuse the implication that Aurelia had something to hide.

"I confess I've not made up my mind yet, but she is a tempting parcel. There is fire to her . . . as you undoubtedly know." That eyebrow winged high again. "On that topic, how well do you know her, Camden?"

Max strode across the room and reached across the desk, grabbing Mackenzie by the edges of his jacket and yanking him halfway across the surface. "Have care how you speak of her. She is more than an *tempting* parcel. If you go near—"

The Scot laughed, seemingly unperturbed at being manhandled in his own home. Was there nothing that affected the bastard? He was cold, to be certain. "This is your brotherly concern, is it?" His eyes fastened on Max, hard as polished malachite. "She is but a lass. A tasty one, but I've not settled on her yet. As I've pointed out, I want position. If could buy a title, believe me, I would. It appears the closest I can get is marrying into a good family. The Earl of Merlton for a brother-in-law would be a nice prize."

"You'll not have Aurelia simply to lift your rank." He flung Mackenzie back in his chair. "She's worth more than that."

She *deserved* more than that.

The idea came to him suddenly. Before he could fathom it or wonder at the origin of such a sentiment.

Mackenzie resettled his weight in his chair, smoothing a hand over the front of his jacket, and then corrected his mussed cravat. He did not reply for some time. He simply stared at Max as he traced the rim of the glass sitting on his desk with idle fingers. "I didna think you have any control over the matter. I've spoken with Aurelia and she would fit nicely into my plans. She has plans of her own, you see."

"What do you know of her plans?" Max demanded, unaccountably angry with her for sharing anything of herself, including her thoughts, with this arrogant ass.

"She has no wish to rusticate in Scotland with her mother and doddering aunt. I know that much. I know she is amenable to the idea of marriage and not opposed to my courtship."

She had shared all of that with him? His stomach cramped, imagining her in Mackenzie's bed. Imaging this man's hands on her, his mouth exploring her as he himself had only ever dreamed.

Hell no.

"It appears we are at a crossroads," Mackenzie said. "I require a wife. Aurelia is amenable." He lifted his glass. "May the best man win."

"You don't have her yet," Max snarled.

Mackenzie shrugged. "You don't want me to have her?" He rubbed his bottom lip before lifting his hand in a mild waving, gesture at Max. "Interesting. What shall we do about this situation?"

"I'm requesting that you leave her alone." He inhaled sharply through his nose, disliking asking this man for anything, though he knew he had to try.

All at once Mackenzie didn't appear so relaxed. He leaned forward, setting his drink down, his dark eyes alert as a hawk closing in on prey. "Are you asking me a favor, Lord Camden?"

Max swallowed against the bitter taste rising up in his throat and gave a hard nod. "Yes."

"Now that's an enticement, Viscount Camden indebted to me. I'm a man who values favors."

"You want position. I can help you achieve that. I have the connections. Important friends."

"That could be . . . useful. That might be the *price* I require." Mackenzie nodded slowly. "Yes. You do." He rose then and moved from around his desk, extending his hand to Max. "I accept your offer. You have my word, Camden. I'll leave your Lady Aurelia alone. In exchange for a future favor."

The words *She's not mine* hovered on his lips, but he could not bring himself to say them. Not to this man. Not with the hot feeling of possession pumping through him.

He looked down at the Scot's proffered hand as though it belonged to the devil himself. It certainly felt as though he were entering into an unholy pact. And yet there was no alternative. "Agreed."

After shaking Mackenzie's hand, Max turned and moved to the door.

"Camden," the Scotsman called out.

Max stopped and turned back to face the blackguard, arching an eyebrow.

"A word of advice?"

"What's that?" he asked warily.

"There is one way to keep the chit out of trouble, you know."

Max stared, waiting for him to elaborate.

"You could just marry her yourself."

He stared at Mackenzie a long moment, those words sinking in before he turned and departed the house.

Chapter 16

Aurelia looked up as a footman led Max into the drawing room. She was careful to school her features into a mask of impassivity despite her surprise at his appearance. After their last encounter, she did not expect to see him for a good while.

Three days had passed since he hauled her from Sodom. Three days since he had kissed and rejected her. Three days since she decided once and for all to move forward with her life and stop doing whatever it was she was doing with Max.

She'd told herself time and distance would be for the best. So truly there was no excuse for her heart to race faster at the sight of him.

His tall length ambled with a casual grace. He conveyed strength and checked power as he greeted her brother and Violet. He cut a fine figure in a dark jacket and buff-colored breeches. She looked away from his impressive physique and glanced to Buckston, sitting across from her. Buckston was still talking, moving his hands animatedly. He had not even noticed the new arrival. Her smile felt brittle as glass but she clung to it, desperate to give no reaction to the inclusion of Max into their dinner party. He'd been around all her life. Tonight should be no different from any other night.

Except it was. She never had to mingle among her family with him so close, with the knowledge of what his lips tasted like, a living, breathing memory.

She clenched her hands together in her lap and followed Buckston's cue, laughing when he laughed even though she had no notion what he had said that he considered so amusing.

Even though she did not glance at Max again, all of her hummed with awareness, her body achingly alert. A marked change from moments ago. She had been fighting to stay awake during Buckston's diatribe as he recounted his latest shopping spree and the new haberdashery that had just opened its doors. Buckston just might enjoy matters of clothing and fashion more than any woman of her acquaintance. He had won Mama over instantly when he complimented her puce turban and matching slippers. Gentlemen so rarely noticed a lady's slippers.

Buckston reached out to stroke the sleeve of her gown. "I must say, Lady Aurelia, I'm a great admirer of jewel tones, and this emerald green is a lovely color on you."

She glanced down at her gown. She was so rattled by Max's presence she could not recall what she was wearing. The awareness of him was still there, a warm hum that flowed along her nerves. Without even looking, she imagined she felt his stare.

A quick glance across the room revealed he was in fact staring at her, his blue eyes dark as a night sky. He watched as Buckston lightly fingered her sleeve, his brows drawn tightly over his deep-set eyes.

Her brother and cousin conversed, oblivious that Max's attention was focused with soul-burning intensity on her. Panic tickled low in her belly when she glanced around the room, catching Violet looking between them curiously. *Blast.* Her sister-in-law had noticed.

She snapped her gaze away. What was he doing looking at her like she had done something wrong? She had not seen fit to visit Sodom again, and she'd refrained from sabotaging any more of his liaisons. Assuming he had any.

That almost made her laugh. This was Max. It had been three days. He'd likely engaged in any number of liaisons.

The very idea that he continued his rakehell ways brought forth her own scowl. *Brilliant.* Now they were both scowling at each other in a roomful of people, displeasure radiating between them in palpable waves.

Blood rushed to her face, and she gave him a slight shake of her head, hopefully signifying that he should stop glowering at her. She forced her attention away. It was a sad state indeed when her body failed to grasp what her mind already had. She needed a husband, and Max was not that man.

She fixated on Buckston's kindly, attentive face and enormous bobbing Adam's apple. She skimmed his rail-thin form and tried to ignore the knotting in her stomach at the idea of Buckston touching her.

"Th-Thank you," she murmured when she realized she had yet to respond to his compliment of her gown.

Even though she did not turn to look, she could see on her periphery that Max had joined Will and Dec at the far side of the room.

She tapped a single foot impatiently beneath her skirts. Tonight was to have been a small dinner party. Aside from Dec and Rosalie, Buckston was the only other person invited. At least that's what she had thought when her mother asked her if she would like to include a suitor. She'd prepared herself for an intimate gathering. She'd had no time to brace herself for seeing Max again so soon. She had convinced herself she would be betrothed before she clapped eyes on him again, and once that happened, she would have forgotten all about Max. Because it was the right thing to do. It was the only thing.

She woke the morning after Sodom with fresh resolve swimming in her veins to welcome whatever suitors came to call. She promised herself that she would be agreeable. Charming even. Well, as charming as possible. She fully expected Struan Mackenzie to call on her, but as it turned out, Buckston was her only suitor to surface. Apparently, Struan Mackenzie had a change of heart after Sodom. It had been an easy enough matter to settle on Buckston when no one else had called on her. It was a jarring reminder that she was no great catch. Penniless with only good bloodlines to recommend her.

Aurelia knew she should have been disappointed, but there was only numbness. Struan or Buckston. It made little difference. She felt nothing for either one of them. In truth, the gangly Buckston was probably the far safer choice. He would expect little. Struan might demand too much from her. She shivered at the thought. He would see past her inane remarks and empty smiles. He would know she thought of another man whenever he touched her.

The thought of Max made her look again. She couldn't help it. He stared back at her over the rim of his glass with eyes far too serious. She was accustomed to derisive laughter and cheeky smiles from him. Not this broody and intense Max. If she thought he was dangerous before, he was downright deadly to her senses now.

Her cheeks burned and she faced forward. Mama urged Buckston to play for them. Everyone else chimed in, clapping encouragingly. Buckston sank behind the pianoforte, flipping out his coattails. "Forgive my blunders," he declared. "I'm no

Chopin." He then began to play with relish. He might not be Chopin but he played a near second.

She took advantage of the reprieve and moved to stand beside her mother. "Mama? What's Camden doing here?"

Mama did not tear her gaze from Buckston at the pianoforte while saying, "Oh, I invited him, dear. It's been a while since he last dined with us." Then, as if a thought occurred to her, she cast a quick frown at Aurelia. "I do hope you won't be a beast, dear. It won't do at all to behave that way in front of Buckston."

"Of course not, Mama," she replied dutifully, sighing as Buckston slid into another song. As well as he played, the loud music beat at her temples. "If you'll pardon me," she murmured. Mama did not spare her a glance, her smiling gaze fixed on Buckston.

Aurelia slipped from the room without a backward glance. She quickly made her way down the corridor, leaving the sounds of the pianoforte behind. For a moment she debated taking refuge in her bedchamber, but Cecily was probably there.

Desperate for a moment's solitude, she slipped inside her brother's study.

Chapter 17

She sank down in an overstuffed armchair beside his desk and gazed unseeingly into the dying embers of the fireplace. Sighing, she rubbed the bridge of her nose, squeezing it between her fingers.

The sudden opening of the door followed by it clicking shut had her sitting upright in her chair, an explanation on her lips. She expected Mama to stand there, ready to chastise her for abandoning their guests . . . especially the favored Buckston. She had not bothered to hide her joy at Aurelia's renewed interest in claiming a suitor.

But it was not her mother. Max stood there, his imposing figure framed against the door. The flickering shadows cast his face into sharp lines and hollows.

She shot to her feet, fisting the fabric of her skirts in both hands. They stared at one another for one long moment against the distant trill of the pianoforte.

"What are you doing in here?" she finally asked. "We shouldn't be alone." Although she knew no one in her family would think askance of the two of them alone in a room together. Mama, Will . . . neither would ever suspect either one of them would behave in a manner that would require supervision.

"What are you doing with that fop Buckston?" he asked, his voice a low rumble in the dark warm space.

"What does it look like?" She lifted her chin defensively. "I'm being *properly* courted."

Why she emphasized the word proper, she had no idea. Perhaps because she and Max were only ever improper with each other and she wanted to fling that at him. She wanted him to know that there existed gentlemen who thought her deserving of courtship. Not a great many, but some.

"Properly courted by that fool dandy? You can't possibly think the two of you will suit?"

And why did that question suddenly make her remember what it felt like to be caught up in Max's arms? The hard sensation of his body against her? The way his lips devoured her mouth? There was more to compatibility than physical attraction.

She flushed hotly. "What concern is it of yours?" Her speech stalled as he started toward her, his strides long and predatory. She swallowed, then resumed speaking. "First you objected to Mr. Mackenzie . . ." She snorted. "You'll be relieved to know that he has ceased to call on me." Something in Max's expression gave her pause. It was as though a veil dropped over his face. He also halted his advance.

"Camden?" She stepped closer, her gaze narrowing as a sinking sensation settled in her belly. "You wouldn't know anything about that, would you?"

He studied her, and she could almost see the calculation behind his eyes. He was trying to decide what to admit to her.

"Camden?" she pressed.

He shrugged one shoulder as if it were of no import.

She crossed the short distance separating them and punched him in the shoulder with her fist, but that probably hurt her hand more than it wounded him. She shook her wrist lightly. He smirked and she was tempted to try again.

"Feel better?" he asked lightly.

"No," she snapped. Her eyes burned. She pressed a hand to her chest. "You know how important this is to me."

He looked uncomfortable for a moment, and she knew she had him. "You didn't want Mackenzie."

Her chest lifted on a quick inhale. "I could have wanted him." In time.

His square jaw clenched. Even in the dim shadows, she detected a muscle feathering along his cheek. "It would have been a mistake."

"And why is that?"

"Because …"

"Why?"

"Because you deserve better," he bit out.

Her mouth closed with a snap, his flattery now mingling with her anger. She pushed the softer sentiment away.

"What was it you said to me?" she whispered, pressing fingers to her suddenly aching temples.

She felt as though he were yanking her left, then right, up, then down. Kissing her. Pushing her away. Chasing her. Running away. "Cease behaving as a child? Well, Camden, why don't you take a bit of your own advice and stay out of my life?"

She stepped around him, giving him wide berth, but his voice stopped her before she reached the door. "The difference between you and me is that you fail to exercise good judgment."

Anger returned in a searing flash. She turned slowly, a red haze filling her vision. "Is that what you call *your* behavior?" She advanced on him. "I've watched you live your life as you please with little thought to decorum or propriety." The words flew from her lips like mortar. Emotion clogged her voice and tightened her chest. "I watched you tup a maid in the greenhouse when I was fifteen years old. I thought I loved you." At his shocked expression, she added, "I know, senseless, yes? It wasn't your fault. You didn't know. I see that now, but back then I was hurt and drew that horrible picture of you. I didn't mean for it to be discovered. You never even heard me out when I tried to apologize." Her voice cracked and she forced a shrug. "Since then we've been at this stupid war, and I'm just weary of it. So very weary. I want it to stop. I want you to stop and leave me alone. Let me live my life."

Color flushed his cheeks. His mouth worked before he asked, "You were there?"

She nodded, the dreaded burn of tears threatening.

"Oh, Aurelia." He stepped toward her and she held up a hand. He stopped as though she had erected an invisible barrier between them with that hand.

"No," she commanded. She couldn't have him touch her again. Not anymore. It addled her head.

He angled his head, looking at her almost tenderly. "Aurelia," he repeated.

She shook her head fiercely, hating herself for having told him. "It doesn't matter. It was a long time ago."

He moved again, cautiously, slowly, as though she were some small animal of prey and he was afraid of startling her.

"Not another step," she warned, hating how her voice shook, how weak she must appear right now.

"No." He nodded yes as though she had not disagreed and closed the distance between them until the flat of her hand met his chest and stopped him. "I'm sorry, Aurelia. I was young and stupid."

"You're still stupid," she charged, her voice cracking, making her feel weak and equally senseless.

He brought a hand up to cup her face, and the tenderness undid her. His thumb stroked her cheek. "I am. I know it."

She closed her eyes at the sensation of his hand on her face, but it did no good. She could still see him looking down at her tenderly. "Stop looking at me like I'm something pathetic to be pitied."

"Open your eyes. Look at me."

She complied. He cupped her face, fingers spearing through her hair as he pinned her with a stark-eyed gaze. "Never. I've never pitied you. It's not possible. You're not pitiable."

Her chest clenched. She shook her head, completely flummoxed. He wasn't supposed to be this. He wasn't supposed to be gentle and kind and sincere. He wasn't supposed to be anything other than a rakehell who burned a path through the hearts and bedrooms of women everywhere. And he was *not* supposed to touch her anymore, affecting her and making her want him in a way she could never have him.

It wasn't right. It wasn't fair that he could be this way. The hot dash of tears tripped down her cheeks. He caught her tears with his fingers in an attempt to rub her cheeks dry. She fought a sob but it escaped, a choked, strangled sound.

"Don't cry, Aurelia," he soothed, still sliding those blunt-tipped fingers over her tear-damp cheeks.

"What are you doing? Please . . . don't touch me."

"I'm sorry." He pressed butterfly kisses to her cheeks. "I can't . . ."

She sniffed, hating and loving his tender ministrations. But it had to stop. It was tearing her apart and wrecking her resolve.

"You can. We have to stop this." She circled his wrists with her fingers and tried to tug his hands down. He wouldn't budge his grip.

He dragged warm lips over the moist tear tracks on her face, ignoring her words and offering the intimacy that made her stomach heat and flutter.

"Stop," she whispered as his mouth inched toward the corner of hers.

Her heart pounded fiercely in her chest. She trembled from the restraint of not lifting her chin that tiny inch and kissing him.

He had no such qualms.

He settled his mouth over hers, his lips loose and open, but not a true kiss.

"You don't want me to stop," he said against her

mouth, lips grazing ever so slightly and spiking sensation straight to every nerve.

"I know." The two words forced her lips to brush against his in a close simulation of a kiss. And perhaps she over-exaggerated the movement, savoring the tantalizing sensation of his mouth. His warm, dry lips softer than she ever thought possible. A shudder racked her.

"Good," he rasped. "Because for three days I've only thought of you. Of this mouth. The things I want to do to it . . . the things I want to teach it."

She moaned softly and his mouth claimed hers. Seized. Completely. Totally. No more tentative dancing around it.

There was no room for breath. His tongue thrust against her tongue. His mouth slanted hotly on hers. A simmer built inside her as his hands buried in her hair, tipping her head back, angling her for his ravaging mouth.

She whimpered, lost, completely at his mercy as he backed her up until she collided with the desk. Something rattled and fell to the floor with a thud. She had a fleeting hope that it wasn't the ink well, and then she did not care. A stampeding herd of llamas could have charged through the room and she wouldn't have stopped kissing Max for a single moment of it.

He loosened his grip for a split second to grab her by the waist and heft her on top of the desk. Then his hands came back for her face, fingers both hard and tender, burrowing through her hair again, scattering pins.

Another thing she didn't care about. She didn't care about having to explain her fallen hair or missing pins. She only cared about his mouth on hers . . . about the deepening ache between her legs that needed assuaging.

He nudged her knees apart and wedged his hips between her thighs, the fabric of her skirts bunching between them. She clutched his waist, her fingers digging deep through fabric to flesh and bone underneath.

His mouth devoured her until she turned into a boneless mass on top of the desk. She slid her hands up, clutching his shoulders, arms, wrists, straining against him, diving headlong into the kiss.

"Aurelia," he gasped into her mouth. "I can't stop this anymore. I can't *not* want you." He sounded aggrieved about it, pained and frustrated.

"Then don't," she heard herself utter back into his mouth. She wanted him to want her. To surrender to the undeniable heat flaring between them. Consequences be damned. She'd worry about that later.

She reveled in this man who was so wrecked for want of her. She never thought it could happen. She never thought she could want him like she did before.

He took one of her hands that wrapped around his wrist and dragged it down between them, placing her palm roughly over the bulge of his manhood. A ragged breath swelled her chest.

"Feel what you do to me. How much I want you, Aurelia."

The core of her throbbed in response. The hard rod pressing against her fingers was because of her.

"I—I want to feel it," she choked against the brand of his searing lips.

His eyes gleamed down at her, never breaking contact even as he opened his breeches and freed his erection. He very deliberately closed her smaller fingers around him, watching her hotly. "Like this," he instructed, showing her what to do, what he liked.

He shook as she stroked him, dropping his forehead against hers. She felt empowered. Holding him in her hand and feeling him shudder with his breath hot on her lips . . . it was the most decadent thing she had ever done. She felt wild and free.

"Oh," she breathed. "It's like silk." Her womanhood tightened almost painfully as she slid her fingers up and down the hard length of him. "It's big."

"I'm hard and hurting and it's all because of you," he accused against her mouth.

She laughed brokenly and wiggled closer on top of the desk, her stocking-clad knees high on his hips.

"I hurt, too," she confessed. Desire pumped through her, pushing her far past any sense of propriety. She guided him between her legs and rubbed the tip of him against her drawers, gasping at this first contact. Shielded by only a layer of cotton, moisture rushed between her legs.

He choked her name, but she didn't stop. She angled her hips and stroked him along her opening. It was a cruel tease, and a broken sob ripped from her throat, as much torment for her as it was for him. If possible, he grew bigger in her hand, and she felt the first stirrings of alarm.

"I don't know . . . would we fit . . ."

"Oh, we'd make it work." Then a pained sound escaped him. "But it can't come to that, Aurelia. Do you understand?"

No, she didn't. With the hard rod of him stroking against her, she didn't understand.

She whimpered again, the throb between her legs twisting, squeezing almost in protest. She tightened her fingers around him and pumped once . . . twice . . .

He gasped. "Aurelia, stop."

"I want it, Camden. I ache so much . . ."

His breathing grew rougher, filling her ears. "Aurelia . . . you don't know . . ." And yet even as his uttered this, he thrust against her sex, molding the fabric to her wetness.

"I do!" Her free hand swept around the curve of his hip, digging into the firm curve of his backside. "I'm no ignorant miss. I want what you give every other woman. I want to feel this . . ." She rolled her thumb over the plump tip of him. A bead of moisture rose to kiss her thumb, and she shuddered with need. " . . . inside me."

He was panting now, and she felt powerful. In control of him for the first time in her life. Before, she had always felt at his mercy, floundering and powerless. Now, in this moment, she felt very much in control.

"Aurelia." He angled his head, studying her. He lifted one hand to brush the hair back from her face.

"Don't you want that?" she whispered, her voice throaty in a way she had never thought herself capable. It was as though she were looking outside herself, watching someone else—a siren confident in her powers of seduction.

"God, yes."

"Then what are you waiting for, Camden?" She hiked her skirts higher around her hips. He slid a hand beneath the ribboned garters holding her stockings in place, and goose bumps broke out on her naked thighs.

She shoved a lifetime of breeding to the wayside and followed the demanding, clenching pulse between her legs, letting it guide her.

She squeezed her thighs around his hips, urging him closer. He obliged, grinding the length of him against her. She gasped at the friction, desperate for more pressure. She knew she should be mortified at the moisture dampening her drawers, but he felt too good against her. The ache low in her belly twisted and tightened. She gasped, rocking against him. Close. So close to something big. Bigger and deeper than even that day against the back of the house. Her breath quickened, noisy pants coming in quick succession.

"Aurelia!"

The shout of her name sounded far away.

"Aurelia!"

She blinked and jerked, noticing then that Max had fallen to disturbing stillness. Her clouded vision focused, crystallizing on his unsmiling face, his handsome features stark and grim in a way she had never seen in him.

Her heart skipped, watching him in dread. Without turning around, he tucked himself back inside his trousers. She quickly shoved her skirts back down and peered over his shoulder.

Her stomach plummeted. Will and Violet stood just inside the study. Will looked like he might be ill, all blood leeched from his face.

Violet placed a hand on Will's shoulder, as though restraining him from moving forward.

Aurelia slid off the desk, but her legs felt like pudding. She started to crumble but Max caught her with a hand on her elbow.

She nodded her thanks, but deliberately avoided looking at him. Right now she couldn't meet his gaze. Not with Will looking at her as though he had never seen her before. From the way her brother's gaze swung and sharpened, she knew Max had turned to face him.

"Will," she began. "I know what this looks like . . ."

Will's gaze flicked to her before returning with burning intensity to Max. "Do you? Good, then.

I'm glad you understand the magnitude of *how* this looks."

"No," she quickly corrected. That's not what she meant . . . "It's *not* what it looks like."

"Indeed?" her brother asked with alarming calm. "Is that true, Max? What do you think? Is this not what it looks like?"

Max replied in a maddeningly calm voice, as though they had not just been caught in a compromising position. "No, Will. It's precisely what it looks like."

She swung a horrified gaze to Max. "What are you doing?" she hissed. This was the moment they should try minimizing their actions.

"Then I expect you know what needs to be done," Will returned.

Horror seeped through her. She shook her head, hair tossing freely around her shoulders.

"Yes," Max replied.

Aurelia swung her gaze between the two of them. "No! Nothing needs to be done. Nothing happened . . . no one knows—"

Violet stepped forward and wrapped an arm around Aurelia's shoulders, guiding her to the center of the room. "Come. Let's go repair your hair . . ."

Aurelia dug in her heels. "No. I'm not leaving

while the two of them discuss me as though I have no say over my life—"

"Aurelia." Will pronounced her name in a way that brought forth memories of a stern tutor she once had. Ms. Turner never smiled and only ever bit out her name like it was something foul tasting in her mouth. "Go with Violet. I need a word with Max."

"About me. You need a word with him about me."

Will frowned at her. "About the *both* of you."

"Then I stay." She crossed her arms.

Her brother sighed. "Aurelia, it isn't done this way—"

"Considering we've gone about things differently, it might as well continue that way," Max announced, a humorless smile playing about his lips.

She shot her brother a satisfied look.

With a snort of disgust, he settled his gaze on Max. "I suppose it was too much too hope that you would have kept your hands off my sister. I should have listened to Violet. She said months ago there was something between the two of you."

Aurelia swung an incredulous gaze to her sister-in-law, who smiled mildly and shrugged. "You seemed to enjoy arguing too much."

"How long has this been going on?" Will asked.

"Not months," Aurelia said hotly.

"Long enough," Max responded.

She looked at him in exasperation again. He was not helping defuse the situation.

Then he went on to add, "I'd recommend a hasty wedding."

She gasped.

Will's jaw clenched, but he nodded.

"Wedding?" Aurelia said. "Who said anything about a wedding? I think we might be overreacting here." She didn't think. She knew it. They were gravely, vastly overreacting.

Will looked at her, and in his gaze she recognized that older brother who had always looked after her. When her father had been distant and not overly concerned with her, Will was the one to care, to visit her in the nursery. It had even been Will who saw to it that Ms. Turner found a different position. "What did you think the outcome of this could possibly be, Aurelia?"

She shook her head. Not this. She had not thought this. With Max, how could she? "Not marriage. I—I . . . Camden doesn't intend to marry." Will especially knew this.

"Plans change," Will bit off tersely.

"No." She looked at Max. "Tell him."

Max stared at her for a long moment before facing Will again. "I shall start the process of acquiring a special license."

Her lungs swelled with a ragged breath.

Will nodded once. "And I shall go explain to my mother why Aurelia is not going to have the monstrous church wedding she always dreamed of." He sent Aurelia a chagrined look. "That shall be your cross to bear, sister."

Aurelia's thoughts spun. Her eyes traveled over the three of them. "Has everyone in this room gone mad?"

Will sighed. Violet rubbed her shoulder in that comforting manner of hers and murmured her name like she was a child who failed to understand. Which wouldn't be an unfair estimate. She did not understand. She didn't understand why she and Max must marry when no one beyond the four of them need ever know what transpired in this room.

"Would you give us a few moments alone?" Max asked.

Will looked ready to object, but Violet approached his side and took his hand. "A few minutes won't do any harm."

At the door, Will sent them each a warning look that seemed to say: *Keep your clothes on.*

When the door clicked shut behind them, Aurelia spun on Max, the words spilling from her in a burning rush, "You don't have to—"

"Don't I?" he retorted.

"I most assuredly won't force you."

"You don't have to force me, Aurelia. It's what we must do. I realize that. Don't you?"

She stared at him for a long moment. "Who knows this even happened? My brother and Violet? *Maybe* he tells my mother. Perhaps. We don't even know—"

"It's enough that they know. I respect them. It's important they respect me. I am only sorry . . . for you. This marriage . . . it can't be what you had dreamed for yourself, Aurelia. I am sorry for that."

That's right. She recalled again that he had warned her. He wasn't made for marriage. "I'll be fine," she promised, but in that moment she wasn't certain if she was promising this to him or herself.

"Why are you doing this?" she whispered miserably, giving him another chance, hoping desperately he would say it wasn't just because of her family. That it was more than that. That marriage to her held some appeal.

"Do you truly think I would not wed you? After

your brother discovered us in such a compromising position?"

It shouldn't hurt, but it did. Her opinion bore little significance to him—*she* bore little—even though it was she he would be marrying and not Will.

"It's the right thing to do," he added, sounding so very sanctimonious she wanted to lash out and hit something.

"And you're all about doing the right thing," she muttered, trying to hide her hurt feelings. Why did he have to be so noble?

"I don't know what you're so upset about."

"Oh, I should be grateful I suppose. I've snared the ever elusive Viscount Camden."

He nodded fiercely, dragging a hand through his hair and sending the dark locks flying in every direction. "You've already proclaimed you need a husband. What difference does it make—"

"Indeed," she said tightly, striking out, wanting to harm him like his words hurt her. "I want to marry. That had been my goal. Only I did not want to marry *you*."

"Don't you? Weren't you just panting in my ear and rubbing my cock? I seem to recollect you begging for it."

He wanted to shock her with his harsh language. She lifted her chin and clung to her composure. "That was something else. Something . . ." her words drifted. She wasn't able to put a name to it. Swallowing against the lump forming in her throat, she lifted her chin and tried again. "It wasn't me wanting to marry you."

"Indeed. Sex and marriage are not mutually inclusive. But have no fear, there will be at least one benefit to this . . ."

"Mistake," she supplied smoothly into his pause, arching an eyebrow. "Is that the word you're searching for?" She walked backward several paces. "You mean 'mistake.' Us. Getting married. It would be a mistake."

He shrugged. "So it's not what I would have planned . . ." His voice faded and his eyes clouded. It wasn't even as though he was looking at her anymore, but something else. Somewhere else. "We shall make the best of it. And I shall at least be the mistake you can readily avail yourself of any time you choose."

Of all the arrogant . . .

She shook her head. "You don't want a marriage. You don't want a wife."

He stared at her, and his silence was all the confirmation she needed, and yet still a bitter thing to swallow.

"Nothing need change. If we must marry, don't let a wife alter your life."

He laughed then. "You jest."

"Not at all." She nodded. "Lead your life as you always do."

His eye narrowed. "You think such a thing possible?"

"You shall have your freedom. I shall have mine. It seems idyllic enough to me."

"Yes. It seems so." He considered for a weighty moment. "Why not?"

She nodded again as if a simple matter of business had been resolved and not the whole course of her life. "I should leave you now. You have a special license to look into procuring."

Without waiting for his reply, she spun and departed the room.

Chapter 18

"You looked beautiful today."

Aurelia looked up and met her mother's gaze in her vanity mirror, offering her a shaky smile in response to the compliment. Cecily unpinned the last curl and set to brushing the mass of crackling dark hair.

"You're certain you were not disappointed, Mama? I know you dreamed of a large wedding."

Her mother smiled whimsically. "I did, but my greatest dream has been for both my children to be happy. Will found that happiness with Violet."

She stopped behind her and set her hands to Aurelia's shoulders. "And now you've found it with dear Maxim. Nothing brings me greater joy. Not even a grand St. James wedding could give me such bliss."

Aurelia returned her mother's smile, wincing inwardly at how her own lips wobbled. Fortunately, Mama did not appear to notice. Instead, she had turned to survey the rather somber and colorless bedchamber. The room that was to be permanently hers as of this very day.

"It's a lovely room," Mama lied. Her mother's tastes ran to colors and frills. There was none of that in this chamber. None of that in this house, for that matter. She gestured to the midnight dark drapes in what was to be her new bedchamber. "Perhaps start with those. A lighter colored counterpane next. More pillows perhaps. I'm certain Aunt Daphne can knit you some. Once you finish in here, you can add more sconces in the halls. A bigger chandelier in the foyer, certainly. It's much too dreary when you first enter the house." She clapped her hands merrily and fairly bounced on her feet. She looked years younger in that moment. "But then, there is no bottom to Max's pockets. You should not limit yourselves to drapes, although it is a fine starting place."

Hands propped on her hips, Mama circled the room assessingly.

Cecily slid Aurelia a knowing look before glancing at the clock on the mantel and clearing her throat. "Lady Merlton," she said. "It grows late."

Mama swung her gaze to the clock and then back to Aurelia. "Oh, indeed, indeed! The time has gotten away with me. We shall discuss remodeling later."

Aurelia opened her mouth to object, to insist that they discuss those renovations now. Anything to delay the inevitable.

Mama pressed a quick kiss to the tip of her nose, gently cupping her face with both hands. "Now I would normally choose this moment to leave you with some parting advice on what to expect in your marital bed, but I'm well aware that you've been reading the medical texts in the library for years."

Aurelia's mouth sagged. *She knew?*

Mama continued. "If there is anything you would like to ask me, just go ahead, my dear. I will endeavor to answer you."

Heat crept up her face. She was not having this conversation with her mother. She shook her head fiercely. "No, thank you, Mama. I think I know what to expect."

Mama nodded and patted her cheek again. "Very good. Now call on me when you're ready and we shall go shopping. I don't want to interrupt your honeymoon."

Honeymoon? She and Max weren't even going anywhere. Could that be termed a honeymoon?

Cecily gave her a quick hug, whispering into her ear, "I'm so very happy for you. I know all will be well. You will see."

She offered her friend what she hoped was a heartening smile. It was a far cry from how she really felt. "I'm sure you are right."

Cecily pulled back and laughed lightly. "You're a terrible liar, but you will see. I'm always right. I have an instinct about these things."

That said, she slipped from the room fast on Mama's heels. The door clicked shut behind them and Aurelia found herself alone in a suddenly echoing silence. She surveyed her new bedchamber. It was a rather grim place. Colorless. Her white nightgown might be the only thing that wasn't drab.

She moved her gaze to the adjoining door. For several moments she watched it. As though it were about to perform some grand trick—such as open. Several moments passed without the door opening. Without a whisper of sound from the other side. Did she think he was waiting for her mother and Cecily to leave to pounce on her?

She paced the length of the massive room. She felt very small and lonely in its great space. The shadows seemed to stretch toward her like long fingers. She missed her old room. Even if it wasn't her room anymore. Not her home. It was Will's and Violet's home. This place. This was her home now.

He had changed his mind.

That was the sole thought burning through her. He had changed his mind and would come to her tonight. He didn't mean the words he had said that night in the library when they had been forced into this marriage. He would certainly want to claim his husbandly rights. Would not any gentleman do as much?

She bit her lip, pacing the chamber, knotting the fine fabric of her nightgown in her hands. Mama had insisted on new bedclothes. Max could afford it, she insisted. Aurelia had not possessed the will to argue. Her head had been too busy, too full of thoughts and bewilderment over the fact that she was marrying Max.

She was Lady Camden now. No longer a burden to her brother and mother.

Max's wife. In name only. At least that was what he had promised.

You wanted it this way.

She stopped pacing and squared her shoulders. That's right. He'd said they were a mistake. This marriage would be a mistake. How could she let him in her bed knowing that was how he felt? She would not let him use her. Even if she was his wife and it was his right, his due as her husband.

She stared out the window through the parted drapes. It was late. The night pressed against the mullioned panes, thick and dark as smoke.

He wasn't coming. He had to know Mama and Cecily had left her by now. All the rest of the guests had long since departed. He simply wasn't coming. She moved to the adjoining door and pressed her ear flat to it. She thought she heard a faint sound from within, but who knew if it was Max or his valet.

Sighing, disgusted with herself, she made her way for the enormous four-post bed. It was hard to miss, even in the dark.

With fresh resolve, she slid beneath the counterpane that Cecily had pulled back for her. Closing her eyes, she rolled onto her side and tried to sleep. Tried to tell herself that she didn't care. That she didn't long for her husband.

That a name-in-only marriage would be enough for her.

She would not wait up for him. After all, she was not certain she wanted this marriage consummated. It felt so false when she knew he had not wanted to marry her. Could she open her bed to him, her body, knowing he regretted taking her to wife? She had seen that glaring truth in his eyes as they made their vows.

She tugged the heavy counterpane higher on her shoulders and rolled onto her side, determined not to wait up like a puppy anxious for the return of its master. Darkness swirled around her, and the chamber hummed as thick and silent as a tomb.

This was her life. Alone in this great bed. In this great, empty mausoleum. At least until she decided to add a few flourishes and modify it to suit her, but even then it would all still belong to Max. She would simply be a stranger living here for perpetuity. Unwelcome and unwanted. He had made certain she understood that.

Her eyes ached from staring into the dark for so long. She closed them, easing their ache, but convinced she would never relax. Never sleep.

Until she slipped into slumber.

"I suppose I should be angry. I've tried to be angry with you. All week I've reminded myself again and again that you dallied with my sister." Will stopped to shudder and then sighed. "And yet I'm not."

Max lifted his gaze from his glass at this declaration from his friend, uncertain how to respond. The week had been awkward. A whirlwind of activity leading up to a wedding that had felt farcical despite its utter gravity.

He had seen Aurelia not at all until the ceremony today, and then she had not even met his gaze during the exchanging of vows. Not until the very end. Until the moment they were pronounced man and wife and the noose he had spent all his life avoiding settled firmly around his neck.

"Er. Thank you?" he offered.

Will nodded. "Once the anger faded, I came to realize that you and Aurelia make sense."

Max's eyes widened. "We do?"

Other than how Aurelia felt in his arms—ardent and responsive to his every touch—there was nothing about either one of them that made much sense.

Thankfully, the ceremony had been brief. They all had agreed to his suggestion of a small service. They'd wed at St. Dominic's, a quaint church he walked by almost every day. Sometimes he would stop and chat with the kindly reverend who officiated there. Reverend Williams had only been too happy to oversee the ceremony.

Max winced. He supposed there was no real mystery as to why the Merlton clan had so readily agreed to a hasty marriage. His insistence that they arrange a quick ceremony with little fanfare had spelled only one thing in their minds.

They thought he had ruined Aurelia.

Because that's what he did. What he was good at doing. He ruined things. Since he lost his family, he had set out to ruin himself. To make himself unfit for any good woman, so that he would never be struck down by the affliction that was love.

He had to admit there had been good women he'd taken to his bed. Women he hurt. Women who offered him their hearts, and he had refused them all like so many unworthy objects.

Will had probably begun counting the days until Aurelia began increasing with child.

That thought chilled him. The idea of being a father was a bloody terrifying thing. Of course, the making of that child had been a fantasy for him for weeks now. Perhaps even longer. He scrubbed a hand over the back of his tightening neck.

In the far back of his mind he had always gravitated toward Aurelia. He told himself it was because her caustic wit amused him, but what sane man subjected himself to such abuse if he wasn't a little aroused by the woman serving such abuse?

A child would be the end of him. He would not be able to withhold himself. He would love a child. His child. His and Aurella's. He dragged his hand around to his face, covering his eyes for a moment. That couldn't happen. Ever.

He realized that Will was still staring at him, waiting for him to say something to his comment about him and Aurelia making sense together.

"It's kind of you to say."

"There's nothing kind about it."

Max winced, imagining a scenario where he was in Will's shoes. If he had caught someone trifling with his sister. Julia had only been seven years old when she left this world. Still an angel in his memories. She'd never had the opportunity to grow up, but he could not imagine reacting with similar tolerance to any man, friend or not, who dallied with her. Just further evidence that Will was a far better man than him. "I don't know if I could be so understanding."

"Well. Initially, I was angry." Will laughed darkly. "Yes. I'll not lie on that score. But I thought about it long and well. And Violet . . . well, my wife helped shed light on matters, too. What we all witnessed these many years and assumed was animosity—" He gestured to himself and Dec, who sat near the fire, as though speaking for the both of them. "Well, Violet viewed it differently. Perhaps with more objectivity since she only recently entered into the family."

"Oh? And how did she view me and Aurelia?" Max lifted his glass to his lips for a drink.

"All the bickering and squabbling . . . it was . . . you both were . . . well, in a manner . . . flirting and seducing each other, as much as it pains me to say it." He winced.

Max coughed as the fiery burn of brandy went down the wrong pipe. Will moved to clap him on the back. He focused tearing eyes on his friend. "That's certainly an interesting theory."

"What I'm saying is that you have my blessing, Max. You and Aurelia . . . have my blessing."

Will's blessing. He didn't deserve it. If he could promise that he was going to make Aurelia happy . . . then, yes. He would perhaps not feel the utter cad sitting before Will. He'd just wed his sister with no intention of making her a wife in truth. He had no intention of being a real husband to her. He would not make Aurelia happy. He knew that. Whatever happiness she found would be at her own instigation. That's what leading separate lives would entail. He leading his life. She leading hers. Separately.

He inhaled a breath that felt too heavy, too blistering for his lungs to hold. It would be a sham of a marriage. Aurelia had laid the groundwork. They would be married, but in name only.

A bitter laugh threatened to overtake him. Had he actually agreed to such a thing? Was he deluding himself? He could scarcely keep his hands off her when they weren't married. And now they were. He didn't have to hold his desires back any longer. He could march upstairs and take his husbandly rights.

Only it wasn't that simple. Even if they were going to try to make a genuine marriage out of this union and she was agreeable to sharing his bed, it wasn't in him to make any one woman happy.

Aurelia would want it all. The kind of happy marriage that Will and Dec had with their wives. He couldn't do that.

"More than my blessing actually," Will clarified, his magnanimous tone a knife to his heart. "I'm happy about this. I'm happy that the both of you have found each other. You've been like a brother to me all these years. I know you'll be the man my sister deserves."

Will be.

A knot formed in his stomach. Even Will knew he wasn't that man presently. Nor could he ever be. Crushing guilt weighed on his chest. How could he tell him not to have such high expectations? Max couldn't change. Not even for Aurelia. True, he did not want her miserable. He'd take care of her. She'd want for nothing. Except love.

He downed the last of his glass, hating himself right now. Hating himself for letting this happen. For being so weak.

As much as he loathed pretending with Will, this wouldn't be the time to make a confession on the true nature of their marriage. Not hours after he had just wed his sister. Hopefully, Aurelia would find contentment enough in their match. She didn't have to move in with her Aunt Daphne at least.

"Thank you," he replied numbly, because he knew some response was expected. Words of some manner. "I will try . . ."

He would *try* not to crush her heart.

He wasn't good enough. He'd seen to that a long time ago. He'd given himself away. Any bit of him that had been good or noble, he had lost long ago. Even if he could be a real husband to her, there was nothing left for her.

Dec rose and refilled his glass, watching him intently, as though he had an inkling of the turmoil inside him. He had said very little while Will talked, after all.

And that turmoil only churned stronger inside of him as he thought of Aurelia asleep upstairs. Alone in a bedchamber that adjoined his room. She was his for the taking. His wife and the woman who filled his every lust-filled fantasy. He could persuade her . . . *seduce* her. She was so responsive, and he knew what she liked. He could do it. It would be natural. Expected. The proper way to begin a marriage.

Not to mention that *being* with her, *having* her, was all he craved.

And yet, as insane as the notion was, he would not venture into her room.

He would not touch her. He would not allow himself that slice of heaven.

Chapter 19

Her first week of marriage passed uneventfully. Each morning, Aurelia arrived ahead of Max to the dining table. She was usually sipping from a cup of steaming tea by the time he entered the room. Polite greetings were exchanged followed with intermittent conversation of only the most banal, meaningless subjects. Of course there was an undercurrent of tension that hummed as tight as a drawn bowstring. The eighth morning of her marriage began in much the same manner.

"Good morning," he greeted.

"Good morning," she returned, watching him over the rim of her cup as he seated himself. A servant stepped up and placed a plate before him as though by magic. She eyed his eggs and kippers. The same breakfast every day. He reached for the blackberry jam and began to liberally slather it on his toast. The same habit there as well. She was learning all his quirks.

It felt intimate, watching him go about his breakfast. This was his regimen, and now she was a part of it, eating her porridge with honey and sipping her tea across from him, trading pleasantries. Almost like husband and wife. Almost. But not quite.

They weren't truly husband and wife. They were more like . . . housemates.

"Did you sleep well?" he asked into the silence of the room.

"Very," she lied.

"The chamber . . . it is to your liking?"

"Quite so."

"Because there are other chambers."

Chambers that did not adjoin his. "It is fine."

He nodded, sipping from his drink and meeting her eyes again.

"However . . ." Her voice faded.

"However?" he prodded, cocking one dark eyebrow.

"Would it be permissible if I made a few changes . . . minor renovations—"

It stuck in her throat to ask anything of him, but this wasn't the kind of thing she could just take upon herself without first consulting him. There would be workmen and expenses. Mama would likely be in and out, voicing her considerable opinions.

"Of course. It's your home now," he replied quickly. "Do as you see fit. Whatever you want." Almost too quickly. She narrowed her gaze on him. Was that relief in his voice?

He averted his eyes, and it dawned on her that he was glad she had asked this of him. A task to occupy herself and forget how less than satisfactory this marriage was for both of them.

A footman arrived holding a tray of correspondence. Max quickly went through them, plucking out one missive and then offering her the tray to browse through the remainder.

"What are these?" she asked.

"Invitations. I have no desire to attend any of them, but by all means, feel free to do so."

Without him.

He really didn't care if she went about Town

without him. Heat slowly crept up her neck. She could just imagine the whispers and titters of those girls who had been so hateful toward her if her first appearance in Society as Lady Camden was *without* Max. The speculation would be vicious and as fast-moving as wildfire.

She swallowed against the thickness of her throat. They truly were going to lead separate lives. She attempted to look on the bright side. She would go where she wanted. She should have reveled in this freedom. Countless other wives would envy her situation.

So why did she feel so bleak? So alone?

She slid the tray closer and began flipping through the mail as a hollow sensation spread throughout her chest. "Thank you," she murmured, focusing her tear-blurred eyes on the neatly penned script, keeping her head carefully bowed so he would not see she was affected. "I believe I will."

The pattern was established.

A routine of actions and behavior that flowed in a comfortable rhythm. Inane chatter over breakfast, and then Max would depart, leaving Aurelia to her own devices.

He busied himself throughout the day—in his

office, meeting with his man of affairs or investors, riding, walking, visiting his club. Essentially anything and everything that took him out of Aurelia's sphere.

He rarely dined at home. His club was good enough for a tasty meal. Mornings, however, were the worst. He couldn't run away entirely. Pride demanded he take his breakfast as he usually did. He insisted on sleeping in the comforting familiarity of his own bed, too.

Fleeing his home completely, eschewing his favored breakfast at his very own table, smacked of fear. Or cruel indifference to his wife. He could not have done any of those either.

The mornings were a torment. Seeing her, knowing she was his and yet not . . . that he could never think of her as belonging to him.

She watched him eat as she nibbled on her porridge and browsed his discarded invitations for any that might strike her interest.

She asked little of him aside from her request to redecorate. She didn't know what he did with himself during the day or where he took himself to at night. She never once asked or seemed to care, and he never volunteered the information. To do so would establish one's claim on the other, and they were quite careful never to cross that invisible line.

It was almost annoying. He'd been with other females who staked more of a claim on him—or attempted to, at any rate. Aurelia did not bother even making the attempt.

He sliced a kipper in half and considered her beneath his lashes. She paused over one invitation, biting her plump bottom lip. The action had him holding back a groan. Even without trying, she managed to entice him.

Max made quick work of finishing his breakfast. Wiping his mouth, he rose to his feet. "If you'll excuse me, I've an appointment."

She looked up at him with those wide eyes of hers, watching him but said nothing as he turned away and strode from the room. He did not return again until the house was shrouded in shadowed silence. Even when he approached the door to her adjoining chamber later that night and pressed his ear to the heavy solidness, he heard nothing.

Chapter 20

Aurelia sighed at her reflection in the mirror. Her slippers tapped anxiously beneath her skirts.

"What's this? A sigh? The day has not begun. What can be so wrong with it already?"

She met Cecily's reflection in the mirror and forced a smile.

Cecily tsked. "Oh, that's scarcely heartfelt."

"What can I say?" Aurelia plucked at a jeweled comb. "I'm restless . . . Very well, I'm bored."

"A matter that can be rectified if you would

only step from these doors and return to the world. Never did I think I would see the day when you cowered—"

"I'm not cowering!" Her gaze snapped fire.

"No? The invitations pour in and yet here you remain day after day."

"I haven't felt the inclination—"

"And why not?"

At this, Aurelia simply stared at herself in the mirror. How could she explain? She did not relish facing the world. Family, friends. The barbed-tongue vipers of the *ton*. She did not want to confront them without her husband at her side.

"Never thought I'd see you afraid—"

"I'm not afraid," she snapped, glaring at Cecily. "I—I . . . it's pride! I have my pride, Cecily."

Cecily squeezed her shoulders and leaned her face close to Aurelia's. "Your pride should not keep you a prisoner in this house. It's your pride that should demand you accept one of those invitations and—"

"Very well." Her chin went up. "I will venture out."

Cecily grinned brightly. "There you are. I recognize you now."

Aurelia felt somewhat better as she finished dressing for the day. Indeed, when she sat down at the dining table, she was almost eager to begin perusing the fresh crop of invitations. She was ready for an end to the monotony. A holiday of sorts from the days of conducting herself politely with Max. The two of them strangers in his great town house.

Perhaps venturing out would help her forget how very much she missed him. She longed for their squabbling. The sniping banter. It wasn't healthy, she supposed. She actually contemplated picking a fight with him, but she couldn't bring herself to do it. She wasn't a child, fighting for his attention anymore. She was his wife, and if that wasn't enough to win his notice, then she wouldn't invent a petty argument.

No, she would live. She would not pick a quarrel. She smiled at him as he seated himself before his plate and returned her attention to the invitations, trying to decide which event would harken the new Lady Camden into Society.

As she was flipping through the invitations, her gaze landed on a familiar name. She must have made a small sound as she came upon the elegant cream-colored envelope.

"What is it?" Max looked up.

She looked up. "Struan Mackenzie is hosting a soiree." Possibly interested, she set the envelope to the side. "It's in a fortnight—"

"You cannot go."

Her gaze shot up to his face. "Pardon me?"

"You will not go. Obviously."

"Why not?"

"Because."

"Because . . ." She let the word hover out there, arching an eyebrow. "Because you simply don't wish me to go?"

"Is that not reason enough?"

"I'm sorry, but no. It's not. We agreed on separate lives. Is that not what we've been doing since I moved in here?"

"Yes, but in this, I cannot budge." He set his fork down on his plate with a clatter. "Pick another invitation. Attend another party," he commanded with all the authority of a father addressing a defiant child.

She rose, tossing her napkin down on the table. Heat crawled over her face, reaching the tips of her ears. "Oh, I *am* going."

It suddenly occurred to her that they were quarreling again. Had she actually missed this? She must be a lunatic to have missed this.

His expression darkened, his eyes going from that gray-blue to deep cobalt. It reminded her of the way he had looked before he kissed her that first time. He'd been so angry at her then, too. A shiver rolled down her spine that she quickly told herself was not anticipation.

He arched one dark brow at her in warning. "I'm your husband and in this matter I am telling you no."

"You don't get to *play* husband with me." She jabbed a finger in the air toward him. "This was a mistake, remember? Separate lives, remember? You gave me my freedom and that means I can chose which parties I wish to attend."

Turning, satisfied she had the last word, she strode from the room, her half-eaten breakfast forgotten. Her hands opened and closed at her sides. Oh, the gall! She was fuming. He could not ignore her when he wished and then impose his will on her when the mood struck him. It wasn't to be borne.

She fled to her bedchamber, determined to venture out for a walk or ride in the park. Perhaps she would call on Rosalie. She only knew that she needed to get out of this house. She immediately started twisting left and right, trying to reach the back of her dress so she might undress and change.

Cecily looked up from where she was putting away garments in her armoire. Her friend took one look at her face and tsked. "What's amiss?"

"That wretch!" She managed to get one button free. Grunting, she continued on to the next.

Cecily approached, hands stretched out to offer assistance. "Allow me."

She continued to writhe, furious and determined to undress herself, for some reason. "He thinks he can bend me to his will . . ."

"Uh-hm." Cecily nodded sympathetically and then froze, her gaze widening as it settled on something beyond her shoulder.

With a sinking sensation, Aurelia turned, her hand pressing to her roiling stomach.

He had followed her, still wearing that dark expression, his lips compressed into an uncompromising line. No doubt he'd just heard her vent her spleen to Cecily.

"You will not go," he repeated, indifferent to the fact that they had an audience.

Cecily whispered beside her, "Aurelia?"

"Leave us, please, Cecily."

There was a long moment of silence before Cecily strode past her, closing the chamber door behind her.

It wasn't until she was gone that Aurelia considered that closed door. This was the first time they were alone in a room—in a bedchamber, no less—since they were married. Her heart pounded, her pulse a loud beat in her ears, even as she reminded herself that theirs was not a marriage of physical intimacy. It didn't matter what had transpired between them in the past. They had agreed on that condition.

Besides. She was so angry . . . desire should be the last thing on her mind when it came to him. "You can't command me—"

"In this, I can. Mackenzie has designs on you—"

"*Had,*" she inserted. "Not 'has.' That is in the past. His interest was in marriage. I'm married now. Sham that it is."

His eyes widened. "Oh, it's real enough. Real enough that I shall not be made a fool, Aurelia."

She frowned. "What do you mean?"

"I won't suffer being made a cuckold."

She sucked in a sharp breath. Was he implying that he thought she would betray her vows? He was not one to cast stones. He who spent every night away from this house. From her. God only knew what time he returned home to his own bed every night. "How many women have you dallied with since we took vows?"

"We are not discussing me."

His jaw clenched. His silence was all the answer she needed. An answer that shouldn't have hurt, but it did.

"No. We never discuss you. Well, rest assured, I'm nothing like you. I won't betray my vows . . . but even if I did, why would you care? We're both free, as I recall. That was our agreement."

"I will not be made a laughingstock."

She laughed then. She could not help it . . . even as his expression burned red. "Oh. You disappoint me, Camden. You're so very typical. For days you care naught for me . . . but now that you imagine some other man has an interest in me you find it necessary to suddenly take notice of me again."

He closed the distance between them until he was looking down at her, his chest practically touching her own. "Make no mistake, Aurelia, I have never *not* noticed you."

She started to step back, but stopped herself. Cecily's accusation rang in her ears. She was not a coward. She would stand her ground and not let him bully her. No matter how her skin shivered and her instincts warned her to flee.

"I will go to Mr. Mackenzie's dinner party . . ." It dawned on her that she didn't care one way or another about Struan Mackenzie's party. This had become about something much bigger. A fight she could not back down from now. "You may always attend with me, of course. Your name was on the invitation."

"The last thing I want to do is attend Mackenzie's party and smile at the bastard as he flirts with my wife."

A flush spread through her that wasn't entirely rooted in displeasure. He behaved almost jealously. She shook her head once, dismissing that notion. There was little logic in that. He had not touched her since their wedding day—and then only a chaste press of his lips to hers. That wasn't the behavior of a man who wanted her for himself.

She folded her hands in front of her. "Then we are at an impasse, I fear."

His hands opened and closed at his sides as though he were restraining himself. She watched in bemusement. She knew he would never harm her. It wasn't in him to be cruel or violent.

He made a low growl of frustration and swung away from her, marching toward the door, stopping and turning back for her, and then stopping again, his hands still working at his sides as though he were tempted to grab something—*her*—and shake it.

She watched him at war with himself. He couldn't control her and it was gnawing at him. She smiled, feeling inordinately pleased with standing her ground as he unraveled. All because he could not get his way. It was gratifying.

And then he caught her expression.

He stilled, looking suddenly dangerous. And that made her nervous. She knew that expression . . . knew what came after it.

Her smug smile slipped, uncertain whether she should run. She held out a hand as if that could ward him off . . . even as a little voice whispered in the back of her mind. *What are you running away from? You want him. You've always wanted him . . .*

Three strides and he caught her up in his arms. His mouth smothered her cry, hard and punishing, but so delicious. She had longed for this. Every night as she lay in her bed, listening for his tread, she had yearned for this. She couldn't lie to herself anymore. Not with his mouth fused to hers. Not with his solid length molded to her.

His hands held her face and then traveled, touching her everywhere. Her hands had minds of their own as well, brushing his cheeks, his shoulders, dragging down the front of his jacket, and then dipping inside, desperate to feel him better.

He did not break his kiss even as he shrugged out of his jacket with anxious, jerky moves. Then his arms went around her, sweeping her against him and lifting her off her feet, carrying her to the bed as if she weighed a feather.

They didn't say anything. They were just mouths and tongues and hands. On the bed, he flipped her over. Face pressed to the counterpane, her breath escaped in noisy pants as he ran a hand slowly down her spine, squeezing her bottom through the folds of her gown. She groaned, arching shamelessly into his touch.

He seized her hem and tossed her skirts up around her waist. Cooler air caressed her stocking-clad legs and seeped inside her drawers. He circled her ankles in strong fingers and guided her legs apart. Breathing heavily, she looked over her shoulder, her breasts heaving against her bodice, the fabric chafing and abrading against her oversensitized flesh.

Max looked wild and rakish, his brown hair falling over his brow, his shirt bare at the throat, a hungry gleam in his eyes as he surveyed her like a feast to be devoured. His hands roamed over her hips and thighs, and then glided between those thighs. He touched her the way he knew would get a response, rubbing against the damp crotch of her drawers, finding that spot that drove her out of her skin. The friction was unbearable and she pushed back against him.

Suddenly his hands left her. She whimpered, bereft and aching at the loss. He unbuttoned her gown, shrugging it up her torso and over her head with quick efficiency. Her undergarments followed.

Then he was rolling her over again, his big hands on her breasts. She cried out, surging into his palms. His gaze scorched her, assessing every exposed inch of her as his thumb rolled her nipples. If his hands weren't driving her out of her mind, she would have felt self-conscious.

And then there was his mouth again. That splendid, brilliant mouth of his could kiss a nun into submission. When his lips covered hers there was nothing gentle or easy about it. It was fire and need . . . as hot and heavy as lava pumping through her veins.

His hands moved over her quickly, roughly, callused palms rasping her sensitive flesh, and she reveled in it. In the way his cobalt-dark eyes tracked over her hungrily as he stripped off the rest of his garments until they were both naked. His hands and mouth followed the path of his eyes, burning caresses, stroking and tasting with his lips, tongue, and teeth until she was arching and moaning, her fingers spearing through his hair and hanging on like he was her lifeline.

His hand delved between them to cover her mound. He pressed the heel of his palm into her as he inserted one finger deep inside. She arched, her hands fisting into the bedding, hanging on tightly as if that was the only thing to keep her from launching off the bed.

He uttered nothing, watching her darkly as he ravaged her, hitting some unknown spot tucked away inside her and sending her flying apart with the stroke of his fingers.

She was still floating back down, her pounding heart slowing, hardly conscious of reality when she felt him at her entrance. The thick head of him entered her a fraction and then stopped.

She sucked in a deep breath, all of her nerves coming to throbbing and aching life where they joined.

Her gaze locked on his. Silence stretched between them, but words passed between them just the same. An unspoken communication. A wordless exchange conveyed in the question in his smoldering gaze.

She answered him by angling her hips and welcoming him into her body. Her hands slid down his back, nails slightly scraping warm flesh to stop at the curve of his spine above his backside. She pushed there, urging him on, propelling him to move over her, in her.

The tendons in his throat worked and his jaw

clenched as he pushed the remaining length of himself inside her. He moved neither fast nor slow. He filled her with a steady thrust until he was lodged to the hilt, pulsing and big and shattering her senses.

Her mouth parted on a gasp at the burning stretch of her body to accommodate him.

Hissing air escaped between her teeth and her fingers ached from clinging to him. It was not entirely pleasant. It was not entirely bad either. He felt so foreign inside her, the sensation alien and a little bewildering.

And then he moved again, withdrawing and burying himself again, making her squeak and clutch, if possible, even tighter to him.

A ragged gasp escaped him and he dropped his head into the crook of her neck, his breath fanning hotly on her flushed skin.

Her thoughts spun, unable to grasp any one thought. There was only feeling. The overwhelming pressure of him locked deep inside her.

He lifted his head and snared her gaze again as he nearly slid all the way free of her body. The slow drag of his hard length made her arch and moan under him, the friction unbearable and not nearly enough.

"Camden," she choked, pleading.

He drove deep again and she cried out in relief, but it was short-lived. She needed more. She didn't understand how something could be so good and so not enough. She felt her core tighten and clench around him and delighted in his gasp.

His face was tense, his expression fixed almost in pain, his arms bracketed on either side of her head

She reached a hand to touch his face, tracing his jaw. "Wh-What's wrong?"

"Nothing. This is the most perfect thing I've ever felt." He followed his words by thrusting faster, harder, a shudder racking him. "You. You are the most perfect thing."

"Oh." Soft whimpers escaped her as his hands swept under her. Palming her back and dragging her closer, crushing her heavy breasts against the solidness of his chest.

She panted his name like someone possessed. Ripples overtook her, tremoring through her body.

He swept her toward that precipice, driving deeper. His hands dove downward and clenched in her bottom, lifting her hips off the bed and angling her in such a way that she felt everything, impossible as it seemed, better. *More*. Deeper. Her mouth opened on a silent cry as she jumped off some invisible cliff and flew out of her skin.

It felt as though she were looking down at herself curled beneath this beautiful man, his big body overtaking hers. He moved several more times until she felt him start to tremble. She stroked a hand down his arm, knowing he neared his own climax.

Then he suddenly pulled from her, gasping. His shoulders shuddered as he surrendered to his release, his head bent. She looked between their bodies, watching in a mixture of fascination and confusion as he spent himself in his hand.

Their breaths slowed in the charged silence. He looked up, his gaze searching her face. A sudden bout of self-consciousness seized her. Too late, she knew, but there nonetheless. She lifted one ankle from around him and dragged her knees together.

He hopped from the bed. She watched, her avid gaze crawling over the lean, muscled lines of his body. He really was beautifully shaped. She drank in the sight of him as he worked at the basin, his biceps and forearms flexing as he washed his hands and wrung out a linen.

She couldn't even look away when he returned, a damp cloth in hand. He lowered himself to the bed beside her and nudged at her legs. "Wh . . . nu-uh." She shook her head, heat swamping her face.

"Come. Let me attend to you. There are no secrets between us anymore. Allow me to do this, Aurelia."

She stiffened, wondering if this was the manner of intimacy shared between all men and women. Had he often done this for other lovers? That though only brought an ugly swipe of jealousy.

"Aurelia." His gaze snared hers, his voice unyielding. "Let me do this for you."

With a resigned nod, she relaxed her knees. He cleaned between her legs with efficient movements. Finished, he rose and disposed of the cloth. Returning, he sank back beside her on the bed. Close, but not touching. His gaze skimmed her, and she must have been seriously confused because she thought she saw heat flare to life in his eyes again. He was utterly at ease with his nudity, and she tried to feel equally as confident.

It didn't work.

She reached for her chemise and pulled it over her head. Feeling somewhat better, a little less vulnerable at least, she curled her knees beneath her and faced him expectantly.

She waited, certain he would say something. This changed everything. This was no longer a name only marriage.

"Why did you do that?" she heard herself asking, motioning to the basin.

He shrugged. "It's the courteous thing."

"No. That's not what I meant." She propped herself up on one elbow so they were at eye level. "You . . . withdrew from me. At the end. I've never heard of a man doing that."

The corner of his mouth quirked. "Do you often discuss such matters?"

She flushed. "Well. No, but I read. I've never come across such a thing in any of the medical texts in the library at Merlton Hall, and those texts have been quite forthcoming on matters such as these. Why would you—"

"It's done to prevent procreation. A child. So that I don't spill my seed inside you."

It took her a long moment to process his words. She understood their meaning, but she still could not *understand*. Once she did, her chest sank. He did not want to have a child with her.

"I don't want children," he added, in case she failed to grasp his meaning.

"What of your line . . . the title—"

"I care not what happens after my death. I'll be dead. The title can pass to some distant relation for all I care."

"But I thought every man wants progeny," she

insisted. She knew that her mother had two miscarriages after her birth and it had been a great disappointment to her father. He had hoped for more children. Sons specifically. That was the way of a nobleman. He wanted sons.

Only this one did not. She had found and married the one man in England who had no wish for progeny.

"Not me," he said evenly, without the faintest doubt or hesitation in his deep voice. "Do not take this as a personal affront, Aurelia," he quickly said, likely reading her uncertainty to this news in her expression. "I would not want a child with any woman. Any wife. It has nothing to do with you."

And yet it did.

It had a great deal to do with her now that they had a true marriage. Now that they had a real marriage and she could have children in her future. Yet he was saying it couldn't happen.

"Oh." She squared her shoulders and tried not to look affronted. It was a difficult thing. She felt dazed and not quite certain how to respond . . . how to *feel*.

"Aurelia." He uttered her name knowingly. "This doesn't have anything to do with you." Apparently she couldn't hide her thoughts entirely.

Nodding numbly, she snatched hold of the rest of her clothes and redressed herself. "I'm your wife. Your decision to never have children impacts me. Does it not?" Even the question fell from her lips tentatively as she looked up at him beneath her lashes.

He winced. "Well. Yes. I gather that it affects you, but I simply don't wish you to take it as a personal slight." He studied her, his bigger body reclining casually on her bed. "Are we all right on this? I don't want to quarrel again."

She nodded. "Neither do I." She forced a smile, her mind spinning as though he had not just dropped news so significant that it would alter the course of her life. Mostly dressed, if not fully buttoned up, she hopped to her feet and faced him as her fingers fumbled at her buttons.

He lifted one brow in that maddening way of his, clearly reading that she was still grappling with this. "Considering that we had little choice in our marriage *and* the fact that we agreed to a strictly platonic relationship, it did not yet occur to me to disclose this."

A valid point, she supposed, but it did not lessen the ache in her heart. "Well, it matters now, does it not?"

"It's not something I will reconsider." He spoke

so matter-of-factly. As though they had not just shared the height of intimacy. "This has long been my position. I will not change for you. I never wanted to marry, however, there was no escaping it. But children, family . . . it won't happen."

Love.

She heard him quite clearly even without the utterance of the word. He was saying love. Her face burned hot. He would not have it. He would not give it. She would be a fool to expect it from him.

He will never love me.

He wasn't cruel enough to fling it at her head that he would never love her, but she understood. Now she knew that it would only ever be meaningless when they came together. Tupping. Sex. It wasn't special. *She* wasn't. She had been deluding herself to ever think she was.

She nodded once. "I understand."

His head angled slightly as he stared at her, as though searching to make certain she understood what he was saying. She arched an eyebrow, crossing her arms in front of her. "I understand," she repeated, her voice strained and tinny to her ears.

He held her gaze for one long moment, his jaw locked, eyes intense. Finally, he stood up from the bed, towering over her, indifferent to his nudity. Unlike her. She was achingly aware of every glorious inch of him on display. The memory of what it felt like to have all that male warmth surrounding her, against her, inside her, was still fresh.

Even staring at him now, she felt the stirrings of desire. A part of her yearned for him to stay. To lose herself in his arms. For things to be right between them . . . for him to say the words that would make everything right . . . better.

For her heart not to feel like a heavy, twisting mass inside her chest.

She glanced to the door, heat itching up her neck, unable to stare at him so proudly exposed before her and know she couldn't ever really have him—that he would always keep his heart from her. One thing, she realized, that she wanted from him.

"I have to leave now, but this wasn't a onetime occurrence. I'm not fool enough to think we can stop this from happening again. There's no going back now. I don't want to." He made quick work of donning his clothes, leaving his shirt off and his hard-contoured chest exposed. A blessing and a torment. Her mouth dried as she eyed him. Was she supposed to disagree? She pasted a tight smile to her lips and lifted her chin a notch, trying to pretend that a physical-only relationship would be enough for her—that she didn't yearn for more.

He laughed low and dark, and the sound sent a shower of gooseflesh along her skin. Her pride asserted itself. Did he think she would languish about, waiting for the moment he turned his gaze to her and decided to bed her again?

"Indeed." She nodded once, squaring her shoulders. "I'll let you know when the mood strikes me."

He chuckled and crossed the distance to her, wrapping an arm around her waist and hauling her against him. Her hands fluttered for a moment before coming to rest on his chest, the expanse of warm bare, satiny flesh stretched over hard muscle.

"Indeed. Let me know." The very mockery lacing his words fueled her determination to prove him wrong. One of his hands seized her bottom, pulling her tighter against him. She gasped. He was ready again, his manhood hard against her belly. "Something tells me I'll be inclined whenever you are." That chuckle again, deep and dark, rolled over her. "Just crook your finger. I'll come running."

Then he released her. She took a staggering step before catching herself.

He stopped at the door, one hand on the latch. "Until then."

She wanted to shout that there would not be a next time, but she would only sound temperamental. Like a child flinging forth a dare. A dare she felt fairly certain she would lose.

Biting her tongue, she watched him pass into the adjoining room, the lean lines of his body disappearing from view.

She backed up and sagged down onto the bed, feeling hot and flushed and achy and bewildered all at once. The memory of what they had done together, how it had felt . . .

It took everything in her not to call him back again for a repeat performance. Pride kept her in check. As well as outrage and crushing disappointment. Love, children . . . she would have none of that with him.

Chapter 21

She didn't crook a finger for him, and after a few days Max was beginning to think she never would.

There was no invitation. Not even a come-hither glance. She was all politeness, to be sure. Pleasant even. But she wasn't the Aurelia he knew. He thought after that morning together she would want him as much as he wanted her. Newly introduced to the delights of the flesh, she wouldn't be able to stay away. No matter what she claimed.

She had proved him wrong.

He strolled about in a constant state of arousal, longing for his wife with a need that made his teeth ache. She avoided him as if a repeat performance were the last thing she desired. Perhaps she had decided that she didn't want him. That he wasn't enough . . . that what he was offering wasn't enough.

A bolt of panic shot through him that he quickly tamped down. He wasn't so desperate that her rejection mattered. He merely hoped to reach some level of contentment in this marriage. For their sake, for his friendship with Will. Yes, he told himself. That was the only reason for that brief stab of panic. He wasn't worried. Truly. He wasn't.

If Aurelia didn't want him again, then he would go on. He would live. There would be other women.

A foul taste coated his mouth. His hand curled into a fist. The mere idea of other women held no appeal. Aurelia was all he could think about it. All he wanted.

There was no arguing between them. No saucy exchange. None of the interaction that got his blood pumping. He missed that. He knew he should be satisfied at such tranquility. She placed no demands. She certainly wasn't a haranguing wife.

No, she was faultless. Ever gracious over breakfast, treating him to easy and courteous conversation, inquiring after his day. And it infuriated him. It was as though he had never bedded her. She was withdrawn, holding herself back, and he wanted to grab her and shake her and kiss her until he had the Aurelia he craved and wanted and . . .

He shook his head, not finishing the thought.

He simply wanted her back.

"If you'll excuse me," she murmured, dabbing at her mouth with a napkin. "I'm meeting Violet in the park."

He didn't need to read her mind to know that this was in reaction to the limitations he had placed on their marriage. She'd understood his expectations. No love. No children.

He watched her intently as she rose from the table, staring at her over his cup. She smiled that smile that did not quite meet her eyes and departed the room. He sat tensely in his chair for some moments, his boot tapping anxiously beneath the table, feeling dismissed. Rebuffed. Even without word or deed, she had made it clear that she didn't need him—crave him—the way he craved her.

"Bloody hell." Max set his cup down and pushed up from the table.

He stomped upstairs, heading directly for her chamber. If this was a game, then she had won. He couldn't stay away from her a moment longer. He couldn't endure her indifference.

He strode into her chamber. She sat on the chaise lounge, her sketch pad in her lap. He had a flash of unreasonable jealousy. She preferred that to him.

Aurelia started at his sudden appearance. "My lord," she murmured as he stopped before her and plucked the pad from her lap.

"Max," he bit out, tossing aside the pad, seizing her by the elbows and dragging her up the length of his body.

His mouth took hers, and he groaned, missing this. Missing her. She tasted even sweeter than he remembered, and it had only been a few days since he last tasted her. It was like she was in his blood.

"I missed this . . . you," he muttered, coming over her on the couch, grabbing fistfuls of her skirts and shoving them out of the way so that he could settle firmly between her thighs.

Her arms snaked around his neck. "Then why didn't you do something about it?" she whispered against his mouth.

"Because I'm a fool." He thought he could be

strong and exhibit control. He thought she would need him first.

Her legs came around his hips, and he dove his hands under her, cupping the swells of her bottom. He growled into her mouth, "If you want me to leave, say it now because in another minute I'm not going to be able to stop."

The sweet breath from her mouth fanned his lips and she shook her head with a muffled whimper.

It was all he needed to hear. The sound spurred him to action.

His hands dove between their bodies, finding the slit in her drawers and touching her sex, caressing her, shuddering at the sensation of her wet heat, ready and weeping for him. He thrust a finger deep inside her, reveling at the sweet clench of her around him.

She gasped and the sound struck him like lightening. He stroked deeper, curling his finger and finding the spot that made her arch and pant. She was so close, but he didn't want to give it to her yet. He wanted to be inside her when she shattered all around him.

He pulled back and she whimpered at the loss of him, biting her lip, the sight of her the most seductive thing he had ever seen. Her hands grabbed onto his hips. "I need—"

"I know." He nodded, dragging his hands up her thighs and hauling her into position beneath him. Leaning down, he lightly bit her throat, overcome with the need to mark her, possess her.

She cried out, arching against him, and he followed the nip with a stroke of his tongue. Her fingers speared through his hair. "Now! I need you in me now."

His hand reached between their bodies again, finding her, gliding against her, teasing her for a moment before pushing a finger deep inside her once more, reveling in her soft, clinging heat. His breath grew hoarse. "You're so wet . . . ready."

She nodded drunkenly. "Please."

Aching hard, he nodded. His body clenched with need. He freed himself and then he was there. Pushing inside her. His hands held tight to her hips, anchoring her as he drove in to the hilt. His body shuddered at the sensation. "God, you're tight."

She whimpered.

"Am I hurting—"

Her eyes blazed up at him. She shook her head furiously, and her inner muscles flexed, milking his cock. "No . . . please, just move."

Thank God. He dropped his head into her neck

with a groan, withdrew and pushed back in again, slamming deep and touching heaven.

Sensation rippled down his spine. He buried himself deep. Again and again. Deeper than he ever thought possible. She came, shuddering, with a shrill cry.

He continued to drive into her, increasing his pace, amazed that he had stayed away this long. Her nails dug into his hips as he worked over her, the sound of their bodies smacking together in sweet song.

Unintelligible sounds choked from her lips. She was close again.

He reached between their bodies and found her sweet bud, rolling it once before pinching it firmly. That's all it took. She came apart in his arms, shuddering and gasping. His arms slipped around her, hugging her close as he followed, his climax rising up in him and tightening his skin. He slammed into her one more time before pulling out and spilling himself into his hand, a jagged cry ripping from his throat.

"Wow," she panted, propping herself up on her elbows.

Max stood and moved to the washstand, feeling shaken and glad for something to do. It had never been like that. Even the last time with her.

As sweet as that had been, this was even better. *Hell, this girl was wrecking him.*

Finished cleaning up, he returned to her and sank back down on the chaise lounge. She studied him warily, and he knew she expected him to take his leave. As though he wanted her only for one thing and now that he'd gotten what he was after he would depart. His stomach knotted. He had done that. He had given her that impression of him.

Settling beside her, he plucked up her sketch pad and said mildly, "What have you been working on?"

Aurelia stared at him in astonishment. "You want to see my sketches?"

He nodded. "They're important to you . . . yes, I want to see them. And you know I've always thought you were brilliant."

She stared at him like she didn't know him at all. "It's been a long time since you—" She cut herself off and shook her head, and he guessed she was forbidding herself from talking about the past.

Blinking, a slow smile curved her lips. "Thank you." Her hand smoothed over the outside of the pad before opening it. "This is my newest sketch . . ."

The days passed in a pleasant blur. Max spent every night in her bed. He loved her with his mouth and hands and body so thoroughly she almost convinced herself that it did not matter that he did not love her with his heart.

She began to convince herself that this was enough. The nights were enough. The fact that he still held himself back, that he kept himself scarce and largely unavailable during the day, would be fine. He didn't need to say the words. She didn't need to hear him profess his eternal love to her. This would work. They could even have a good life together.

Until the third morning she woke up sick to her stomach and had to face the fact that a good life with Max might not be her fate.

It had been over two weeks since that morning with him, but a sinking realization rooted inside Aurelia.

It might be too soon to know with any certainty, but she was late. Late when she was never late. And she was not the only one who noticed.

Cecily knew Aurelia's habits as well as Aurelia herself, and she had voiced the possibility a week ago, making it nearly impossible for Aurelia to stick her head in the sand and ignore the possibility.

Aurelia swung between elation and misery. She had never overly contemplated motherhood, and following Max's revelation that he had no intention of being a father, she had accepted that motherhood would not be in her future. And now this.

With every day that passed and no arrival of her menses, her certainty grew, squashing the denial. Apparently, Max's preventive measures did not work. She would have to tell him eventually, but dread held her back. She would say nothing for now. Cowardly, perhaps, but she was not eager to ruin the delicate harmony between them. It would shatter the instant he learned of her condition. Besides, she could be mistaken.

"You truly think this is wise?" Cecily asked, standing to the side as Aurelia searched among the gowns in her wardrobe. "Considering your condition . . ."

Aurelia whipped through dress after dress, scarcely seeing them.

"Wisdom has naught to do with it . . . nor does my *possible* condition prevent me from attending a dinner party. I'm not trekking across Great Britain on some great journey, Cecily. Max said he would not be home for dinner. Why should I stay home when I could spend an evening out?"

"Possible? You are clockwork with your cycles."

"Possible," Aurelia repeated, pulling a dress from the armoire and glaring at her friend.

"When will you tell him?" Cecily pressed.

Her stomach twisted sickly. Tell Max? She shook her head. Tell him that he was going to be a father when the very last thing he wanted in life was to have a child? Watch as their peaceful existence crumbled to ash? No. No, she couldn't. She wouldn't. Not yet.

"When I know for certain," she replied vaguely.

Cecily made a humming sound, refraining from insisting they already knew for certain. Instead, after a few moments watching Aurelia tap her lip and blindly study her assortment of slippers, she asked yet again, "You truly mean to go, then?"

"Yes. Why not? I've been stuck in this house long enough . . ."

"No one has forced you to stay here. And you haven't. You've called on your family . . . your mother, Rosalie and Violet. Walked in the park yesterday."

"You know what I mean. Society, Cecily."

Out of the corner of her eye she caught Cecily shaking her head. "Even though your husband expressly told you not to go?"

"He is not the final authority on everything.

Especially not on the matter of where I can and cannot go."

If she remained in these walls, fretting about the future, about Max, the child—*their* child . . . she would go stark mad. She needed a diversion. And there was that part of her that chafed at Max forbidding her to go to Struan Mackenzie's dinner party. He didn't get to issue ultimatums and then ignore her day after day, coming to her bed only at night, effectively reminding her precisely how low her importance was in his life.

"I think it's a mistake," Cecily said. "You should just talk to him, Aurelia."

He had said everything there was to say. Theirs would be a marriage without love. Without children. She shivered, thinking of his reaction when she revealed that one part of his grand plan was no longer even possible.

"Perhaps," she allowed, looking her friend squarely in the eyes, and shrugged. "But then it wouldn't be my first mistake."

Max returned home early. He couldn't help himself. Staying away from her a moment longer felt like punishment, and he wasn't keen on punishing himself. He'd never been one to refrain from taking his pleasures where he saw fit, and it turned out that his wife was a great pleasure indeed.

He nodded to a footman positioned in the foyer near the base of the stairs as he headed up the steps to his chamber, his boots biting into the plush runner with dogged resolve. Silence hummed through the house. The dinner hour had passed. Aurelia would likely be in her chamber by now.

Entering his room, he tugged his cravat loose with an aggravated yank. Things could not continue as they were. Avoiding her during the day. It was ridiculous. He wanted her. She wanted him. They were married. There was no reason why they couldn't be enjoying each other more frequently.

He rubbed a hand against the back of his neck. God knew he didn't want any other woman. He'd tried. He hadn't returned to Sodom, but that didn't mean opportunities hadn't presented themselves in the course of his daily customs. Except there was only Aurelia. In his mind. Under his skin. In his blood. He wanted her in his bed. Even after these weeks, they'd barely scratched the surface of all the things he wanted to do to her.

He stopped and caught sight of himself in

the cheval mirror. He looked like hell. Eyes red-rimmed. Face drawn, hair mussed from constantly running his hands through it. He couldn't go on this way. He'd been with many women . . . but none had ever reached inside him. None had rooted so deeply.

The problem was that Aurelia wanted everything. She wanted the fairy tale. She was still the little girl with big dreams chasing puppies. He'd seen that dreamy look in her eyes these past weeks. Even though he had put their relationship into perspective at the beginning. No children. No love. She still hoped for it. He knew that. She wanted what he couldn't give—the kind of marriage Dec and Will shared with their wives. He wouldn't be like his father, quick to eat a bullet at the inevitable loss of love. He wouldn't.

He stopped before their adjoining door. They could still have a good life without love. They could have a life in which they came together and enjoyed each other. Only, perspective must not be lost. It wouldn't be right for either one of them to come to expect or rely on each other in any regard. Even shagging. It didn't have to be messy or complicated.

He was certain if they just spent more time

together—in bed—he could purge her from his blood. And that would be best. For both of them. He knocked once at the adjoining room door and entered.

"Oh," Cecily softly exclaimed as he stopped in the threshold. She straightened from where she held a stack of linens, her big brown eyes blinking owlishly.

"Pardon me." His gaze flicked around the chamber as though he would find Aurelia lurking in some corner. "I was searching for my wife."

Cecily cast her eyes downward, her hand smoothing over the linens. "She is not here, my lord."

He took one step deeper into the room. "Where is she?"

"She went out for the evening, my lord."

"Out where?" he persisted, feeling unaccountably annoyed. This wasn't what he had anticipated. She was supposed to be here.

She looked at him and away again. "Oh . . . I believe she mentioned a dinner party . . ."

"A dinner party?" His nape prickled, even though a dinner party sounded innocent enough. It was the woman's manner. The hesitation in her voice.

He knew Aurelia had ventured out before.

She had called on her family, as well as Rosalie and Violet, of course. She often took tea with her mother, who would be leaving for Scotland soon.

"What dinner party?" he demanded. "Whose?"

Sighing, Cecily lifted her gaze and faced him, grim acceptance in her eyes. He knew the answer then. She didn't need to say it. He could read it all over her face.

He was beside himself with fury. He had expressly told her not to attend, and she had anyway. He would settle this once and for all. He wasn't a caveman. He simply did not trust Mackenzie . . . nor did he like the man knowing any of their secrets. And Aurelia frequenting Sodom's was very much a secret. One word would fan the rumor mills and she could be ruined. It pained him to think of Aurelia subjected to Society's cruel judgments. He'd spare her that. Even if meant he had to suffer through a dinner party and endure the likes of Mackenzie eyeing his wife as though he would like to get a glimpse beneath her skirts.

An uncomfortable hardness rose in his trousers at the thought of Aurelia naked. She was magnificent. Her body was lush and sweet and as tempting as Botticelli's Venus. That dark hair . . .

those ripe breasts. Groaning, he shifting himself, trying to restrain his cock. How could he keep his hands off her now that he knew how truly brilliant it could be between them?

Without a word, he spun around and strode from the room, knowing exactly where he could find her.

Chapter 22

The gentle hum of conversation mingled with the chords of a pianoforte and a gentleman's drifting baritone. Aurelia sat very straight upon her chair, telling herself to relax. Venturing out from the house, beyond the comfort of her close circle of family, was good for her. She couldn't cloister herself away forever.

The evening hadn't been so bad. The food was delicious. Even the company had been pleasing. It was good for her. At least that's what she continued to tell herself. Getting out of her comfort zone and engaging with Society. Taking her mind off the shambles of her life.

Struan Mackenzie's Mayfair mansion was the height of opulence. The dinner had been no less lavish, a meal fit for the Queen consisting of too many courses to count. The finest food and drink for a couple dozen guests, all titled. All of whom she knew either in name or acquaintance. Clearly the gentleman was all about making connections in the highest echelons of Society. There were at least three marriageable young ladies present, all of whom cast admiring glances his way. She had no doubt he would soon find himself a bride to his liking.

The young ladies in attendance were actually kind to her. That was a novel experience she credited to the fact that she was married now and not a threat to their prospects with Mackenzie. They were no longer competing. And he was clearly the catch they were all vying for.

"I'm sorry that Lord Camden couldn't attend tonight."

With a fixed smile, she looked away from the young lady playing the pianoforte to Struan Mackenzie as he stepped beside her. "He was most sorry to miss it as well," she managed to say without choking on the lie.

Mr. Mackenzie stared at her overly long, and she was almost certain he sensed the falsehood . . . that he knew Max knew nothing about her being here tonight.

"I confess I am a little surprised to be included in your dinner party, Mr. Mackenzie."

"And why is that?"

She shrugged lightly. "You could have invited an eligible young lady rather than me." That would have better served his interest.

He smiled slowly, his teeth a blinding flash of white against his golden skin. "I invited you and your husband because I find you both interesting."

"Interesting?"

"Amusing," he amended. She frowned, not sure she liked that any better than being called interesting.

"I did not realize we were the subject of your amusement."

"I was curious to see how the two of ye are getting along in your new marriage."

And she had come here alone. Without Max. What must he think? She stifled a cringe and told herself she did not care what Mackenzie or anyone else thought of her.

"We are doing quite well. Thank you for your

well wishes." She smiled tightly, well aware that he had not precisely wished them well.

He angled his head. "Your husband is an interesting man."

Interesting? Max? That was a fair assessment. He had long fascinated her.

Mackenzie continued, "I was not at all surprised when I learned the news of your marriage. Not after Lord Camden paid me a call."

She whipped her head around, scrutinizing him anew. "My husband paid you a visit?" Max made no attempt to disguise his dislike for Mackenzie. Why would he call on him?

The Scotsman nodded as though it were of no real significance. "Yes. Following our encounter at . . ." His voice faded but she knew to what he was referring. Max had called on him after he returned her home from Sodom. It would have been very late. Practically the middle of the night. Why would he have done such a thing?

Mackenzie must have read her bewilderment. He stepped closer, his deep burr a low whisper. "I believe he wanted to guarantee my discretion on your behalf. I assured him he need not concern himself on that account. It is no' a hobby of mine to ruin young ladies."

She flushed and nodded once. Max had done

that? She supposed she shouldn't be surprised. He had always expressed concern for her reputation. Perhaps she should have been more concerned about Mackenzie's inclination to keep her secret.

"Lord Camden takes his responsibilities very seriously." If her voice sounded strained, she was hopeful he did not notice.

"Verra seriously indeed." He chuckled, his gaze skimming her appreciatively. "And ye were one of his responsibilities even before marriage? Now that is what I find most interesting."

Her flush burned deeper, and she knew she must be blushing bright red. She watched as his moss green eyes traveled over the length of her before settling on her face.

"Then I suppose you weren't surprised to learn we had wed."

He chuckled deeply again. "Ah, no. Not at all. Considering the real purpose of his visit was to warn me off you—"

"What?" She turned and faced him fully, not even pretending interest in the couple at the front of the room anymore.

"Are you so astonished? He warned me to stay away . . ."

"Away?"

"Yes. He warned me away from you."

Aurelia blinked and stared unseeingly at the elegant folds of his cravat for a long moment, trying to understand what he was saying. Max had warned Struan Mackenzie to stay away from her? It all clicked into place then. "That's why you did not call on me again?"

Mackenzie shrugged. "We came to a gentlemen's agreement."

About her. They came to an agreement about *her.* As though she weren't a person but a piece of meat to be *fought* over? A matter—not a person—upon which to be negotiated. It wasn't to be borne.

"He wanted my promise not to marry you," he elaborated. "I gave him my word."

As if it was only up to Struan Mackenzie. As if she possessed no say . . . no brain.

"In exchange for what?" she bit out, and then shook her head, waving a hand. "Never mind. It doesn't matter."

Hot indignation bubbled up inside her. An awkward stretch of silence fell between them. She groped for something to say to fill the void when all she really wanted to do was storm from the room and corner Max somewhere so she could unleash her ire.

"The young Lady Camille is lovely," she offered to the Scotsman.

The girl had been perfectly cordial to Aurelia, congratulating her on her marriage. Camille was also one of the few present who had been kind to her prior to her marriage.

"I suppose. A little thin. I prefer my ladies with curves."

Not missing the flirtation, heat scored her cheeks. She felt a frisson of guilt. Max had insisted the man's interest would not have dissipated because they were now married. Perhaps she should not have scoffed at him.

Then she recalled how angry she was at him. She quickly repressed her guilt.

"Are you happy, Aurelia?" Mackenzie asked, rolling her name in that gravelly burr of his.

She shifted uncomfortably on her feet and blinked at him. "You are blunt, and I don't recall giving you leave to use my Christian name. It's Lady Camden now, Mr. Mackenzie."

"Come. As a former suitor? Are we not permitted a little familiarity?"

She didn't reply, instead sipped her punch and scanned the drawing room, hoping one of the guests milling about would choose that moment to join them so she did not have to answer Mackenzie's discomfiting questions.

His burr was low and silky near her ear and his hand brushed her elbow. "Is it too much to think I might care for you?"

She lifted her gaze, reading the seduction in his eyes. This was more than friendly interest.

"Step away from my wife."

Chapter 23

It all felt hotly familiar to Max. Walking up on Aurelia with Mackenzie hovering close, his big hand on her like he had every right to touch her. If possible, this time he felt closer to unraveling. Here, in Struan Mackenzie's drawing room, he wanted to tear the bastard apart.

Aurelia's eyes widened and then narrowed. "Camden," she said with a calm at odds with the spitting fire in her brown eyes.

There she went again. Calling him Camden as if they weren't lovers.

And why did she look so angry to see him? She was here against his wishes. He had done nothing to her. She was the one in error here.

"This is a surprise." Her lips curved into a brittle smile. "I did not think you could make it tonight."

Oh, the cheek of the girl!

Mackenzie slid his hand off her arm, and some of the tension ebbed from Max's shoulders. Until the bastard opened his mouth.

"Your delightful wife and I were just having a fascinating conversation." He slid her an appreciative glance. "She always proves diverting."

Max shook his head, despising that way he spoke about Aurelia. As if she and he were the most intimate of friends. He stepped closer, almost nose-to-nose with the Scotsman. He might not give a bloody damn about the curious stares shooting their way, but he would speak low so they would not be overheard. "You gave your word to stay away from her."

"I promised I would give up my pursuit to marry her." Mackenzie shot him a cocky smile. "I did no' say I would no speak to her again . . . no' touch her—"

Max's fist flew out before he could stop himself, his knuckles contacting with the man's jaw.

Mackenzie went down. Chaos erupted, which included Aurelia shouting his name. *Max.* Not Camden, and for that he was perversely satisfied. Even as several men lunged across the room to restrain him, he was gratified to know that in the heat of passion she thought of him as Max and not Camden as everyone else in the world. She was it, the only one, and for some reason that mattered to him for reasons he refused to examine.

"I'm fine," he growled, shaking off hands.

The big Scot rose to his feet, gingerly touching his jaw. The crowd shrank back, no doubt assuming Mackenzie would want a crack at him now.

Aurelia was of the same assumption, too. She stepped between them, holding out a hand as though to ward off Mackenzie. "Don't . . . please . . ."

Something snapped inside Max at having her intervene as though he couldn't defend himself. Or her.

He stepped around Aurelia, closing his hand around hers and pulling her to his side. "We're leaving." He held Mackenzie's gaze, conveying all his fury, all his possessiveness. In a single look he let the Scotsman know that he would not have his way. He would not have her.

A long moment passed and then something

passed over Mackenzie's eyes. He nodded. One nearly imperceptible nod. He understood.

With one hand still flexing his jaw, he stepped to the side and gestured for them to pass.

Adjusting his clasp on Aurelia's hand, Max pulled her after him and out of the drawing room. Every pair of eyes followed them and he didn't care. He didn't give a bloody damn.

He was going home and he was taking his wife with him.

In moments they were in the carriage. She launched herself into the seat across from him. It was reminiscent of the night he fetched her from Sodom. Now, as then, she didn't want to touch him.

"Are you out of your mind?" she demanded.

"I told you not to come here." He shrugged. "What did expect me to do when I learned where you were?"

"Not that! You hit him! In front of all those people! What will people say—"

"Come now." He tsked. "What others think of you has never mattered."

She crossed her arms over her chest, which only pushed the generous swell of her breasts higher. The sight made him ache. He wanted to touch her there again. Taste her. Close his mouth around—

"Perhaps it matters now."

He studied her in the shadowy interior of his rocking carriage. "Oh? What's changed?"

She said nothing. Her eyes gleamed at him across the distance, deep and full with emotion. The anger was still there but something else lurked, too. Something he had never seen in her before. Whatever it was it made him want to haul her across the carriage and into his arms so she didn't look that way anymore.

She must have realized she was revealing something of herself because she averted her gaze, looking downward. Her lashes cast dark crescents on her cheeks. "He told me what you did," she whispered, and damned if she didn't sound wounded. As though he had damaged her somehow.

She lifted her gaze and there it was. The hurt in her eyes.

"What did he tell you?" Immediately he wondered if Mackenzie had made up some lies.

"You went to see him. After Sodom."

Not lies, then. The truth. The truth had upset her. A flicker of uncertainty curled in his chest that perhaps he had something to feel guilty about. A feeling he quickly squashed. He would not change his actions, so there was no sense regretting them. "Yes. I did," he admitted.

She inhaled, lifting her breasts higher against her bodice. He tried not to stare. Staring only made him want her more, and she clearly wasn't in the mood to have him. No, she looked as though she would rather have his head on a pike. "How could you do that?"

He frowned. "I was looking out for you—"

"You made him promise not to court me . . . not to ask to marry me." She shook her head. "That left me with Buckston."

"What does any of this matter now? You're married to me."

"It matters because you don't trust me. I won't have you control me . . . my own family never treated me like that. I was twenty-three and unwed because they trusted me to make my own choices. Something you—my own husband—can't even do!"

Helplessness washed over him looking at her, listening to her. This was new. Listening to a female. Trying to understand the workings of her mind and how not to behave in a wholly selfish manner. He'd never come near to this intimacy with another female. He was gone before things ever became even close to this. Aurelia was the only woman he ever argued with . . . the only one who mattered.

A lump rose in his throat and he inwardly cursed. "Has it occurred to you that I did it for myself?"

She nodded fiercely, scooting to the edge of her seat in the heat of her indignation. "Well, you certainly weren't thinking of me."

He nodded back just as fiercely, leaning forward, feeling dangerous right then. As though he might admit anything. *Do* anything. "My own selfish reasons drove me."

She sucked in a tiny breath and jerked back ever so slightly.

He closed in, moving closer. A few inches separated them. It would be so easy to grab her, touch her, kiss her.

Instead, he continued talking. "I went to Mackenzie's because I couldn't stand the thought of you with him. I probably would have put an end to you and Buckston, too, no matter that he was but a harmless fop . . ." He was breathing harshly now, his hands curling around the edges of the squabs. "Because the idea of you being with anyone but me makes me want to hit something."

There was no sound save the rasp of their breaths and the creak of the rolling wheels on the street.

She blinked, her brown eyes owlishly big in her face.

"Don't tell me I silenced you." Such a thing he would have never thought possible.

She opened her mouth. Her lips worked, but no sound emerged except a strangled, "I—I—"

"It's all right," he growled. "You don't have to say anything." He reached out, curved a hand around the back of her neck and hauled her onto his lap.

Her sweet breath escaped in a puff against his mouth as they gazed into each other's eyes in the dim interior. They were so close. Their mouths practically touching, but not. Not kissing. Not yet. Everything in him quivered from the restraint. Another one of those whimpery sounds escaped her lips.

He speared a hand through her hair, scattering the pins so that the dark mass tumbled loose. A small sound escaped her. God. He loved all those little sounds she made.

He pulled her head back, bringing his nose to the arch of her throat and inhaling. He missed her smell. He loved it. He caught whiffs of it throughout the house. Especially when he passed her door. He wanted to roll over in his bed and be able to breathe it in all the time.

He dragged his mouth and nose up her throat, loving the way she shuddered in his arms. He flexed his hand in her hair, forcing her face back down, his mouth taking hers. Claiming it in a crushing kiss.

She was eager, ready. Her mouth opened instantly for his and his tongue swept inside, colliding with hers, tasting all her sweetness. All her warmth.

Her fingers dug into his shoulders and she pushed herself up on his lap so she could straddle him. She settled back down then, pressing her sex against his cock. Even with clothing between them, she scorched him.

Her skirts pooled around them in a giant puddle of silk. His hands roamed her bottom, buried beneath layers of fabric, and he growled, frustrated at the bulk of material in his way. His palms moved around to her front. He yanked her bodice down, not caring at the rip of seams. He tugged down her corset and broke their kiss to look at her. To feast his gaze on the erotic bounty of her breasts spilling free, pushed up high over her corset. His cock jumped against the front of his trousers. Groaning, he bent his head and seized a dusky nipple, drawing it deep into his mouth.

She cried out, arching against him, fingers diving into his hair, urging him on. He sucked and laved her nipple with his tongue and then scraped it with his teeth until it sprang into a hard, distended tip. She went wild in his arms, her hips undulating on him. She knew what was coming now and it made her hotter, ready and eager.

She pulled on his hair, yanking him to her neglected breast. "Camden," she growled.

"No. Say it, damn it. Say my name." Camden was his father. And his grandfather and the sire before him. She used to say his name. Long ago. He'd hear it from her lips again.

Her lips pressed into a flirty, mutinous line. "No."

He smiled slowly. "I'll hear it from you."

She shook her head, her dark hair tossing around her.

"Shall I make you?" he said in his most silky voice, stroking a finger so softly against her neglected nipple.

She shivered slightly. "Please . . ."

He arched a dark brow. "Say it."

"Max," she choked.

He ducked his head and sucked her into his mouth, loving the sweet taste of her on his tongue. He bit down. Just enough pressure to sting sweetly.

She screamed and shuddered, coming apart in his arms.

He couldn't wait another moment. His hands dove between them, working his trousers open. He was so anxious he was shaking. He freed himself, and then she was there, her hand closing around him.

He cursed and dropped his head back on the squabs at the sensation of her cool fingers around his swollen length.

"Aurelia," he ground out as her thumb rolled over the tip of him. He lifted his head. "I need to be inside you. Now."

Her eyes settled on his face. They were beautiful. Clouded and hazy with desire. She smiled slowly. A siren's smile and she didn't even know it. Her lips were moist and bruised . . . plumper than usual. They were the kind of lips a man fantasized closing around his cock. He groaned again. He was so hard he actually hurt. He wanted her to do that to him. He wanted to act out his every fantasy with her.

But right now he wanted to be inside her more. He needed to sink inside her. It was as imperative as his next breath.

She rose up on her knees. Then she was guiding him through the slit in her drawers and sinking down, lowering her weight and impaling herself on him.

They moaned simultaneously. Her snug channel hugged him like a fist. And then she started to move, clumsy at first until she gained her own rhythm. She used his shoulders for leverage, fingers digging into his jacket. She pumped over him, stroking him in and out of her.

She was the most beautiful thing he had ever seen. A dark temptress. Her face flushed. Eyes liquid-dark as she worked toward her own climax. Pressure gathered at the base of his cock. He was close.

He gripped her hips, helping her along now, setting her at a faster clip. Harder. Their flesh met with satisfying smacks that grew louder as their movements became wilder. She was so close. She shook in his arms . . .

Then she cried out, dropping all her weight down on him. Her channel tightened and convulsed around him and he was lost. His hands curled around her shoulders, pulling her down, holding her tight as he spilled himself inside her.

They remained just so for several moments, trembling in the aftermath. Air escaped their lungs in ragged saws of breath. He felt dazed. In a fuzzy state of euphoria. He wanted to roll over, pull her against him and fall asleep buried inside her.

A curse exploded from him.

She jerked in his arms.

There was a frozen moment in which he could not say anything. Or move.

And then, horrified, he was moving, yanking her off him and depositing her on the seat across from him. Tucking himself back into his trousers, he stared at her as though he didn't know her. Or rather . . . as though he didn't know himself.

She worked to set her clothing to rights, too. The front of her gown sagged loose and he recalled the sound of ripping seams. She pulled her cloak around her shoulders, shielding herself from his view.

Something softened inside him when he noticed how her hands shook. Until what he had done, once again, hit him like a brick in the face.

He dragged a hand over his head, rubbing at the back of his neck. He had released his seed inside Aurelia. He had never down that before. He had never even come close to losing himself before.

This just proved what he already had accepted. She was different. Special.

He brought both hands to cover his face and

expelled a heavy breath. How could he have forgotten? He lived by a code.

"We're here," she said abruptly.

Then she was out of the carriage. She didn't wait for the groom to open the door and assist her. He barely had time to lower his hands before she was gone. A blue blur of silk and streaming dark hair.

He took off after her. "Aurelia."

She didn't stop. She ascended the front steps, rushing past the butler. He sent him a nod of greeting and then followed at a more sedate pace. He didn't want to alarm the servants by running her to ground. But catch her he would. They needed to talk about this. They needed to make sure it never happened again.

He stopped her in the empty corridor outside her chamber, circling a hand around her wrist and forcing her around.

"Aurelia—" He stopped at the wrecked expression of her face.

She shook her head, her dark waves tossing wildly. "That was the most humiliating . . . the smallest I've ever felt—"

"No." He cupped her face, pushing strands of hair back off her face. "It wasn't you . . . it was me. I lost control because it was so good. Perfect." He kissed her softly, something twisting inside him at her unresponsive lips. "I reacted badly. You know how I feel about—" He cut himself off, feeling as though he were drowning in the ocean of her eyes. "I realize it's unlikely just this once, but the risk that we could have created a child—"

"You don't have to worry about that," she said in a flat voice, her eyes like flint. "Ease your mind. You have nothing to worry about on that score. You didn't get me with child tonight."

"No? And how do you know that?"

"Because I already am," she blurted. "Your sure-fired way all the other times we came together . . . well, it's not quite one hundred percent effective. Given my lateness, it probably happened the first time we were together."

Ice swept over him. "You lie."

She gasped and staggered a step back. Hellfire. Had he just accused her of lying? Of something like this?

He shook his head, feeling the warmth return to his face. "No. That is to say . . . you're *mistaken.* It cannot be."

"Oh. It can be. It is. I'm having our child."

"You can't know that yet," he insisted.

"Oh, I know. I've been in denial, wanting to prolong telling you, but I am."

He angled his head, an uneasy feeling stirring in the pit of his stomach. Something in her face. In her voice. She never looked so hard before. So untouchable.

She exhaled, a brittle smile playing about her mouth. "I'm already with child," she repeated.

"You can't be. I didn't . . ."

"Yes, well, *that* apparently didn't work."

He grabbed her by the arms and gave her a gentle shake. "You are certain?"

"Fairly certain. I'm late . . ." She sighed. "I'm never late."

He dropped his hands from her and took a step back. Then another one.

The idea of having a child . . . being a father . . .

He couldn't wrap his mind around it. He had long rejected it as a choice or a possibility. He could not fathom it.

"This . . ." He couldn't think what to say. How to react. It had only been two weeks since that night. She could be mistaken. "So you are not absolutely positive."

She stared at him, the light fading from her eyes. A candle snuffed out, her brown eyes gazed flatly at him. "You can always hope."

She turned then and continued to her room. She moved like she was tired. A tired, beaten woman.

Not the vibrant lover who had moved over him just moments ago.

He opened his mouth to call out to her but no sound escaped. Nor could he force his legs to move to go after her. He watched her disappear inside her chamber. And still he stood in the center of the corridor.

The ground was no longer solid beneath his feet. Everything he ever thought he knew. Gone.

Aurelia carried his child. He was going to be a father. With a curse, he charged into his bedchamber and headed for the decanter of whiskey. He didn't bother with a glass.

Chapter 24

The following morning, Aurelia didn't wait for Cecily before she was up. Awake, dressed, and already packed.

The moment she entered her bedchamber last night, she had flung herself on the bed and had a long, bitter cry.

She had wept for herself. She wept for her unborn child. And she wept for Max. Because he would never allow himself the love she or this child could give him. One look at his face and she knew. He was horrified. He could not hide it. He could not pretend otherwise.

In a short time she had become his worst nightmare. Both his wife and the mother of his child. Neither two things he ever wanted.

Oh, she loved him. She knew it now. She doubted she had ever stopped. Not since she was nine. She slapped a rogue tear trailing down her cheek. Apparently she had not spent all her tears yet. But he wouldn't let himself love or be loved. And she wouldn't stay here, taking whatever scraps he tossed at her. She certainly couldn't allow her child to feel that way. Ignored. Neglected. Occasionally acknowledged with just enough attention for he or she to know what she was missing.

Cecily entered the room, her eyes widening when she took in the packed trunk. "What's happening?"

"I'm going to Scotland. To Aunt Daphne. Mama will be venturing there soon. I'm just departing sooner to get settled in," she said with forced brightness.

"Very well," Cecily said slowly. "Discounting the fact that you are married now and might be expected to reside with your husband, I thought you didn't want to live with your Aunt Daphne."

Aurelia shrugged. "I thought it would be lonely." And boring. But then, she wouldn't mind a little tedium. She'd endured enough excitement and upheaval. She stroked her stomach as though she could already feel the child growing there. "I won't be lonely. I'll have Aunt Daphne, Mama, the baby . . ." Her gaze locked on Cecily. "And you. I hope I'll have you."

Cecily hesitated, and it occurred to Aurelia that perhaps she had plans of her own that did not include rusticating in an obscure corner of Scotland. Then her friend smiled. "Of course. Of course I'll go with you."

They embraced. "Now," Cecily said, "you look about finished here. I'll send a footman for the trunk and then go pack my things." She started to leave, but hesitated at the door. "Have you told your husband yet? Does he know you're leaving?"

Aurelia shook her head. "I'll leave a note."

Cecily looked uncertain. "Perhaps you should talk. There could be a chance—"

"No. There's no chance. He doesn't want this child." Again her hand went to her stomach. The prospect of the baby saved her from total bleakness. "And he never wanted me."

Her heart was broken, but it had not stopped beating. She was not like Max, unable to love. She would love this baby enough for both of them. She had to.

Max woke with a raging headache. The afternoon sunlight streaming into the room felt like knives in his eyeballs. It only took a few moments for the events of the night before to flood over him, and then he knew he deserved every bit of the agony he was experiencing.

Had he actually reacted like such a bloody bastard when Aurelia told him she was increasing? She had to be frightened, dreading the moment she told him. She knew he didn't want children. He had made that abundantly clear. And then he had gone and acted like he'd been dealt a death blow.

He rose, pressing the base of his palm to one eye and then the other as pain spiked through his skull. He had to see Aurelia. He had to apologize.

He staggered to his feet and made his way to the basin. Splashing water on his face, he studied his red-rimmed eyes in the mirror. He had to apologize and tell her . . .

He looked at himself, wondering if this was the man he wanted to be. Someone who drank himself into a stupor because he'd been given news that would overjoy most husbands. Gazing at himself, he saw a weak man in the mirror.

Weak like his father.

Weak like the man he swore he would never become.

"Hell." He pushed himself up from the basin, ready to find his wife. Ready to hold her and tell her he was going to be a good father.

He knocked once before opening the door to her chamber. She wasn't there, which wasn't so unusual for the middle of the day. He started to turn away when he noticed the doors to her armoire wide-open. He inched forward, his stomach tightening. It was empty. No clothes.

His gaze swung around the room, his stomach now pitching violently. He caught sight of the dressing table. It, too, was clear of items. No brush or perfumes. There was nothing left of her here.

She was gone.

They had been traveling most of the morning when it started to rain. Wind whistled. The normal gentle rocking of the carriage soon grew uneven and jerky. Aurelia began to feel queasy. Typically, her stomach wasn't so sensitive. She knew the cause could be her condition, but she suspected it had more to do with the turbulence of her feelings.

She was conflicted. As much as she believed she needed to leave for her sake—and her unborn child—it left her slightly ill. She thought of Max's face when he learned she left. She imagined the shock followed swiftly by tears of regret. She snorted. It was a ridiculous image. Max wallowing in grief because of her was as likely as him loving her.

"Are you all right?" Cecily asked when she noticed her holding her stomach.

Aurelia nodded. "Just a little bumpy."

"It's the wind." She nodded, her gaze skimming the walls of the carriage pensively. "Perhaps we should signal the driver to stop?"

"We're still a distance from the next town. Even if we stop we'll still be buffeted with wind and rain," she reasoned.

The wind howled shrilly then, lifting over the sound of rain. Cecily's eyes rounded and she angled her head, gazing at Aurelia in a way that seemed to say, *Are you certain of that?*

"Surely the driver would stop if it's too dangerous to continue on." A thin thread of doubt hung to her words.

They held silent for a moment, swaying where they sat on the squabs. The carriage gave a little lurch and Aurelia grasped the strap that hung near her head to keep her balance. She sent Cecily a nervous smile she had intended to be reassuring.

"Perhaps we could find a crofter's cottage and—" Cecily's suggestion was cut off as a sudden howl punched through the steady beat of rain.

A thunderous crack followed, reminiscent of bone cracking. When she was a girl, Will had fallen from a tree and broken his arm. She remembered the terrible snapping sound of the bone breaking in that spilt second. This was like that. Ugly and sharp. Only louder.

The carriage slammed into a wall. At least that was how it felt. She knew there were no walls on the north road, but the impact jarred her to the teeth. Her head snapped on her neck as the carriage heaved sideways. She and Cecily tumbled from their seats in a flurry of skirts and tangling limbs. Fear lodged in her throat. Everything slowed to a grinding crawl as they were tossed around the inside of the carriage like marbles in a box. Her chest clenched. Squeezed. Air ceased to flow. Pain scraped her elbow and her mouth opened wide.

A scream reverberated in her ears. Shrill and as endless as the rolling carriage.

It registered dimly. As though she were someone else, somewhere else. Looking down at the scene from afar.

However, the ringing scream was her own.

Chapter 25

She hadn't bothered to cover her tracks. She took one of his coachmen and carriages. Which only indicated to him that she didn't think he would care. She didn't think he would give pursuit.

She was wrong.

Max rejected taking a carriage himself, knowing he would catch up with her faster on horseback. An hour after departing, with London well behind him, it started to rain. A steady downpour that soon soaked him to the bone.

He didn't let the rain stop him. If anything, it would slow her down. He knew she couldn't be far ahead. He pushed himself harder through the deluge. Fortunately there was no lightning, so he didn't have to concern himself with that danger.

Time crawled. His thoughts spun to the rhythm of rain and pounding hooves. She left him. She was his wife. She carried his child.

His life . . . his future was rushing away from him and it was his fault. He had to get it back. He had to get *her* back.

Aurelia. She'd always been there. Larger than life.

Desperation hummed inside him, an anxious energy that propelled him, coating his mouth with bitter panic.

He loved her. He was *in* love with her. He'd loved her for a long time, but recently that love had changed, grown into something so fierce and consuming. Elation swelled inside him. Fear was there, coupled with the memory of his family—his father, but for the first time the prospect did not cripple him.

Loss was a part of life. An undeniable absolute. There was no escaping it. Only learning to accept the inevitability of it—and live well and fully in the interim—that was reaching contentment and happiness. Finding someone, joy, love . . . that was never a guarantee. But he had found it. He'd found it with Aurelia. And he turned his back on it. On her.

Never again. No more.

He nudged his heels and urged his mount faster.

The wind howled. Several branches snapped off trees and littered the road. He stayed alert, watching the ground ahead of him, making sure his mount avoided some of the bigger branches that could trip him. He was so busy studying the ground immediately before him that he wasn't looking into the far distance. Not until he heard the wild whinny of a horse.

His gaze snapped up, spotting the mangled corpse of a carriage ahead. He pulled up on his reins, everything in him clamping down hard as he recognized his own carriage. Bile surged in his throat. One of the doors was ripped from its moors, hanging askew. The sight of his family's crest was a slap in the face. A haunting reminder. Nearly two decades ago another carriage bearing his family's crest had met such a fate. His mother and sister had died inside it.

"Aurelia," he choked, digging in his heels and launching his mount forward.

He jumped from the horse before it came to a full stop. "Aurelia!" He ran to the carriage and grabbed hold of the door, ducking his head to look within. Empty.

"My lord!"

He turned to face Thomas, the coachman. The man looked hale except for the gash in his forehead. Blood welled up from the wound before the rain washed it clean.

He grabbed the man by the shoulders. "Where is she? My wife—"

The coachman looked over his shoulder and gestured toward the tree line.

Max turned. The moment seemed to drag on into infinity as his eyes searched for his wife, dreading what he would find, what he would see. He begged to God to spare her and thereby him. To give him this.

To not take her, too.

Aurelia stared at Max through a gray wash of rain. She blinked, convinced her eyes deceived her. *Why was he here?*

He bounded across the distance and reached for her, his hands gentle on her arms, as though she were some fragile piece of crystal. "Are you hurt?"

He'd come for her.

She shook her head, trying to shake sense into herself. Her knee ached where she had banged it into the side paneling of the carriage, but she was otherwise unharmed. "I banged my knee and scraped my elbow . . . nothing more." She motioned to Cecily where she sat at the base of the tree. "Cecily hurt her ankle."

Cecily waved her hand. "It's nothing."

Before Aurelia could speak again, Max scooped her up in his arms and lowered her to the ground beneath the tree. They had taken shelter under it, the thick canopy of branches and leaves blocking most of the rain.

Her hand fluttered to his shoulder. "I'm not hurt, Max."

He lifted her skirt and peered up her stocking-clad leg to examine her knee. A bruise was already beginning to form there. He tested it gingerly with his fingers.

"It's not broken," she assured him.

His stormy eyes settled back on her face, searching her features. "You're fine?"

A smile tugged on her face. "Yes. I promise."

His gaze dropped to her stomach, and his expression was both tender and terrified. "The babe?"

Her breath shuddered out of her. His hand moved to cover her stomach then and she jerked at the contact. At the burning imprint of his hand on her. Something passed over his eyes that looked very close to pain.

"I'm sorry," he whispered, shaking his head, his voice ripe with misery. "I was afraid to love you . . . to love this baby, but it's too late for that." He paused, his gaze locking in on her face. Moisture brimmed there, and if she wasn't sitting down she felt certain her legs would have given out.

He continued, "I do. I do love you . . . I love you." His voice seemed to gain strength each time he uttered it. "I love you. I already love our baby and can't wait to meet her."

She couldn't speak. She could only stare, trying to reconcile his words with what she knew. With what she *thought* she knew.

"You can't love me," she whispered. "Because . . . you can't."

"That's what I always thought. It's what I wanted you to think. But how—" His voice choked on a sob. He stopped and swallowed, his rain-damp throat working. "How could I not fall in love with you?" He brought his other hand to cup her cheek, pushing back wet snarls of her hair. "Say you love me. Say you'll come home with me. That we will be a family."

She moistened her lips, the lump in her throat blocking her words. "Max . . ."

He nodded, one hand still caressing her stomach, the other holding her face.

"How do you know we're having a girl?"

He laughed roughly, throwing back his head. "Wishful thinking. A little girl just like you . . . The world would be so lucky to have her."

"Lucky indeed," Cecily chimed in.

Max flashed her a grin before looking back at Aurelia. His grin faded as his eyes searched her face, his expression turning grave, and she realized she had not said anything in response to his declaration.

She moistened her lips. "I've loved you, Maxim Alexander Chandler," she said, "fourth Viscount of Camden, Max to your familiars, since the first moment I clapped eyes on you."

"And then you hated me," he reminded her with a wry twist to his lips.

"No. I was just waiting for this. Waiting for you . . . for me. For the both of us to get to this point. To get it right."

His chest lifted on a deep breath. "I'm here now, Aurelia."

She crushed her mouth to his, kissing him deeply, her hands curling around his shoulders.

She was here, too.

Epilogue

Max opened the door of his bedchamber and fell back against the hard length of the door with a gust of breath. He'd been in meetings all morning with his man of affairs and barrister regarding a new investment prospect. Typically, before his marriage, the prospect would have diverted him, but he'd been anxious to wrap up the meeting and return home. To Aurelia.

His gaze scanned the chamber for her. Now he was free, and only one thing weighed on his mind. Or to be more accurate, only one thing *burned* through his blood like scalded cinders.

He tugged the cravat loose from around his neck as his gaze landed on his wife where she sat before the dressing table. Her gaze lifted and collided with his in the mirror. Color flooded her cheeks. He loved that. Loved that she still blushed when their eyes met. He loved that he still had the ability to make the color rush to her face.

Her lush mouth curved into a slow smile as he took his time assessing her. It was almost shy, beguiling, and that made the skin tighten at the back of his neck. She still had this effect on him. Even after months of marriage. After countless days and nights together where they had each loved and explored each other with unhurried leisure, using their hearts alongside their bodies, he knew it would never be any other way between them.

Still staring at him in her dressing table mirror, she settled back a bit on the bench, her hand drifting to the well-rounded curve of her belly.

Aurelia, ripe with child, was impossibly beautiful. He ached at the sight of her. Garbed in a rich blue dressing robe, her dark hair flowing in waves over her shoulders and down her back, she radiated life and vitality.

His chest clenched when he thought she had tried to leave him. Then it clenched even tighter when he recalled the sight of that carriage tossed on its side. He could have lost her that day. Both of them. Aurelia and their child.

His dark thoughts must have crossed his face.

She pouted at him and angled her head to the side. *Come here,* she mouthed at him in the mirror, crooking her finger.

He didn't need to be told twice. He pushed off the door and crossed the room to her in a few quick strides. At the bench, he dropped to his knees and wrapped his arms around her. She turned to meet him and he rested his cheek against her swollen belly.

From the corner of his eye he spotted a new sketch on her dressing table. "Is that for me?" he asked mildly, picking it up and admiring her work. Watching her sketch had become a favorite pastime. She was brilliant and amusing and he enjoyed offering her his perspectives on the goings-on around Town, honored when she often took his ideas and incorporated them into her drawings. He only insisted that he be the one to leave the drawings around London. If discovered, he would weather the storm better than she. It wasn't fair, but it was the reality. And she was his wife. He would protect her from anything, small or large.

"I thought we might leave this at the musicale—"

"At Mackenzie's?" He frowned. "Must we go?"

"Come. Don't you want to see Mackenzie properly domesticated? She's a lovely girl—"

"She has my utmost pity." He snorted.

She swatted his shoulder. "Be nice, Max. You got what you wanted."

"That's right." He folded his arms around her again and returned his cheek to her stomach, turning to press a kiss on the swell of her belly. Glancing up, his heart squeezed at the sight of her glowing face. "I've got you. Forever."

Next month, don't miss these exciting new love stories only from Avon Books

When a Scot Ties the Knot by Tessa Dare

To avoid the pressures of London society, Miss Madeline Gracechurch invented a sweetheart who was conveniently never around. Maddie wrote the imaginary Captain MacKenzie letter after letter until his (pretend) death in battle. Then years later, the real Captain Logan MacKenzie arrives on her doorstep, ready to make good on every promise Maddie never expected to keep.

Even Vampires Get the Blues by Sandra Hill

Viking vampire angel Harek Sigurdsson's otherworldly mission teams him with a Navy SEAL who's more than his match—she's his predestined mate. The SEALs call her "Camo" for her ability to blend in—yet her sensual energy draws Harek's gaze like a white-hot spotlight. Just Camille's luck that the sexiest man she's ever met may also be a vampire!

Her Lucky Cowboy by Jennifer Ryan

Bull rider Dane Bowden is eight seconds from winning the championship, but his bull has other plans. When Dane wakes up, he's sure he's gone to heaven . . . because his doctor is the girl who saved his life and disappeared years ago. Despite becoming a surgeon, Bell still sees herself as the awkward girl who's never had a boyfriend. But when a rodeo rivalry turns deadly, it's Dane's turn to save Bell's life.

Available wherever books are sold or please call 1-800-331-3761 to order.

REL 0815